Praise for Me
Talking Underwater

"*Talking Underwater* unfolds with the slow, sinuous rhythms of summer. We taste salt on the skin, we smell the ozone of fast-moving storms. Melissa Corliss DeLorenzo is a master at tracing the currents that run beneath the closest relationships and how sudden riptides can swallow them whole. By turns tender and tragic, this is the most generous and genuine story of sisterly love I've read in ages."—SHERI HOLMAN, author of THE DRESS LODGER and WITCHES ON THE ROAD TONIGHT

"Writing in confident, musical prose, Melissa Corliss DeLorenzo weaves a story of youth and what it means to come of age in a world whose perfection cannot last. With their beloved childhood beach as a backdrop, two sisters learn to overcome longing and loss and, ultimately, to find redemption."—NAOMI BENARON, author of RUNNING THE RIFT, winner of the Bellwether Prize for Fiction

"Melissa Corliss DeLorenzo is quickly becoming one of my favorite authors. *Talking Underwater* is a literary gift, filled with characters you want to spend time with. As a fellow New England author, I especially appreciate her scene settings—which are rich and vivid. Deep character connections and family intrigue frame a plot that makes for a definite page-turner. I highly recommend *Talking Underwater* to anyone looking to devour the next great read."—STEVEN MANCHESTER, #1 Bestselling author of THE ROCKIN' CHAIR and TWELVE MONTHS

"Melissa Corliss DeLorenzo's *Talking Underwater* is the searing, heartfelt story of two sisters and the tragedy that tests their lifelong bond. Told with evocative prose, this powerful novel will have you rooting for Amy and Heather to find their way back to each other. Book clubs will love this."—KRISTYN KUSEK LEWIS, author of SAVE ME and HOW LUCKY YOU ARE

Talking Underwater

A Novel

Melissa Corliss DeLorenzo

Thorncraft Publishing
Clarksville, Tennessee

First Edition, 2015

Published in the United States by Thorncraft Publishing. No part
of this book may be reproduced, by any means, without written
permission from the author and/or Thorncraft Publishing.
Requests for permission to reproduce material from this work
should be sent to Thorncraft Publishing, P.O. Box 31121,
Clarksville, TN 37040.

ISBN-13: 978-0-9857947-6-7
ISBN-10: 0985794763

Cover Design by etcetera...
Cover photos by Shana Thornton
Author photo by Jim DeLorenzo

Library of Congress Control Number: 2015938787

Thorncraft Publishing
P.O. Box 31121
Clarksville, TN 37040
http://www.thorncraftpublishing.com
thorncraftpublishing@gmail.com

Printed and Bound in the United States of America

10 9 8 7 6 5 4 3 2 1

For my sister, Rebecca, who always gets it.

ACKNOWLEDGMENTS

Thank you to everyone who repeatedly asked when this book would be published—your support and enthusiasm are part of the reason you hold it in your hands. Many friends have read *Talking Underwater* in at least one of its incarnations and although a blanket "thank you" is less than you deserve, please know it comes straight from my heart.

Thank you to my amazing and supportive team of editors: Kitty Madden, Beverly Fisher, Jennifer Goode Stevens and Rita Yerrington. Your diligence shaped this book for the better.

Thank you, Laura LaTour, for all the support from Partners Village Store and you especially.

A mountain of thanks to Kate Robinson. Your reading is always thoughtful and your cheering endless! I am so very grateful for your friendship.

Thank you, Nicole Daly, for not only reading the manuscript and offering valuable feedback, but also for ordering my Matilda Jane Fins in Peacock Blue when I was too busy writing to use the Internet. I love those pants.

Thank you, Shana Thornton, for believing in this book so deeply. Your friendship and enthusiasm are invaluable to me!

Thank you, Mom and Dad, for giving me so much, the beach included.

Thank you, Rebecca—for everything.

And, of course, thank you, Jim. I love our little life.

Talking Underwater

"Life must go on;
I forget just why."
—Edna St. Vincent Millay,
from "Lament"

MELISSA CORLISS DELORENZO

"Amy! Amy!" Heather calls. "Come listen!" Amy and her sister sink under, hands clasped, heads close together.

And they try to talk to each other underwater.

The way it works is that one of them thinks of a phrase before they dip beneath the surface together. Their little girl bottoms hit the packed sand of the ocean floor, their bodies bounce back up and the water suspends them.

It sounds like *blub blub blub blub blub*.

They emerge.

"Did you hear me?"

"Yeah, but I didn't really get it."

"Oh. Well, maybe if we hold our noses, less bubbles will mess it up."

"Okay." They dip under again.

Blub blub blub blub blub. Then rapidly *blub blub blub blub*.

Their heads pop above the surface—they choke out laughter and salt water. The girl who spoke laughs at the funny thing she said; the listener laughs because even though she couldn't make out the words, she *knows* it was funny. They laugh because it's not really working and somehow that is especially funny. They never understand the other. They keep trying.

They sink under again and again.

Part 1

MELISSA CORLISS DELORENZO

After

She pushes the sharp, fine needle into the taut fabric. She holds the wooden embroidery hoop in one hand, the needle in the other, the exquisite indigo material pooling on her lap like water, and she stitches a cluster of French knots with a startling yellow thread. A body of stars appears. She rests her hands for a moment and looks out over the railing of the ferry. Even though it is high summer—near to the solstice—the air coming off the ocean is cool. Amy's skin has gone to gooseflesh and she pulls her light cotton cardigan closer.

"Are you cold?" asks Heather.

Amy nods her head slightly, looks back down at the embroidery work she holds. She takes her stitching back up. She finds solace in busy hands. "Yes, a little."

"Well, you know...the water..." Heather says.

Amy nods again, but doesn't look up at her sister. Heather looks at Amy's hands, too. Amy watches her sister peripherally from the inside of her eyelashes. She moves her eyes back to the blue fabric and stitches a new constellation.

This time is "after," is what she is thinking. There was a before, and this is after.

There is always a before and there is always an after. Sometimes the line between the two is subtle. Barely noticed. When this happens, no note is taken because the effects are inconsiderable, passing imperceptibly. These kinds of changes alter people, but blend in gently, naturally brushing the edges of the self. But then there are the moments that delineate life; moments that draw the lines.

She often thinks of the life before. Her mind wanders there and she is helpless to stop it. She wonders what her "after" might have been if not for this unbearable one. Maybe it would have been her parents' deaths or Matt's, but not until they all had grown old, which would be fair. Right and orderly. Maybe Heather's death once she and Amy had aged into doddering old widows, sitting on a porch swing, making fun of their children, sneaking foods they shouldn't eat.

Amy and her sister had planned to be old ladies together. There had been plans for aging as there had been intentions for everything leading to old age.

"I can't imagine how neurotic you'll be," Heather has said to Amy many times.

"Well, can you imagine how bitchy you'll be? No one will be safe," Amy always tells her in return.

They imagined they were prepared to witness the deterioration of their bodies and find the humor in it. They were convinced they would be ready for it when the time arrived, certain it would be good in its own way, as everything before had always been.

Before, the future was not fluid; Amy thought it as nearly solid as the past. It was so simple—what was to be was exactly what she expected, that for which she had always wished. And this vision was shared by her sister. Amy wonders now if these were arrogant assumptions or merely ignorant ones. She finds herself working toward what is yet to come as though history has not woven them, she and her sister, into an intricate pattern of blood and bone and skin, of stance, of ornate history. They are roots of ancient trees wound and wound, coiled and curled, inextricable, and now they must forge a future, when before it was as set as all that had come before; as though before, they were gypsies with cards to tell the stories not yet written.

Once, when they were both still living at home, their parents went on a vacation, and they sent the girls out on the ferry to Martha's Vineyard.

"That way you can have a vacation, too," their mother had said cheerfully, her voice bright.

"They just don't want us alone in the house," Heather said to Amy later when they were alone. "They don't trust what we might do."

She was nineteen and home for the summer from college. Amy was almost eighteen and anticipating her freshman year. They were on the edge of a nebulous before and after, their twenties, and following soon, adulthood. Something was uncoiling, opening. They could speak of it only in the smallest of words. The vaguest. It was more a shared feeling that passed between them. An energy.

They were only half-heartedly offended by their mother's insinuations because although they weren't likely to have done anything too worrisome, they wouldn't have been entirely innocent, either.

"What do they think we're going to do?" Heather said as they stood at the bow of the ferry, the salted air curling their hair.

"Have sex every waking moment," Amy said.

"All over the house," Heather added.

"Well, maybe not in their bed..."

"No, especially in their bed."

"That is beyond disgusting." And they laughed at their own undone mischief.

As the boat passed through the harbor and into the bigger mouth of the ocean, the horizon opened out past the familiar and moved into unexplored territory. A feeling of promise rose up in Amy. It was one of those sublime mornings in July when the sky is a piercing blue, the sun still low on the horizon. She felt good for no reason other than the particular blue of the sky, the sun right there where it was in the blue. She felt full and ripe and unstoppable with possibility.

"They even gave us money for food. God. We do have jobs," Heather said and rolled her eyes. Not that either of them had refused the cash their father had placed in their hands.

They pulled their long, misbehaving hair into haphazard buns, tangled with colorful scrunchies. They wore ripped-up jeans and tee shirts. Sweatshirts emblazoned with the names of their respective colleges staved off the late summer chill. Heather walked the deck barefoot, her flip-flops discarded near the heap of their bags. Amy's hand caught the breeze through the flowing air around them—as through an open car window—up and down, up and down. The air had substance, heft.

"Careful, Amy, you might get stung by a bee," Heather told her and they laughed, as young girls do when making fun of their mothers.

Amy could hear her mother's voice as clearly in her head now as she did when a child. "Don't ever stick your hand out the open car window, especially when the car is on the highway."

"Why?" Heather's favorite word, the one their mother often took for sass.

In this instance, their mom postulated mishaps with small stones springing from rubber tires and burrowing into delicate flesh. Flying insects winging past open car windows, their mean stingers poised. Amy's small heart had tightened. She settled more deeply into the safety of the backseat of their two-door hatchback.

"Even if it's just your fingers and not your whole arm?" Heather had asked.

"Maybe. Do you really want to take that chance?" Their mother had glanced at her for a moment before her eyes returned to the road. Two hands held the wheel, palms and fingers curled, gripped.

"But I like the way it feels," Heather had said. Her fingers fluttered at the edge of the open window.

"Hand in, Heather." Mom had grown stern.

"Fine," she'd muttered, her pinkie clinging to the edge.

Amy's belly had leapt at that small finger. Not only because of the dangers of which their mother spoke, but because of Heather's defiant bravery. Amy admired it deeply, yet always cried for her when Heather pushed their parents to anger.

There on the ferry with Heather on their way to the Vineyard, their childhoods newly behind them, they remembered their mother's warnings as their hands fluttered in the wind.

"I'm always going to let my kids put their hands out the window," Heather said. "Anyway, Mom's a science teacher, for God's sake. It's virtually impossible that a bee flying toward a car driving toward a bee..." Heather trailed.

"I hate word problems," Amy interrupted.

They stayed in Oak Bluffs, at an old inn—the ocean sparkled outside the windows of their room, the fanciest they had ever seen. The sheets were the softest, the furniture antique, the halls plushly carpeted in deep red. Amy ran her hand along the curving rich cherry bed frame, fell back into the mounds of down and spongy chenille.

"How can Mom and Dad afford this?"

"She must have had a coupon," Heather said, referencing their mother's penchant for bargains.

Amy snorted. "Still," she said.

Heather wandered the room, checking out the bathroom, the closets. "Hey, I don't think there's a TV." She looked around some more. Opened the armoire. "Nope." She flopped down on the bed next to Amy. They were quiet, staring at the ceiling.

"It's cooler here than at home."

"Yeah. Before we know it, it'll be fall." Amy thought of school with a mixture of excitement and fear.

She watched patterns emerge on the ceiling. Heard a gentle hum from somewhere nearby and the crunch of crushed shells on the driveway. The light dimmed and crickets started up tentatively, haltingly. She had the sensation of settling deeper into the bed while at the same time her body grew weightless. The light in the room, a pale filtered orange, mixed with dancing blackness across her eyes. Time passed only in terms of the shifting light. Heather's hand brushed against her arm and broke the spell. She was suddenly aware of the chill in the room. Goosebumps rose on her bare skin. She turned her head toward her sister.

"What should we do?" Heather asked.

They both realized at the same moment that they were famished. "Find a place for dinner?"

"Yeah, good idea."

They wandered the cobblestone streets, peeking at menus displayed outside restaurants, not embarrassed with each other at their shared unfamiliarity with the cuisines, shocked at the prices attached to the strange food. Finally, they found a dimly lit steakhouse and ordered filet mignon and baked potatoes, salads smothered in French dressing—food, at the time, they considered cultured. They asked for beers and were served without question. They never thought they would get *away with it. They toasted themselves—they lauded their adventure.*

Every day of the four-day trip they stayed up late into the nights talking, as if they hadn't seen each other practically every day of their lives. There were always new secrets, new revelations and discoveries. Things whispered in darkness as though written in black ink onto the surface of the lightless night sky. Ideas and intentions, beliefs and inklings, perceptions and plans—shared mind to mind and tucked away. Always safe.

Now Amy and her sister, fifteen years older, ride the ferry again, back to the inn. It is early evening, the sun again low on the horizon, not rising this time, but sinking fast. It is cool on the open ocean, cooler even than at the shores of Cattail Beach. They left Boston in late afternoon, turning their children over to their husbands, to commence the drive to the ferry. It is Friday. They will return home Sunday, day or night, depending. This is Amy's thinking at least. She doesn't know Heather's thoughts. They agreed to return on Sunday, the day—Sunday, not a specific time. They came here to see what could be salvaged.

This is an island. The symbolism has not been lost on Amy and she doubts that Heather has not thought of it herself.

Coming to the Vineyard was Amy's idea. Heather readily accepted, her happiness rolling out in waves. But Amy knew, even with that which Heather expressed, that she was holding back her excitement. Her joy. Amy knows Heather's face, her expressions, very well. Better than she knows her own which she never sees except reflected in the mirror or in the responding expressions of the ones she loves.

Amy is less ready to forgive than she expected to be by now. As if there is a scale somewhere. A means of measuring this. She is trying. She has reached the brittle point where she is not quite ready to let go but bone-tired of where she stands, mired in her pain and outrage. She is beginning to want happiness again. She is almost ready to accept the idea that happiness is once more a thing she is allowed. She is tangled with the ghosts of the past, but almost ready to allow the idea that life will go on into her being. Allow it to pour in slowly and coat the inside of her body.

Life goes on. It is the phrase people tell one another when something is lost and those who are left must carry on. It is meant to be a salve, this little dose of truth. But it is cold honesty drizzled with honeyed kindness. These words are intended to soothe, but for those who have lost, the words are a definitive line to cross. Simple: life goes on. Breakfast happens day after day. Weekends crop up every seven. There is a new moon every twenty-nine days or so. Time continues to pass. And those who have lost cannot believe this can be possible. This level of cruelty. Life goes on means you go with it: live in the present, face the future, long and wide and black with the unknown. Leave the past behind. But it is impossible to do this when something irreplaceable has been lost. At least not right away.

But Amy has glimpsed the other side. She is beginning to remember the good.

Almost a year since that changing day on the shores of Cattail Beach, she can almost see the other side of the definitive line. She can almost imagine crossing it. "Life goes on" used to make her furious; used to make her cry. Sometimes it still does. But she is beginning to see it reveal its truth.

The ferry crosses through the bay into open water on the last scheduled trip of the day. The sun has just slipped into the ocean. It is dark this time as they approach Martha's Vineyard.

She looks away from her embroidery and up at Heather, who senses it and turns and smiles tentatively.

Amy looks the other way, out at the blackening ocean, the deepening blue of nightfall.

Things to count on.

Swimming in warm water as the sun goes down, sandpipers pecking the shore when beach-goers begin to leave for the day, dune grass yellow-green flowing waves in the breeze, brilliant blue hydrangeas like soft jewels, footprints in the sand hinting their silent stories, the grains arranged in intricate random patterns on ankles and toes like bridal henna, beach glass, the Point, riptides and undertows, seagulls fighting over leftovers late in the day, a warm shower at day's end, seaweed and sand stuck to the white skin under your bathing suit.

Before

When they were small, there was school (their least favorite), after school and weekends (they liked these more) and summer which was better than any other time—even Christmas—because they spent every day they could at the beach. There was no place in the world Amy and Heather loved more than the beach.

Heather was older, so for Amy there was never *me* without *her*. There was their mother, too, of course, and their father on weekends and vacations. But when Amy thought of the *we* of her childhood, it was Heather and she who created the plural.

Amy wondered at their mother becoming pregnant with her when Heather was merely seven months old. Amy always thought she would follow suit, but when her daughter, Rachel, reached seven months, she found herself entirely unready. Neither for pregnancy, for labor and birth, nor for another small being who needed her. Rachel was so young and she and Rachel belonged so deeply to each other, mother to child, child to mother. There could not be another. Amy's second child was conceived only when Rachel began to be more her own person than just Amy's baby. Rachel was nearly three when Sage was born. *Their* experience of sisterhood, Amy knew and mourned (although it was her own doing) would be different from Heather's and hers.

For Amy and Heather, *sister* was a sacred word.

A childhood of summers on the beach was a blessed one, they believed. Their beach, Cattail, a sacred place. They loved it unequivocally. There was no other thing to do in summer that could equal time spent there. Sleep-away camp or crafts classes, trips to far geographies, days spent with school friends—not for them. For someone who had never laid eyes on that stretch of sand, that expanse of blue moving water, Amy could not be sure how they might perceive it, how it might affect them. She was not sure just how special their beach actually was, but to Amy and Heather there was no other place whose measure came close. And if there were flaws—as she was sure there must be—they didn't see them.

There were two ways to get to Cattail. One, a series of highways, the final being Route 88, a two-way stretch of road shrouded on both sides by dense greenery. It led to the bridge that crossed the river that flowed into open water. One side of the bridge, salt marsh and the other, ocean. As they crossed the bridge, the harbor came into view on the right, boats swaying at the docks, seagulls and black cormorants perched on the boulders protruding from the water. On the left, marshy grass. Route 88 was efficient and direct. Cars whizzed past each other going in opposite directions. Their mother, ever-cautious, was comfortable enough with that on the way in. But going home was different. When Amy and Heather were children, the Commonwealth had lax rules about alcohol on the beach and after a long afternoon, the ride home on 88 became more perilous. Recklessly immortal kids drunkenly weaving, driving too fast. Their mother drove carefully, both hands on the wheel, her tiny girls nibbling grapes in the backseat. She was most likely thinking of supper, was preparing it in her head, coordinating baths, laundry, chopping, and sautéing, bestowing order, when a maroon car pulled up very close behind. A blue blur passed on the left. The maroon car pulled into the breakdown lane and drew up on their right. The blue car drove in the lane of on-coming traffic, racing the maroon car in the breakdown lane, their car in the middle, all three flanked together. Amy only remembered the startled and choked sound her mother exhaled. Then a rushed sliding from the slippery vinyl seat as her mother braked hard to a stop. The blue car and the maroon car roared past them.

Later that night in bed, under cool sunshine-drenched sheets in her ruffled baby-doll pajamas, Amy listened as her parents talked in the living room.

"Never again! They could have killed all of us! Drunk drag-racing kids!" she hissed in a fury. Mom was strong in the ways she must be, but at the core she harbored small seeds of fear. She did not tend and nurture them, but tried instead to bury them. And although without sun and water the seeds could not grow, neither did they disappear. And fear made her mother angry.

"I know, honey. But you're all okay," Dad said in his calm way. His deep voice resonated warmly.

"Never again!" she resolved, as he uttered soothing sounds in the background.

The other way to Cattail was a longer ride through rural back roads. Winding, bending, largely unmarked roads that were learned by landmarks: a house, a wide curve or the straight-back spine of a tree. Houses covered with graying shingles and white painted trim were set back off the road behind scatterings of trees. Farm stands selling sweet corn, peaches and tomatoes cropped up here and there. Fields of strawberries, alfalfa and silver queen and butter and sugar corn spread out back from the road, pushed into the blue of the sky hung here and there with puffy white, non-threatening clouds. As they drew closer to the ocean, the air flowing into the car became cooler, as though a mystical line had been crossed. The cooled air was how Amy and Heather knew they were almost there. Sometimes in that same spot, the sky would shift to gray, a fog engulfing the car, a cold dampness penetrating. But most days the blue skies and sun prevailed. They followed the road until it curved sharply to the right and the rocky shoreline came into view. The girls craned to look.

"Big waves!"

"No seaweed!"

That first glance of ocean water spoke to them of the water they would find at Cattail that day. Waves in the small inlet meant much bigger waves at Cattail. No seaweed and there was a good chance that Cattail was the same. They didn't like seaweed. The brown and stringy curling ribbon sort was endurable. Although it was annoying and itchy when it wrapped around the ankles, it was tolerable. But not so for the soft, furry clumps the color of clotted blood. Some days the small chunks floated sparsely. Other days it was dense, the waves breaking red and thick. It accumulated on the shore, its smell strong. Flies buzzed and hovered over it as it baked in the sun. The girls wouldn't swim in that water. On those days, they found other things to do, but felt cheated, for swimming was the best part of the beach.

Most days, the water was clear and clean, and they were happy.

"Mom, we're going to go test the water," they announced each day then ran down to the shore. The water lapped at their ankles.

"It's warmer than yesterday," one of them would say.

The other shrugging, "Maybe." They ran back to their mother.

"Lunch?" she said. They nodded eagerly. Their mom never made them wait the perfunctory half hour after eating to go swimming. She trusted that they knew their own limits. In the insular world she created for them, she possessed an innate sense of what was safe. She believed in instincts.

They ate quickly then headed straight to the shore.

"Jill's mother makes her wait almost an hour," Amy told Heather as they walked to the water.

"That's so unfair." Sadness lapped the edges of her voice.

The water rushed to their ankles. Heather jumped right in. Amy made her way in agonizingly, inch by inch, hating that cold shock to her warm skin. Once she made it in up to her waist, Heather came bounding over.

"Be careful! You're splashing!" Amy yelled.

"Come on, Amy! You take so long!" And she began to count.

"No!" Amy screamed, scampering away gingerly, careful not to splash dry areas of her body. Heather ran after her, much faster since she was already wet.

"Four...five...six..." she chanted slowly.

"No, Heather! I'll get in! I'll get in! I promise!"

"Seven...eight-nine-ten!" she said much faster. She lunged at Amy, wrapped her arms and legs around her, toppling them over into the water together. They emerged sputtering and laughing.

"I hate that!" Amy said. But not really. They laughed. Both fully wet, now they could play games. Their games had specific objectives, mostly made up. There was embellished swimming and diving. Each wave was rated.

"Dive in this one," and looking beyond it toward the deep ocean where new waves came into view, a bigger one. "No, no, that one, that one!" Bigger was better.

Amy dived into one as it curled. The sound of the wave roared underwater, the rushing foam tickled the heels of her feet. Floating underwater she felt completely alone, but without fear or discomfort. A hand or a foot grazed her outer thigh and she emerged. Heather was a few feet away.

"They're big today!" Amy stood still to gauge the pull of the water. It dragged her where it wanted her to go. It knew what it wanted, with purpose and meaning. *No, this way. No. I said this way.* Here. People were fearful of it. But understanding this pull and release made body surfing possible.

How did she acquire the knowledge? She couldn't recall. She simply innately learned where to position her body, when to merge it with the wave.

They loved to ride the waves.

They'd walk out until the water was no higher than their hip bones. They turned to evaluate the swells moving in lines toward them—too small, too small, too small. There. The right one. A tug on the lower part of her body and she waited. Waited. Waited for the precise moment—there was a precise moment—the pull released and she leapt right on top just as the wave broke and curled under her belly and rushed to shore in a burst of energy and white foam. Felt the sand beneath her outstretched hands and the ride was over. The water rushed back out into itself and she was left in the shallows. She stood, adjusted the bottom of her bathing suit, pushed the wet hair out of her eyes. Galloped back out to wait for another.

A wave, when caught just right, carried them to shore. It had to be sensed. Keep their bodies in front of the wave until it started to curl. Feel the pull down near their feet grow stronger and stronger. As the wave started to pass, jump right on top, feel it break under their bellies and ride it as far as it would take them.

As far back as Amy's memory reached, they had gone to the beach in summer, but not always to

Cattail. When she and Heather were little, their mother stuck closer to home at the local beaches. But then one day they pulled a little boy, blue and slack, from the water near the end of the jetty. Amy was four, but even when grown, she could recall the deep blue of the uniforms the emergency workers wore, the slant of the sun in the sky. Her mother's brown bathing suit with orange and yellow flowers all over it.

The ambulance screamed up to the curb of the road that flanked West Beach. Amy's mother sat on a low chair in the sand, one eye in her fat summer novel, the other on her tiny girls playing in the sand near her feet. The men in blue raced out to the end of the jetty. People stood to see what was going on, made their hands into visors across their foreheads. Amy's mother stood, too. Only then did Amy pay any attention to what was going on and got up to stand near her mother. The men in blue climbed back up the far end of the jetty. One of them carried the little boy, clad only in his swim trunks. He was limp and blue and bouncing with the movements of the man who carried him across his big arms, running toward the ambulance. Foamy stuff oozed from the little boy's nose. It looked like the sudsy bubbles at the edge of the surf on rough days.

Amy stood close to her mother, leaned up against her smooth, bare legs. Amy remembered her mother's warmth against her own body. She had tried to cover Amy's eyes as the men in blue got closer. Later that night, on the news, they said the little boy died at the hospital.

It was the last day they went to the city beach.

"I will never take them there again!" Amy heard her mother vow to her father with tears in her voice later that night when she was supposed to be asleep. "It was bad enough with all my students constantly pestering me, but this was the last straw! Do you know the mother of that child left him in the care of his nine-year-old brother while she went off God knows where?"

That was when they started going to Cattail Beach.

Amy was four, Heather six. Mom had been hesitant to bring her young children to Cattail—the waves were large, the undertow and riptides local legend. She worried they would be dragged out to sea. But after a little boy died at West Beach, presumably the safer span of shoreline and closer to home, she must have realized anywhere else was just as safe.

"Why is it called Cattail?" Amy asked her mother.

"Um, I think it's because of the shape," Mom said.

Amy puzzled at this. What shape? What about the cat—its tail? She'd never seen any cats there. They didn't even allow dogs at all.

"What about the cat?"

Mom was busy packing up the beach stuff as Amy clung to the edge of the kitchen in the doorway watching her. "The cat?" Mom said. "Um, I'm not sure." That was the end of that.

"Oh." But this was not an acceptable answer. It made Amy think of the song "Wildfire," the horse who ran away on the cold winter night.

She sang along with the radio, filled with sadness for the horse and the girl who lost her. "Mom, what happened to Wildfire?"

"Who?" she said. She was distracted, her eyebrows slightly furrowed.

"The horse in the song. 'Wildfire.' The horse." Amy was exasperated. It was playing on the radio at that very moment, for crying out loud. "Why'd she run away?"

Mom shook her head a little, Amy watched her face as it softened in the rear view mirror, relieved it was not a problem she would have to consider genuine in her grown-up state of mind. One less thing she would have to remedy.

"Oh, I don't know, love. It's just a silly song."

Amy couldn't understand why her mother didn't simply ache to know the way she did.

Amy couldn't pinpoint in her memory the very first time they went to Cattail, but eventually the summer and this beach became inextricably entwined.

Cattail sat in the bay underneath the crooked arm of Massachusetts. Warm bay water, perfect swimming temperature, lapped its shores. While the water of the Atlantic coast up north stayed cold all summer, by late June, Cattail waters were within twenty degrees of human body temperature—refreshing from the hot sun, but not cramping cold like the waters of the northern coast. The sand was fine as sugar, the color of pale butter. Soft and sweet on hands and toes as Amy dug them in deep. Hot, warm, cool the deeper she went. They drove up to Cattail every day they could, their father joined on his days off.

Every summer morning Amy got up, ate breakfast, helped Mom pack the beach stuff. She stirred the powdered lemonade mix with water poured from the kitchen tap into the yellow plastic drink cooler. She gathered the beach towels and did anything else Mom asked her to do. Amy placed some of their things into the trunk of the car—the cooler would be last—then went in to change her clothes. The kitchen linoleum was cool and smooth as she passed over it on the way to her room.

"Car's packed, Mom!" she said as she trotted past Mom's back. Mom faced the counter, sandwich baggies, bread, jar of mayonnaise, cantaloupe all spread out before her.

"Thanks! Get changed!" she called back.

In her room, Amy pulled out a bathing suit, her favorite, and the things to wear on top which weren't that important—they'd be discarded quickly.

They drove the back roads, parked in the far south lot, carried all the stuff particularly balanced up the uneven splintering wooden boardwalk to the same spot in the sand. They set up three chairs in a row, the cooler within Mom's reach.

"Let's go feel the water," Amy said to Heather, or she to Amy. The girls tugged their clothes off, folded them loosely, handed them to Mom and ran down to check the water. It pooled around their ankles, swiftly flowed back out, their feet engulfed in soft, wet, gray-brown sand. Amy always imagined it as wet cement—she would never break away!—until Heather called, "Amy!" and she pulled her feet free and ran through the surf after her sister.

Swim, lunch, run through the dunes, swim, snack, walk to the Point, maybe one more swim if they could talk Mom into it. Home to make supper for Dad.

Their routine meandered in its same, sweet pattern. The current was gentle and they bobbed along, Amy and her mother and sister. There was a comfort in the stability, the solidity.

Amy and Heather swam until their fingers wrinkled and their lips purpled. When they grew tired of swimming, they ran to their spot in the sand and drank lemonade from the waxed paper cups their Mom brought. With the long fingernail of her right index finger, Mom scraped their initials on the bottom of the cups. "H" and "A." They blew the salt water from their noses into the tissues she handed them and took turns combing their snarly hair with a wide-tooth comb. They lay in the sun on towels, trying to be like the older girls around them who devoted entire afternoons to their tans. But they soon grew bored.

"You girls want lunch?" Mom asked. They nodded. She passed sandwiches wrapped in waxed paper, baggies of crackers, more lemonade. Amy ate her lunch, balanced her cup the same way she always did and shared the crackers with Heather, making sure they had an equal amount. She watched the ocean pulling in and out. The sugary sand leading to the water. Heard the gulls cry. Felt the mesh chair beneath her. The cooler, the towels, the little wooden slat table.

When they had to pee, they walked up past several tall lifeguard chairs. That's how they kept track of where they were. They sat at station eight— six stations away from the bathrooms.

They hopped across the hot tar of the path, scuttling to dry patches of blown sand. They tried to tolerate the hotness on their bare feet, but had to give up and put on the sandals that dangled from their fingers. Mom would not allow them to enter the bathroom without footwear. They scrambled between two small dunes, their secret short-cut, and walked into the dark, cool bathroom. Their eyes worked to adjust. Amy slipped into a stall. When she came out, Heather was looking at herself in the rust-spotted, hazy mirror. Amy watched her. Watched Heather's eyes scan her own body, her own face. Amy knew what Heather was thinking about and it sent a wave of coldness through her.

In moments like these, Amy began to have the feeling that if she turned her head and looked behind her, everything she was sure of would be there in a heap, staring back at her.

As she watched Heather in the mirror, she knew that things would change and she could do nothing to stop it. She thought about their conversation the day before after coming home from Cattail. The tar of their driveway was still hot but bearable beneath their bare feet. While Mom started supper, Amy and Heather lay on their backs in the driveway. The tar felt good and warm on their cooled skin. The sun was low in the sky. Their fingers touched from their outstretched arms.

"What do you want to be when you grow up?" Heather asked.

"I don't know." Heather already knew this.

"I want to be an actress." They both already knew this, too. She said "actress" all breathy as she struck a pose, one hand on her hip, the other at her ear, her elbow pointing at the sky.

Amy didn't want to grow up. She thought about the girls in her class. At slumber parties all they talked about was growing up. Their mothers had ordered them kits about their changing bodies. The kits had pamphlets and samples of Stayfree. They were excited about it. They were just heading into sixth grade. They wanted boys and breasts. Amy sat silently; she didn't wish for any of it, but didn't want the other girls to know. Inside, she prayed every night to put it all off. *Please, God, just one more day.*

But Heather was eager for it, too. "I wish we had boobs," Heather said wistfully. "Then we could wear bras and look really good in shirts."

Amy took in the blue of the sky above her. "Come on, Heather, no you don't," she said lightly.

"Sure I do. Don't you want to be older?"

Panic rumbled through Amy's belly. She swallowed hard against it. *Don't,* she thought, panicked. *Don't.* She breathed in the blue of the sky. She touched the soft skin of Heather's hand, and thought *don't* as a non-word. Just a feeling, *don't*. The moment drew out long and frozen.

But that was yesterday. Here and now in the bathroom at Cattail, Amy banged out of the stall and broke the spell, dropped the cold feelings in her wake.

Heather turned as Amy pushed open the stall door and walked to the sink. Heather skipped toward the exit.

"Heather! You didn't wash your hands!" Amy said.

She stopped, her back to Amy, sighed heavily, her shoulders heaving.

"They'll get clean when we go swimming," Heather replied with exasperation.

"You're so gross," Amy said, but followed her out. Heather headed toward the concession stand instead of the secret short-cut.

"Hey, where're you going?" Amy said.

"Let's see what ice cream they have."

"Heather, Mom'll never let us get any." But she went to look with her anyway. They looked at the ice cream they wouldn't have and as they walked back to the tar path, they decided which flavor they would get if they could. Amy decided on cherry vanilla. Heather was stuck between mint chocolate chip and coffee chocolate swirl. They discussed which would be better and why.

When they returned, Mom was reading her thick novel. They couldn't understand why grown-ups wasted perfectly good beach days with their faces in books. They shook their heads at their misguided folly. So they swam, played in the dunes, checked in with Mom, swam again, ate some cantaloupe. A walk down the shore.

Then it was time to go home.

Mom promised corn on the cob and they stopped at the farm stand they liked the most, the one owned by the farmer they called "the old man." A sign told them to choose their own, which involved a considerable amount of debate between the sisters. They put the money in the rusty Maxwell House coffee can, two dollars and fifty cents a dozen, paid for by the honor system. But a dozen really meant thirteen. *Why, Mom?*

Back in the car, Amy listened to the radio. She and Heather liked pop stations and Mom usually tuned into one as they drove around. Sometimes she grew tired of that music and hit the button for the adult station and they'd listen to Barry Manilow or Seals and Crofts' "Summer Breeze." Amy really liked that song. It played in the car and she settled down in the backseat, looking out at the trees that she knew in a way deeper than knowing as the cool air rushed at her from the open windows.

Later, she and Heather husked the corn and then rinsed sand from their legs and feet, the tiny grains stuck there with invisible glue. They used the garden hose and threatened each other with the cold water. "Don't!" they squealed running away from the other. They argued over who would shower first, as they dawdled and sucked salt from their fingers and hair, stiffened to little points.

"Someone get in the shower!" Mom called from the kitchen window.

They lingered a little longer, hesitant to wash it all off for another day.

~~~

Amy and Heather drove down to Cattail as the stirrings of summer coiled more deeply into spring. The inseparableness of their childhood summers long gone, seized by the obligations of work and motherhood, they promised each other one day out of the month to spend together. No excuses. They called it "our day."

"We should be working," Amy said, as the city spread out smaller and smaller in the rearview mirror.

"Not on a day like this," Heather said. "It's a benefit of being your own boss. And you know there's no working on our day."

Today, lunch at their favorite local restaurant, a long walk on the beach all the way to the Point and a look at the renovations being done to their parents' new retirement house. Mom and Dad had recently sold Amy and Heather's childhood home and moved into the beach cottage they'd bought years ago as a rental investment. It was the site, too, of their beloved shared family vacations—two weeks every August. Now, their parents were renovating it and moving in for good.

All the flowers of spring had fallen from their stems and drifted away and the green that flanked the rural road was spreading out, rowdy and multi-hued. Unstoppable. It also signaled that wedding season was upon her. Upon them. Her husband, Matt, as well as her sister, all of whom made their living from those big events of life: bar and bat mitzvahs, sweet sixteen parties, silver anniversaries, New Year's Eve galas, corporate Christmas functions. And weddings. Although June was no longer the most favored month for brides, it was still an extremely popular one. There were autumn brides and Christmas brides and Valentine's Day brides, but the June brides still reigned. June was a busy month for them with nine to twelve weddings in that four-week span. Weddings weren't only for Saturdays anymore. A good June meant a dozen weddings: every weekend—Friday, Saturday and Sunday—filled.

This day late in May, Amy and Heather made their way through Boston traffic, over the Expressway and down to Buzzards Bay where they would spend one leisurely weekday afternoon before June crashed in full-force.

"Are you ready for the hoedown?" Amy asked.

An important event was coming up this June at the Park Plaza in Boston. An elaborate and extremely upscale wedding—the daughter of a prominent Boston politician. The vendors secretly and ironically, but not without affection, referred to it as "the hoedown." With nearly two years of planning in the making, this was the kind of wedding that was distressingly high-maintenance. Each and every detail weighted equally with utter, exquisite importance.

"Donna is outwardly cool as can be, but I know she must be freaking out about it," said Heather, as if reading Amy's thoughts. Donna was the premier event coordinator in Boston and in charge of this monumental event. If you were brought in as a vendor, it meant you were premier in your chosen field, too.

"Yeah, well, this bride isn't exactly your typical bride," Amy said.

"Our brides are never typical brides," said Heather as she leaned back in the passenger seat. She closed her eyes; her hand floated outside the window up and down in the fast-moving air.

"No, they definitely are not," Amy agreed. Their brides possessed wedding budgets in the triple-digits. Their brides spent a slick thirty thousand on flowers alone, from the singular flower shop in Boston where all brides with thirty thousand to spend on flowers spent it, *de rigueur*. A single bride's flowers equaled the entire cost of Amy's and Heather's weddings combined, they often noted. "But this one is especially atypical. This will be our first bride for whose wedding Secret Service is present."

"Do you know who's working this little get-together?" asked Heather.

"Boulangerie on cake and pastries, Soirée on specialty linens, you-know-who on flowers...of course..." they said in unison. "Oh, and they are bringing in a celebrity guest-chef for catering. But no one we know knows who—it's a big secret, apparently. And, as you know, Glimmer, Inc. on lighting and Déguiser on decoration." The last being Heather's and Amy's companies.

"That's a fun group." Her eyes were still closed.

"Yeah, it is." These vendors had worked together in and around events for years—they were one big, flamboyant, neurotic family with their own language and shared legendary events.

Heather ran Glimmer, Inc. which provided specialized lighting—soft colors, precision pin-lights, lighted columns, faux flame. Heather, a theatre design major in college, worked many of the theaters in Boston and did private events as well. Amy had worked for Heather a couple of years out of art school, when she finally had to admit that the paying market for textile artists was not vast.

"Come work with me. Aren't you tired of slinging cheese yet?" Heather asked her repeatedly back then. Glimmer, Inc. was in its earliest days and just beginning to flourish. "Call me when you are."

Amy worked in the cheese department at the health food supermarket throughout college and a few years after graduation while "real" work eluded her. She told Heather no, no, no, believing her dream job would emerge. She knew it simply must.

Then one day: "Where is the soy mozzarella?"

Amy sank. Was that out of stock again? She walked over to the shelf. Empty.

"I'll check out back for you, ma'am." Amy slowly made her way across the store to the giant walk-in refrigerator shared by the cheese and dairy departments. No soy mozzarella. She stood inside the insulated walk-in, the cold penetrating the stiff white smock she wore, the whir of the motor masking all sound from the busy store outside the heavy metal door. She leaned against the shelf of milk, stared at some soft point in front of her eyes, seeing nothing in particular. The dairy guy came in and collected crates of milk on a two-wheeler.

"Hiding?" he said.

"Yes."

"Some asshole?"

Amy nodded. "Yup." She sighed, stood up straight and steeled herself.

The customer—as Amy foresaw—grew irate. "This item is almost never in stock." She spit malevolence. "I don't think you understand anything about the difficulty of dietary restrictions." Amy was accused of being inexcusably insensitive. She stood in silence, nodded sympathetically, apologized. She was not responsible for ordering (or not) any of their products. Finally, the woman left to complain to the store manager.

After that, Amy started working for Heather. It wasn't much yet—Glimmer, Inc. was just starting out. But it wasn't cheese. Amy often reflected on the funny things that lead life. In this instance, soy mozzarella. Who knew? A bland lump of terrible-tasting fake cheese led to the founding of Déguiser and everything that followed—the moves that are made, the wake they stir, the small ripples.

One lovely June day, at a wedding on the Cape, as Amy threaded electrical cord to power the lights that the staff of Glimmer, Inc. were setting in the apex, she suddenly saw the tent for what it was: a vast canvas. A blank, white breadth of space calling for grace, pleading for adornment.

Later, as Amy and Heather shared cold bottles of beer at a bar in Allston down the street from the apartment they had shared since college, Amy told her sister her business idea.

"What are you going to call it?" said Heather.

"Déguiser," Amy said. "It means 'to disguise' in French."

"You know French?"

"No. You know I took Spanish. I looked it up," said Amy.

"Ah."

"But do you get it?"

"Yeah—it's a totally great idea, Amy." Heather was twenty-six and Amy twenty-four and anything was possible.

These grand ballrooms and broad white tents where Amy and Heather worked were raw material, big white blank spaces waiting to be dressed up, to be made lovely.

"I tried to find a verb for 'dolled up,' but I don't think I understand enough French to get that right."

"You don't understand any French."

"I know *fromage*," Amy said. "But I used a French/English dictionary for this."

Heather nodded as she sipped her beer.

Amy looked at those blank spaces and corners and imagined vast amounts of cloth draped and gathered, gossamer and muted—a softening of the hard edges, a drawing in of the space, a gathering. And to make it beautiful.

"Think I'm pronouncing it right?"

"Probably," said Heather.

"What the hell do you know? You didn't take French, either!" She drank her beer and got quiet. "Am I crazy?"

Heather nodded yes but said, "Nope."

"What if no one wants this?"

"They will. If they want pin lights *just so* on their tables, they will want this. Anything to make the extraordinary moment just that much..." she paused to locate the word. "More," she said.

And Amy thought, *Isn't that what everyone wants?*

~~~

Amy and Heather lived just outside of Boston. Amy's home flanked the B line in Allston and Heather's the C line in Brookline—quick rides up the Green train from the city. A mere fifteen-minute walk lay between one of their respective homes and the other, each in brick-on-brick condos cobbled together in old brownstones. Amy was a sucker for old charm, and so was her sister. Cattail was less than a ninety-minute car ride from Boston, but the distance seemed vast. Not simply the vista—skyscrapers and concrete to yellow-green meadows and the sprawling endless ocean—but the sentiment that descended upon Amy when she was there. A calm that slid through her, like rain down a glass pane. A brief reprieve from her troubles and worries—deadlines and to-dos. When she was there, she was some smoother version of herself. She became sleek and light. More herself in some essential way than anyplace else.

The May sky was a saturated, unblemished blue and the sun warm on their faces with the late spring promise of summer lushness as Amy and Heather drew closer to Cattail.

"I love it when the sun shines on our day," said Amy.

The ocean burst out over the expanse of the horizon as they descended Old Pine Hill Road. Green hills spread out on either side, waiting for seed. The town, one part old families, steeped in salty history, and one part new money, was a beloved place—as beloved as Cattail. They thought it beautiful nearly beyond words. Amy could speak of it, yet never was certain the words didn't fall short of the feelings this expanse of sand and salted water, roving meadow, swaying marsh grass conjured. Grown up, it was still her idea of perfection. It was her home. Perhaps not her physical home, but her heart-home. That it was her home was a simple and unadorned knowing in her bones; in the way the seasons felt right and every view some form of sublime perfection. In the way nothing was missing. All was nameable without the necessity of words. It was the place she would reclaim again and again. It was the place that always called her back. She often reflected that if you are lucky, there is a place on Earth that says home to you. When your eyes are filled with this place, it is akin to religion. You get what is meant by "heaven." In this place, you are more you than you can understand or articulate. When the sun began setting and the beach cleared of people, the light at a particular slant, a singular butter color still sparkling on the waves, the air a touch cool, Amy would put on a long-sleeve shirt, and abide in perfect peace. It was *she*. She was *it*. Her soul clean, her heart slow and steady. It was her place. Her family's place.

They drove past the short stretch of shoreline that faced the open ocean. On a clear day, the Elizabeth Islands were visible and beyond them, the Vineyard. They both looked out over the water, the brown and green of the islands humped in the ocean.

Amy checked the clock as she switched the radio station to her favorite broadcast from Martha's Vineyard. "It's early," she said. "Want to go for a walk before we head over to the house?"

Heather, eyes still closed, nodded affirmatively and Amy followed the curve in the road that led past the shore lined with trailers and mobile summer homes, swung slightly north toward their beach. She parked the car and they got out and stretched their limbs.

Today, without their small children in tow, they had as much time as they wanted. They could walk all the way to the Point. They left their shoes in the car and walked the length of the graying wood boardwalk. When they reached its end, they swiveled their feet in the warm, soft sand, then walked down to the shore and tentatively allowed the water to flow over their feet.

"Oh!" Amy yelped. "Cold."

"Oh my God," Heather said and rolled her eyes, but smiled.

When they were kids, a walk down the shore always capped their beach days. They'd set out together just as the sun began to lose its intensity, while the people around them packed up to go home. Their leaving was how Amy knew the best part of the day was about to begin. People didn't know any better and missed it, but Amy and Heather and their mother did know better, so every day when the sun slanted its mid-afternoon angle, they headed down the shore on one of their long walks.

"Should we go for a walk and then pack up? We need to get home and start supper soon," Mom would say, her back to them as she shook sand from towels, tri-folded and stacked them on her chair.

They always left all their stuff. No one would touch it. And anyway, Mom never brought her wallet onto the beach. "We don't invite trouble," she said.

The breeze grew cool as the sun moved across the sky. The long-sleeve shirts they pulled over their bathing suits cut the afternoon breeze. The water moved in and out over their feet as they walked, and Amy and Heather told their mother about Alison at school who liked Jimmy, but he thought she was gross and he really liked Pam and she said she couldn't stand him, but, really, they believed she secretly liked him. They expanded upon theories about their classmates' behavior and then dismissed them as easily as they changed the topic of conversation to *what are we gonna have for supper, Mom?*

The sun was in their eyes on the way to the Point, but rested warm on their backs on their return.

A walk was a loved thing.

There were seagull tracks at the end of every day, when the beach had cleared of most people. The imprints crisscrossed, weaving complex patterns in the soft sand. Amy noticed them every day before their walk. She imagined the sound of the gulls' step on the sand as soft. She imagined the way the sand felt to the seagulls' feet, webbed and rubbery-looking.

Should we go for a walk? Mom always said, then stood up. She wore her long white button-down collared shirt. She reached into her little cloth bag and removed her coral lipstick, applied a coat to her lips. She didn't need a mirror. Her hands pulled off the cap and swiveled the coral cylinder up. Mom's hands were beautiful, delicate and seemingly fragile, but they weren't. When Amy learned about the hollowness of birds' bones, she thought immediately of her mother's hands. Light, like birds' bones. Flying, touching, walking lightly on sand. Mom's skin looked creamy pink against the white of her shirt and the white of her teeth in her coral smile. They walked to the shore together.

At the Point, the sand curved up to the right around the dunes. Tucked on the other side of the curve was the harbor. Sailing and fishing boats and tiny dinghies were tied to the weathered gray of the docks.

Along the way, they watched sandpipers dart in and out of the surf on their fast little stick legs. They scanned the shore for pretty shells and beach glass. They watched the sun sparkle on the waves. Listened to the surf, regular and strong like a solid heartbeat. They talked or they didn't. They laughed and splashed or they enjoyed the suspension of their voices. They didn't notice the time pass, except for the shift in the sunlight. They turned and went back, once they reached the Point.

When it first touched them, the water felt cold on their sun-warmed skin, but before they knew it their feet and shins became accustomed and the water felt comfortable and warm. The transition happened without making itself apparent; suddenly they'd simply be aware of the change. They never experienced the change itself.

Walks to the Point, once she'd reached adulthood, didn't feel much different to Amy, even if the topics of conversation seemed much weightier. She recalled that their childhood concerns felt important at one time, too. Amy could easily imagine looking back someday with Heather at their conversations and laughing for ever taking themselves so seriously.

"I love 'our day,'" Heather said now.

"Me, too," Amy said and threaded her arm through her sister's. "So," she said.

"What?" Heather looked over at Amy sharply. "Are you pregnant?" Her eyes were wide.

Amy laughed. "No! God, no."

"What then?"

"So," Amy repeated.

"Cut the crap!"

"I finally got my slides over to the gallery. They're considering me for a show."

"Amy! Holy shit! When?"

"Early fall, next year. But they want to see several more pieces..." Amy trailed off.

"So?"

"I don't know if I can get that much work finished in that amount of time. Between Déguiser and the kids, I mean, when will I get it done?"

"You have to. Somehow. You can do it. I can help with the kids whenever you need."

Amy squeezed Heather's hand. "I know. Thank you." She shook her head and squinted out over the water. "But still."

"No, 'but still' anything. I'm so excited for you! You've wanted this for so long."

When she first left art school, Amy worked on her pieces every free waking moment that she possessed. If she wasn't weaving or sewing, she was schlepping her portfolio up and down Newbury Street to all the galleries. And once she had a car, to any gallery in the limited driving distance of her old beater VW. She'd never made a dent in the Boston art scene. But that didn't mean she'd stopped trying.

Heather worked in theater, just as she always said she would. Maybe it wasn't Broadway and maybe she ran a side-business to supplement her theater work. But she did it—she never wavered in this vision of her future life. Amy had never been able to answer the question adults always lob at children: *what do you want to be when you grow up?* There was a time when she also wanted to do theater and Heather claimed that was only because Amy was copying. Which was exactly right, even if at the time Amy insisted Heather was wrong. At different points, she wanted to be a marine biologist, an orthodontist, a veterinarian and a ballet dancer. She discovered art on a school field trip to the Museum of Fine Arts in Boston. She walked by the paintings and many were lovely but it was a special exhibit of textile art that captivated her. The fabrics, ranging from gossamer chiffon to coarse gunny, textures and saturated or muted colors overlapped and integrated, and she was enchanted.

Amy finally knew what she wanted to be. And with passion.

They walked back from the Point enjoying the sun on their backs. As they walked slowly to the car, Amy felt the unavoidable hesitancy to walk away from the beach she had always experienced. Knowing she would always come back never made it easier to leave.

As they drove to their parents' cottage, Amy wiggled sand between her toes, and they rounded the sharp turn in the road that curved away from the shore, followed it to the sandy crushed-shell street that led to their parents' house. She parked the car along the line of grass and cut the engine. Gulls and the sounds of the surf replaced the noise of the engine and the car radio. Amy and Heather peered out the window.

"Whoa," Heather breathed.

"Holy shit," Amy said.

They got out and walked closer to the shell of the cottage. The old footprint was intact, but its new frame reached three stories into the blue, cloudless sky.

"There's nothing left but the basic shape," Amy said.

The cottage in its original form had been a single-floor, tiny weathered-shingle place. When Amy and Heather were children, their parents rented the cottage every summer for their family vacation. They bought the place, furniture and all, when the owner had finally had it with renters in summer and snow in general. He moved to Florida, a thing many old New Englanders did when they'd had enough of damp, raw winters by the ocean. Mom and Dad had rented it out a week at a time all summer and the rental fees paid the mortgage. But they always intended to make it their year-'round home one day. Their dreams were no longer wishes and visions, but solid beams, walls, roof.

"Where is everything?" Amy asked Heather. "The tables, the old sink...all of it."

"In that dumpster, I would assume." Heather tiptoed over and peered inside. "There's that old rickety table," Heather said. "Oh, and the nasty rag rug!"

"Nasty!" Amy exclaimed. She tiptoed to have a look, too. "Oh my God!"

There in the dumpster sprawled the odd eclectic collection of furniture and decor that had persisted forever. The mismatched tables that had lined the walls—one painted red, whole chips flaking off, revealing a turquoise coat underneath, another stained dark brown, yet another a light oak. The chairs with missing parts. But Amy had loved every disparate bit of it. Even the dubious living room decoration. "Y'know, girls, a lot of these..." Mom told them once, pausing, distaste shaping her face as she gazed up at the colored and striped buoys in the rafters of the living room, "...ornamentations are going when we renovate someday. People who aren't from the coast *like* this sort of thing, but I can do without the buoys and lobster traps." They were arrayed at odd angles and interwoven with heavy rope. They looked as though they'd just washed up haphazardly into the rafters from the sea.

On the floor had been a large, old braided rag rug. At one time it may have been brightly colored, but so many sandy, damp feet had mashed it to dull brown-gray, only glimpses of blue or red here and there revealed its one-time glory. All of it, rejected items from someone's basement or garage—the kind of furnishings that made up summer beach cottages.

There had been bedrooms enough for everyone in the back. Tiny little rooms with little extra space left once furniture was introduced. A person simply scooted around as best as she could. The walls in the living room were a warm honey color coated in shellac, so they gleamed and reflected the light. The bedroom walls were painted white boards. Not paneling; they looked like walls look before sheetrock was put up. Neatly spaced rows of two-by-fours coated with thick white paint. Shorter pieces of wood were nailed in to make small shelves here and there. There was no pattern or order to it. Books lined some of the shelves and on others were tucked seashells and rocks. Every bedroom had had different style stuff in it. The theme tying it all together: old.

Amy had loved every broken piece of furniture, every ugly decoration. "They are distinctive," she always said, to which both her mother and sister snorted. "Hey, who's the artist in this family?"

"Yeah, it's the artist in you and not the metathesiophobe in you who likes this junk!" said Heather.

"What in the world is that?" Amy said. Heather only cocked her head and raised a single eyebrow.

"Look it up."

"Isn't that what Lucy accused Charlie Brown of being? Afraid of everything?" said Amy.

"It's the fear of change."

"How do you know this?"

"I'm the smart one. You're the metathesiophobic one and I'm the smart one."

"I can think of other adjectives to describe you..."

"Girls..." Mom warned.

"We're being good, Mommy. We swear," said Heather.

But when Amy had looked at everything in the cottage, she'd felt right. Everything in its mysteriously good place. It was an unknowable thing, the kind of flawlessness she saw. The idea of it being changed, torn apart, made her ache.

Today, Amy stood on the grass near the crushed-shell road and viewed the bones of the renovated cottage in disbelief. It was all gone. She turned her attention to the small beach house next door where Mom and Dad were staying during the renovations. Music bellowed from its open windows. "Statesboro Blues," one of their all-time favorites, as Dad referred to it. Amy and Heather walked into the tiny kitchen where Mom waggled her bottom. She turned in time to the music and when her rotation brought her to face them, she waved her hands and yelled, "Hello, girls!" over the music.

As they greeted her, Amy looked out the window and saw their dad walking away from his garden. He wore worn, dirt-stained khakis and an old Grateful Dead T-shirt. And his battered old Red Sox cap. His olive skin was already well on its way to its smooth summer amber. She could hear his rich voice singing along. "Woke up this morning...," his singing voice was terrible. He didn't care. He loved to sing.

Amy loved it when he did. His gait was quick, and although he lacked in stature, he was thin and fit.

He walked into the kitchen. "Women!" he said and opened his arms wide.

"Daddy," Amy shook her head as she hugged him.

"You know, Pops, it's not actually better to say 'women' ironically than it is to call us 'ladies,'" said Heather. They may have trained him out of calling them "ladies," but now they got this instead.

"Your mother never gave me nearly as much trouble as you two." He pulled Mom close to him. Spun her to the music.

"I'll be your lady," she said. "I don't mind it one bit."

"M'lady," he bowed to her. He turned to his girls. "Did you take a look at the house?" He led them outside.

"What do you girls think?" Mom asked.

"It's so different," Amy said. "I mean, I can't even picture what it will be like."

"I can!" said Heather. She gazed up at the skeleton of the house, its newborn bones exposed to the familiar ocean air. "Space for everyone, gorgeous kitchen, TWO bathrooms! An up-to-code septic system. Lots of windows—it'll be like floating."

"Exactly!" said Mom.

"You don't like it, Amy?" said Dad.

She stared up at the house. She tried to remember everything she could about their old house and was sad to discover that it was already fading in her memory. Where did everything fit? All of the things in their just-right places? They were gone.

"Sweetheart? What do you think?" Mom repeated.

The buoys were gone, the braided rag rug, too. What she thought about was what was undone and erased. Never to be again.

~~~

There would be no more summer renters coming in and out every week, but every summer Saturday for years, Mom cleaned the cottage for the vacationing families—one family out at ten in the morning, another in at noon. Mom was precise about cleanliness, organization and the guidelines she recited to each new vacationing family.

She'd enumerate in her upbeat manner, as rapt women, their children buzzing excitedly around them, took her instruction. "Now, the septic is the original and it works, but this is an old place and things can get...temperamental." Her delicate way of informing them that if they weren't careful with flushing and showering, they might find themselves wading in their own sewage. She pointed out the amenities, which didn't take long, and asked them to be careful with the amount of noise they made.

"Many of those left in this little neighborhood are old-timers who live here all year. They don't possess a great deal of patience for drunken rowdiness," she'd say. It was a script Amy and Heather knew by heart. As they stood out of their mother's sight, Heather would mouth nearly word-for-word her mother's weekly speech, Amy stifling giggles. Heather could duplicate their mother's expressions and gestures. Amy's favorite part was when Heather pinched her face at the word *temperamental.*

Before the noon renters arrived, the family whose vacation was coming to an end turned over the keys to Mom and were bid farewell and told to *enjoy the rest of your summer*, most often after penciling themselves into Mom's planner for the same week next year.

Then the cleaning began.

No one possessed cleaning standards quite as sturdy as Mom's, which grew even more stringent when their own family vacation arrived. Amy was twenty before fully realizing that much of what her mother had taught her when it came to house cleaning was not necessarily the way most people went about it. Very few, actually. When they were kids, Amy and Heather griped, but some part of them liked to clean the cottage. By the time they were grown, they loved it, especially when it was time for their own vacation.

Even when they were kids, cottage cleaning was decidedly more fun than regular weekly home cleanings and vastly more fun than the seasonal cleanings imposed on them which Mom referred to as Spring Cleaning and Fall Cleaning.

"Girls, guess what we're going to do today?" Mom would say.

Her tone promising, the girls were immediately excited.

"What?" they asked together.

"Spring Clean the kitchen!" she'd announce. Capital S, capital C.

Cold dread coursed through Amy's blood. Hours of scouring cabinets with Murphy's Oil Soap, vacuuming the walls with that brush attachment for which normal people never found a use, toothbrushes scrubbing metal handles. Hours would pass with no detail going unconsidered.

When they were growing up, this happened in every room. Twice a year.

Every fall, Amy and Heather groaned. Fall Cleaning.

"We just did this in May, Mom."

"Things gets really dirty over the summer with the windows open all day." She said the same thing in spring about the windows being closed all winter.

As children, the girls vowed they would never subject their own offspring to the rituals of Spring and Fall Cleaning.

Mom's cleaning methods did not diminish over the years and were as hardy as ever once her daughters were grown, married and mothers themselves. When the first Saturday of their vacation arrived, Amy and Heather's children were left with their fathers, the men given strict orders to arrive no sooner than noon. The women needed quiet, undistracted time to clean.

"And if you're a little later than noon, all the better," Mom told them.

Amy brought a radio from home—the same one she'd had since college. Then they battled it out over which CD they'd play while they cleaned. Every year their cleaning ritual the same.

"It's my year to choose!" Mom declared every year.

"It cannot be your year every year."

"I gave you life, can't you at least listen to *Eat A Peach* in return? That one came out smack in the middle between your births."

"I am the one who keeps track and, sorry Mommy-dear, but it's Heather's year."

"Yay! Okay, no *Eat A Peach* for you, Mommy-dearest!" said Heather.

Mom protested loudly. "Please no Guns and stinkin' Roses!"

"Nope," Heather said as she popped a CD in the player and pressed the play button. "But..." she said as a slide-guitar keened through the speakers. "How about *At Filmore East*?"

Mom cackled and waggled her bottom. "You're a good, good daughter!"

They started with the kitchen and the bathroom. Their reasoning: get the worst over with first. Most renters left the cottage at a typical level of disarray and griminess. Usual amounts of sand and seaweed gathered in corners of the shower and bathroom floor. The sink, a little toothpaste-speckled. The toilet, a little dingy. The kitchen floor needed a wash, the counters and stove needed a wipe-down and the white ceramic sink contained little particles of food stuck here and there.

They surveyed the damage. *Not too bad*, Amy always thought. "Could be a lot worse," Heather always murmured to her as they stood in the kitchen. Mom emerged from the bathroom, her nose puckered.

"Would you ever leave a place in this condition?" she always muttered. She grabbed three pairs of rubber gloves, handed out a pair each to Amy and Heather and donned a pair herself. "Let's get going. I'll get at that bathroom, you two work in here."

This was the price for two glorious weeks each year. *I can live with this arrangement*, Amy thought, but only after Mom's final approval of their efforts.

Amy scrubbed out the fridge, Heather worked at the sink, a challenge since there was no mixer on the kitchen plumbing—only a choice between scalding her hands or freezing them.

"Did you think it'd turn out like this, Heather?" Amy asked her sister once as they cleaned the cottage for their two weeks together.

"Like what?"

"I don't know. Everything. All this."

"I don't know. I guess I never planned out things as much as you did."

As she scrubbed out the fridge, Amy thought back to college when she took the Peter Pan bus from Boston to Providence to visit Heather. It was the farthest and longest they'd ever been apart. Frequent visits were arranged, as often as their meager budgets could sustain the cost of a bus ticket. Sometimes it meant ramen noodles for a week, sometimes the phone bill had to be neglected for a bit. Because not visiting wasn't an option.

Heather had the same dorm room all four years, while Amy moved around more often. Heather's room looked lived-in—felt settled. Amy liked going to see her.

Heather would meet Amy at the bus station with a borrowed car. Bundled up against the cold in scarf, mittens, fluffy hooded parka, Heather bounced from foot to foot outside the bus. Always one of the first off, Amy bounded down the stairs and the girls embraced as though they hadn't seen each other in ages. They drove toward campus, stopping for a six-pack and a pizza to bring back with them.

It was just after New Year's when classes had resumed from winter break.

"It's so freakin' cold!" Heather said.

"No shit. God, it's hard to even remember the beach right now. How're your classes going?"

It was Heather's final semester. "Fine. But I wish to shit I'd gotten my stupid language requirement out of the way sooner."

"I thought you liked languages?" Amy asked her.

"I do, I just have so much else to do and memorizing verb conjugations always gets last priority. How 'bout you?"

"Fine," Amy shrugged.

They were quiet for a moment, their breath visible as they exhaled in the cold car. It was dark on the roads from the bus station to the campus once they left the city. No cars passed by as they floated together over the roads, in shared silence.

"Didn't you think this would be more exciting or something?" Heather said into the silence. "It was at first. But everything gets normal." She seemed disappointed.

"Yeah, I know. You're lucky, though—you're almost done," Amy said.

"True, but then it's the real world..." she joked, but Amy recognized an apprehension in her voice.

They pulled up to the dorms and parked the car. Amy started to get out, but Heather placed a mittened hand on her arm to stop her. Amy turned her head to face her.

"What?"

"Let's just never be regular, Amy." Heather was very serious.

"Regular?"

"You know, like everybody else. Like we never had dreams. Like we never sat around saying what we really wanted."

"You mean settle."

"Yeah. I guess," she answered.

Amy smiled. "I promise." They went inside, drank beer, ate pizza and dreamed up the future, gossiped the present.

Amy thought about those younger times as she cleaned out the sticky fridge.

"God, what do these people do in here?" she asked. "Come look, I'm serious. Mom's got to see this. Mom!" Amy called.

"What is it?" Mom called back in a muffled voice.

"C'mere."

Amy and Heather laughed at their mother's revulsion to the brown, impossibly sticky spot. "What the hell is it?" They took turns scrubbing it out and moved on to the living room and bedrooms, vacuuming, changing linens.

"How can so much sand end up in here?" Mom asked no one in particular. "Don't they brush off before coming in?" It did not require an answer. You were supposed to take a beach towel and run it over your legs and feet before you went in the house. Simple.

"Not everyone is as smart as we are, Mommy," said Amy. "Maybe you should offer a class."

"You could call it 'Beach Cottage Maintenance and Etiquette: Creative Ideas for Keeping the Sand Where It's Supposed To Be,'" said Heather.

"Oh! And, 'Innovative Uses for Vacuum Attachments 101.'"

"'Q-Tips: They're Not Just for Ears! That might be graduate level...'"

"Brats," said Mom. "You mock me but I know you appreciate the lack of sand in your bed sheets."

Amy couldn't deny that there were the simple ways life was supposed to be lived. And those things were never supposed to change.

~~~

Now Amy stood in the yard in the shadow of the new heights and depths of the cottage.

"Are you sure you don't want to stay for lunch, girls?" Mom said. "I have a nice pasta salad and grilled fish." Mom's food was always nice.

"Have you spent any time with that salad, Mom? How do you know for sure it's genuinely nice?" Heather would say.

"I heard that 'nice' soup committed at least two felonies and never calls its mother on Mother's Day," Amy would say.

Today, Amy said, "Thanks, Mom, but..."

Her mother cut her off, "Yes, I know. That pasta salad is truly an asshole and cheats on its taxes."

Amy and Heather laughed. "I was going to say we're craving fish and chips."

"Alright," said Mom and she gave them each a hug and a kiss.

Amy knew without asking that Heather loved the new house. She never shied from new things—she embraced them. She was the one who thought up new ideas. Amy initially rejected them and then, once accepted, clung to them more and more fiercely year after year. Amy liked the worn-in grooves of their childhood. She liked the worn-in grooves of her life now.

After they left their parents and the new house, Amy and Heather stopped at their favorite summer place and shared a platter of fish and chips between sweating glasses of beer.

"I love it," Heather said.

Amy knew Heather meant the house. She asked, "The beer or the fish and chips?"

"Both. But I meant the house. It's going to be something else."

"Yes, it is."

"I knew you'd freak out about this!" she teased. "But I'll bet you'll love it when it's done. Imagine all the space? A toilet that works. Two toilets that work! Even you must be happy about that one."

Amy sighed. "Yeah. I just..."

"I know," she said. "We'll make a whole new thing of it and then you'll love it."

"I don't want to go through the process!" Amy whined.

"You are so fussy." She dipped a piece of fish in tartar sauce. "Just think of all the stuff you love now that you resisted at first."

"You make me sound like such a freak."

"Middle school, high school, college, new babysitters, new couch, color television, every different haircut I ever got, skinny dipping..." she listed.

"Okay, okay," Amy said. "You are hilarious." But she couldn't help but smile.

Heather was right, of course. Amy did eventually come around to new things and most of Heather's brainstorms. And she had to admit that some of them turned into traditions she grew to love. Like the tradition of skinny dipping.

Heather came up with it when they were teenagers on vacation. "Tomorrow morning let's get up early and go for a swim before breakfast."

They whispered in the dark of the cottage, from the small bedroom they shared.

"Okay," Amy said.

They slipped out early the next morning before their mom and dad woke. They carried towels over their arms, their bathing suits on under sweatpants and baggy shirts.

They giggled.

"Shhhhhhh!" which only made them giggle more. A tickling feeling that started in the belly and moved into the throat, came out and tingled around the face.

"Come on!" They closed the door quietly and skipped across the dew-wet grass, followed the stone and crushed-shell road to the tarred street that led to the beach.

"You have to get right in," Heather warned. "Promise." Amy dipped her toe at the edge of the surf.

"Frigid," she stated.

"Promise."

"Oh, fine."

They shed their clothes, Amy steeled herself and they ran without stopping into the water, dived in, emerged laughing. She floated on her back, the air a touch cool, the sun beginning its rise. The water was warm against the chilly morning air. Amy floated on her back, her ears underwater, her face cradled by the surface. Heather splashed her and she popped up.

"Hey!" Amy splashed her back. She floated on her stomach. "This was a good idea, Heather."

"Those are the only kind I ever have." Amy guffawed at that. "I have another one," she grinned. "Let's skinny dip."

Amy looked up and down the beach. Deserted. But still. "No way! What if someone sees us?"

"Who's around?"

"Well, no one, but what if someone comes?"

"Well, what if no one does?"

"Ugh. You drive me crazy!"

"Just do it!"

"Fine! But if we get caught I am going to kill you."

They tugged and snapped at their suits underwater, triumphantly held them up over their heads. The suits dripped back down at them. They gripped them tightly in one hand as they swam around. Heather mooned Amy and she laughed in a big mouthful of salt water, choked and laughed some more.

It was free and luscious and they didn't want to get out. Finally they did after wrestling their bathing suits back on underwater, laughter making the task more difficult. Reluctantly, they headed back to the cottage.

The skinny dipping became a tradition. At least once every year while on vacation, they'd creep away, leaving babies sleeping. Over the years, they found a perfect spot where huge boulders protruded from the sand in the shallows, providing perfect cover. Eventually they stopped bothering with the pretense of suits and wore cotton pants and loose T-shirts over their naked bodies. When they emerged from the water, they'd pull the clothes over their wet bodies, hair dripping. The pants stuck to their legs in patches, their bodies almost dry by the time they reached the cottage to start breakfast.

"Admit it—you like all those things now, right?" said Heather.

"Well, a couple of those haircuts never grew on me...No pun intended."

"Said the woman who's had the same hairstyle since third grade."

They drove home as the sun set and the top of the sky colored itself a deep indigo speckled with stars, dimly illuminated by a sliver moon. Heather drove and Amy grew sleepy as the mild May evening air blew in through the car window and the lights of the city grew closer.

She genuinely tried for a moment to imagine that new house her parents were building. She could draw no concrete images. She tried and instead her mind was only clear and dark. No sliver of moonlight to illuminate. She thought, *maybe I just don't want to see.*

~~~

The large industrial elevator shuddered as it slowly climbed the three flights to the top floor of the old mill building that housed Déguiser. Amy opened the door to her studio. It was early—the sun just rising up and flowing through the floor-to-ceiling windows that ran along two full walls of the corner unit. Amy was lucky, but only in retrospect. Everyone had thought she was crazy to rent this space several years ago when it was empty and newly retrofitted as artists' studios.

Even Heather had been skeptical. "An abandoned mill on the sketchy edge of Charlestown. Seriously, Amy? There are all kinds of places for the murderers and rapists to hide in here," she said as she peered around corners in the hallway.

"Yeah, but wait until you see it," Amy said, unlocking the door. The morning light poured in over the pitted wide-board wood floors. The ceiling stretched two stories high. Exposed brick and ductwork decorated the walls and ceiling.

Amy walked briskly to the wall to their left, the one with no windows. "I'll line up rolling rack after rolling rack for my fabrics here," she motioned along the wall with her hands. "Then when there's an event, all I have to do is roll the rack to the elevator, push it to the loading dock and onto the van!" She felt triumphant. "There's space for our office over here," Amy walked to the corner, "and I can install a huge cutting table here and my sewing machine here," she pointed and smiled largely. "And the rent is dirt-cheap."

"Yeah, it's great, but you'll be all alone here."

"I have Matt now." Matt had just left his job downtown to run the business end of Déguiser. He hated that job downtown, but this was scary, this leap they were taking. Exhilarating and terrifying. "Since when am I the adventurous one?"

Heather laughed. "You're right—it's fantastic. There is space in my building, though. You know, if you wanted to come over to Back Bay."

Amy shook her head. "I can't afford it. Plus I need way more space than you do. My inventory is already huge and it's only going to grow. My stuff needs more space than your stuff." At that point, the small apartment she shared with Matt was stuffed with the yards and yards of fabric she used to transform the mundane into the beautiful. Not that the Park Plaza or Copley Square Hotel ballrooms were dull—far from it—but she added the softness, the romance. The ambiance. It was as if, for one magical and lovely moment, the outside world absolutely mirrored the inside. And the other way around.

"And you can do your art here, too," said Heather.

"And I can do my art here, too!"

Now, the building was full, with a lengthy waiting list. Amy heard that artists tried to keep tabs on the inner scoop about which business might be ready to bite the dust. Or which artist.

Amy was still one of the first to arrive most mornings, so at the early hour, it almost felt like those early days when she was the only one. She was grateful every day for listening to her instincts on this place.

She had a lot to do today. Along with weddings and holiday events, Déguiser had expanded into bar and bat mitzvahs, baptisms, engagement parties, extravagant birthday parties, baby showers even. Today Amy had meetings with two mothers, one for a sweet sixteen party and the other a high school graduation. Almost no one possessed moderate perspective when it came to these milestone events of their lives. So she had to offer them some balance while equally honoring the magnitude of the event from her clients' point of view.

Along with the meetings, Amy had fabric to prepare for the three weddings scheduled for the weekend, four days away.

She was deep in the racks of voile when she heard Matt come in. "Amy?" he called out. "I have coffee!"

He dropped the girls off to the sitter and then joined Amy at their space, always with her second cup of coffee. Decaf, since she was still nursing Sage. They had made this arrangement because the girls cried less when he dropped them off and so did Amy. In this manner, the heavy guilt Amy felt for leaving them to come to work was lightened somewhat. While Matt came to Déguiser every day, Amy crammed her work into three days, doing some at home if necessary. That was the most she could bear to be away from her girls. The worst thing mothers ever told their daughters was that they could do it all. The worst thing peers told women was that they must. This is where Amy—and she certainly was not alone—found herself, wanting two disparate things equally desperately. She had no idea how to balance career and motherhood. No one else did, either, although that was nothing but cold comfort.

She was grateful to Matt for gifting her this small reprieve from the joyous and painful tearing of motherhood.

Amy crawled out from under all that soft, sheer fabric, her hair a frizzy tangle, and made her way to the office. Matt placed her coffee in her hand.

"Hello," she said. She caught a glimpse of herself in the mirror. "Oh, lord," she said, touching her hair. "I've got a mom coming in about a sweet sixteen and look at me!"

He smoothed it out a little. "Looks fine." She took his hand in hers.

The sun had fully risen, the morning light angled in through their big windows. Nothing was easy but some things were certain. In that moment, she wanted for nothing.

Sanctuary.

Those small spaces or broad places of sand, of salt water, of curtained windows, of a cherished laugh, of a mother's cool hands on warm foreheads and round bellies and in between shoulder blades. A room. A closet. A boat. A liquid. In stories told and not told; written and not written. Behind closed eyes. Cracked-wide heart. Truest, wisest, open self. Fearless.

This is called safe haven.

Safe Harbor

Each spring, Amy tried to be mindful of the blooming lilacs. They were the sweetest and shortest aspect of the season, or perhaps seemed so since she loved them so dearly. Their buds slow to form, slower to open; their scented presence a blink. And if she failed to make the time to pay attention, the purple would have disappeared into the green and she would have missed it. This past spring she had been busy, and, as happened too often, the lilacs came and went and she could not recall having really noticed them except in passing. Even of that she could not be sure. Was it merely a memory from some other year?

I am too busy, Amy thought. She found herself in a constant state of thinking—of things that needed to be done, that were not getting done, lists and spiraling priorities. *There is always too much to do*, she thought. Whenever her thoughts steered toward that which she needed to accomplish, they never failed to follow into a wash—sometimes shallow and other times vast—of anxiety. Her work, the care of her children, the care of her home and always relegated to the back-burner, her art.

All of it together seemed impossible to balance. Presence in her own life was often hampered by the nagging list of things to be done, even as she craved it and yearned to be living now with her two small daughters, the anxiety of keeping everything going crept in to tarnish those moments, a black smudge. She tried to hug her babies often, inhale their scents, touch their bare skin and hair, listen to them talk to her and watch them sleep. She hoped that something of the essence of their being would stay with her, especially in the spaces where memory might fail, some impression of them would remain, intangible but very real. Then she wouldn't feel she had missed everything once they were grown and gone. She attempted never to make up for some dearth of a genuine feeling of presence by attempting to capture the salient moments digitally. The Internet was bloated with all the ways mothers should document then display those bits of their children's lives, but she ached for something more visceral.

Too often her life resembled a bag of slippery satin ribbon—lovely in its array of bright colors, but prop the silky mass up in one area and it drooped in another. Grant attention to the slack and she'd drop that which she'd just shored up.

And there was the ever-present worry that she simply wasn't measuring up—not getting any of it right. This one exact and elusive right way to do every single thing to ensure—what? Nothing she thought of precisely as perfection. More like some evasive rightness upon which everything hinged in some crucial and precarious way. It was a puzzle she could not solve, which made it even more worrisome. Yet she forged on as if the forward motion alone would lead her to the answer.

"You worry too much," Heather told her.

"That is not helpful."

"Perhaps not, but it is true."

"That isn't helpful, either."

"You need to stop and smell the roses."

"Holy shit, did you just say that?"

"A journey of a thousand miles begins with the first step," Heather quoted.

"What?"

"You can only do what you can do. Stop freaking out."

"I know you mean to be helpful..."

"A spoon full of sugar helps the medicine go down."

"Now you're just saying things."

"Haste makes waste! A bird in the hand is worth two in the bush! Put one foot in front of the other!"

"That last one's from a Christmas cartoon."

And so, Amy had mostly missed the lilacs this year. Except for one moment.

In the car, in transit, seemed to be one of the times her mind slowed and she was able to fill the present space fully. She was grateful that both of her children still napped and there were times in the car going from one place to another when they dozed off, their sleepy heads tipped over, necessitating a longer ride for the sake of a lengthy rest. "Snooze cruise" she and Heather called these car rides. Held captive in her car by her sleeping children, Amy settled into a quietness of mind and spirit. The voices of talk radio whispered through the speakers and she drove aimlessly, the only goal to prolong sleep.

One rainy day in the recent spring, in the liminal moment before summer came rolling in, head over feet, Amy was on a snooze cruise up through the twisting back roads of Brighton, past the green of Boston College, through Newton and then a loop back to their brownstone in Allston. It was one of the last cool and wet days of spring when the sky was milky all day, and from that sky drifted a pervasive mist that insisted its damp way into everything. The green had been sprouting for weeks but she was only beginning to take notice with a sudden realization that spring had indeed arrived—not the hope of it or the promise, but the green reality. And the wet coating over all those varied greens of the trees and flowering shrubs and the flush of soft grass on the lawns of the houses, that mist made the green seem more so. The green, densely hued, up against the soft white of the sky which draped itself in all the open spaces, wide and narrow. It occurred to her that it was easy to see the prettiness of the world on a sunny, blue-skied day. The kind with harmless, white-fluffed clouds floating through. But this—this wet green, this milk and gray sky—the kind of day that is often simply endured, evoked its own loveliness and truth.

And then she noticed that the purpled buds of the lilacs were wide open. Amy told herself she would remember to smell them. She would stop her car on a sunny day when the children were not asleep and push her face into the soft, sweet buds. She would pluck a small branch and share the smell with her daughters and then take it home, put the flowers in a jar and place it on the kitchen table.

But then she forgot or grew too busy, or some combination of both.

Maybe that one moment of seeing will be enough, she thought. It would have to be because suddenly it was late June.

Summer rolled in under the door, cool and dewy in the mornings, growing hot and sultry as it stretched out its drowsy arms across the days. Another summer. And now Amy's daughters were three and one.

She sat in her kitchen and nursed Sage who had just woken up for the day. Amy hummed to her, as a cool breeze floated in from Commonwealth Avenue. The trolley rounded the corner noisily and Sage pointed toward the window and with wide eyes said, "T'ain."

"Yes, train," said Amy. Sage closed her eyes and resumed nursing.

Rachel tottered into the kitchen, her feet clicking against the tile. Amy wondered at the sound and turned to look. This morning, Rachel wore pink plastic high heels and a bridal veil with her pajamas. "Wow. Very understated," Amy said. She had wanted girls. She wouldn't have said it but it had been her secret wish. Boys would have been loved equally, but little girls were what she dreamed of. She brushed Rachel's bare arm with the backs of her own fingers simply to touch her little girl skin.

"I want yogurt and granola for supper," Rachel said.

Amy stood, placed Sage on the floor and handed her several wooden spoons to keep her busy. "Breakfast," Amy said automatically, moving to the refrigerator.

"Breakfast," Rachel repeated.

"Can you think of a better way to ask?" Amy said as she spooned yogurt into a bowl.

"Please."

"Peeeeeeease," Sage echoed. "Pease pease pease," and she tapped the wooden spoons together.

Amy handed Rachel the bowl with a flourish.

"But, Mommy. I need the other bowl," she wailed.

"Well, this one's good, right? It's the nice flowery one."

A howl, "Nooooo!" Amy sighed as the phone rang. She picked it up on the third ring, grabbed Sage from the floor, placed the baby on her hip. Amy took the offending bowl from Rachel.

"Hello? Hi! What am I doing? I'm glad you asked—I'm happily transferring yogurt from one bowl to another for my eldest child. Right—wrong bowl first time. Sage has eaten. She is satisfied with all the utensils and bowls I pick out—at least for another few months. We'll be ready soon." Amy placed the baby on the clean kitchen floor and moved to the counter where the open cooler sat, the phone cradled at her neck. "Cooler's just about packed. See you in an hour." Amy hung up the phone. She packed sandwiches for herself, and for Rachel, raisins and crackers, and yogurt for Sage. Fruit for all of them. Amy placed everything in the cooler purposefully. She felt small hands on her calves. Sage said, "Up, up." Amy reached down and lifted her baby to her hip. She wrinkled her nose at Sage. "Can you make funny face for Mama?" Sage puckered her lips tightly and wrinkled her nose. Amy laughed. "Mama!" Sage exclaimed and buried her face in Amy's neck.

"Mommy, what're you doing?" Rachel asked.

"Getting ready for the beach, sweetie. Are you finished with your yogurt?" Rachel nodded. Amy took the bowl, rinsed it and placed it in the dishwasher, then steered Rachel down the hall to her room. She wrestled the wriggling, protesting baby into a bathing suit while supervising Rachel's clumsy attempts at dressing herself.

"Legs in first. Now pull it over your bum. Right. No. Okay, here; let me help a little."

"I can do it myself!" she hollered.

"I know you can do it yourself, but Auntie Heather will be here to get us in a minute."

"I have to go pee-pee," she said. Of course. She was fully dressed. If Heather had already been there, they would have laughed. Amy sighed but smiled at her little girl. She peeled off Rachel's layers of clothes, put her on the toilet and waited. "Auntie Heather has the good toilet paper," Rachel said.

"Good toilet paper?"

"Yeah. It's fancy. I like Auntie Heather's toilet paper."

Amy heard a beep from out front. She ran to the kitchen, opened the window and called to her, "Be down in a sec!" The first time Amy saw Heather's van she laughed. A minivan. "We always said 'never.' And look at this thing!"

"It'll hold everyone," Heather had declared. It did, with a load of baby seats of varying sizes strapped in the back.

Amy managed her beach stuff and her children down the two flights of stairs to the carriage road outside her brownstone. She slid open the van door and three little faces turned toward her.

"Hi, guys!" she said to Heather's children. Three more little girls: Lauren, Amber and baby Tara. Heather loaded Amy's beach stuff at the back. Rachel scrambled expertly into her seat. Amy tucked Sage into hers, turned and threaded Rachel's arms through the straps, ending the task with a kiss. "I want to click it," she declared, as she did every time she got into the car. Amy helped her without being obvious about it. "Good job!" she said when Rachel worked the clasp. She slid the door closed and hopped into the front seat, leaned over and kissed Heather.

"Hello."

"Hi. How're you?"

"Better now! Is Mom meeting us there?"

"I'm not sure. I didn't actually talk to her. But she's always there." The chatter in the backseat quieted as the children drifted and bobbed into sleep.

"Car coma," Amy sighed.

"Shall we drive forever?" Heather said, looked over at Amy and smiled. They rode on in silence, the familiar roads washing over them, their body memories swaying with every curve.

They parked in the south lot and set about maneuvering everyone onto the beach. Laurel, Amber and Rachel, the three upright children, were put to work carrying the lightest, least breakable items. Into a red wagon the babies, Sage and Tara, were packed with towels and soft diaper bags. Heather pulled it with one hand and carried two beach chairs in the other. Amy managed whatever was left and steered the kids and they made their way to their spot in the sand. Mom was already there, reading a book, sunglasses perched on her face. Her bare feet had dug out little holes in which to rest themselves.

"There's Mom," Amy said, gesturing with her chin. "By the way. What fancy toilet paper do you buy?"

"Fancy toilet paper?"

"Yes. Apparently my child likes your brand more than ours."

She laughed. "It's the kind with the little flowers sort of puffed on it."

"Right."

"Grammy!" one of the children called. She turned and waved, got up and helped the girls haul the stuff. They opened their chairs in line with Mom's, set up their babies and their stuff.

Amy and Heather's bare feet dug out their own little holes in which to rest themselves.

~~~

Amy left home when the sun was just rising on a Sunday. She left her sleeping husband and babies, and drove to Déguiser. She rode the wobbling elevator that made many nervous, yet always reached its destination, and opened her studio door. She locked it behind her and headed straight for the enormous work table. She tenderly touched the fabric she was embroidering for her latest piece. Most of her pieces were large—around ten feet by twelve feet—but this piece was smaller. It was so delicate. It confounded her, with its size and its sharp departure from her usual large, exuberant work. She liked color clashing and merging. This was watercolor-washed silk, opaque yet sheer. She had no clear plan for it.

She was enjoying the tension of not knowing where it was going. Being an artist was everything and nothing like she imagined it would be when she started out.

She and her college friends once believed they were going to change the world. They possessed endless energy toward this endeavor and unwavering confidence in the possibility that it could be achieved. She participated in long, beer-soaked conversations about how it would be accomplished with paint, with clay, with a fuck-society-as-we-know-it bravado.

Changing the world.

Heather thought they were crazy.

"Change what? How are you going to do that?" She tipped her bottle of beer back to her mouth, emptied it.

When Amy wasn't visiting Heather in Rhode Island, Heather was visiting Amy in Boston. Always there was a group of college girls sitting cross-legged on the floor of one or another's room, incense burning at the cracked-open window, ashtray in the center of the circle gradually filling, mini-fridge in the corner packed with beer. Candles burned, a lava lamp bubbled, music from the sixties in the CD player. They were hippies, twenty years after.

They were going to set the world on fire.

"No patchouli," Heather barked into the phone before getting on the bus in Providence. "I will leave if anyone lights up patchouli."

When they sat in a circle, Heather was one of them even in her sporty clothes that rubbed up against Amy's friends' gauzy skirts and thin, colorfully patched jeans. Heather had cut her long hair into a short softly curled strawberry blond bob she kept tucked behind her ears. Little wisps always escaping, so she was forever tucking, tucking, tucking. The gesture had become a part of her natural motion. She got up to get another beer. URI in white block letters stretched down the right leg of her sweats, vibrant against the navy blue fabric. Her right hand pushed a stray strand of hair into place, her thumb curled against the length of her jaw. One deft, unthinking motion. Amy watched her move across the room, her small, wiry frame so much like Amy's own. In motion, Heather was all energy snapping to escape through her limbs. She strode, strong and lissome. Amy measured her own movements, of fluid or fire—subtle, slipping around like a shadow.

"You girls talk about this all the time. How, precisely, do you hope to achieve it?" She twisted the cap off her beer, deftly tossed it across the room into the waste basket, and sank down to the floor, legs crossed, all grace.

"Well, Heather, someone has to do it," said one of the girls, echoing the collective voice. "AIDS, nukes, suburban bullshit, mindless drones running the show..."

"You have that power?" Heather teased. "That's a lot of pressure, holding the world in your hands like that." She took another sip of beer.

"You're an artist, too," one of the girls said.

"Theatre," she barked. "Not some artsy-fartsy bullshit. Not that I don't like art. I just don't take myself so seriously."

"Right. Thespians never take themselves seriously!"

Once Amy started walking Newbury Street, she realized changing the world with scraps of fabric might be more difficult than she'd imagined. And they surely did not pay the rent.

When Amy began working with Heather, she'd take the T to Glimmer, Inc. and use the studio to spend her mornings working on her textile pieces. Afternoons and evenings were for productions and parties. Amy loved the cool early summer mornings. The sun just warm enough to chase the chill from her skin. On those sunny mornings, as cars and buses began jamming the streets, she left her apartment early for the luxury of leisurely making her way to work, coffee in hand.

In those lean days, a trip to the small second-run movie theater in Back Bay was Amy's favorite guilty pleasure. She could scarcely afford it—even with the half-rate ticket prices—but it was worth it. She couldn't afford the snacks, though—that would have been too strenuous a blow to her meager budget—and carefully sneaked in her own. Sometimes she went by herself and other times Heather accompanied her when she could get away from work.

"You sneak candy into the movies?" Heather stage-whispered at her. "Shame on you!"

"Sssshhhhhh!" Amy looked around furtively. "Be quiet."

"Why? Because you snuck food into the movies? You're not supposed to do that, right?" She poked Amy. "Right?" She poked her again. "You never used to do things like this. What happened to you? And what have you got in there?" She dug her hand in Amy's bag and rustled the contents around.

"Stop!" Amy hissed. "Must you always embarrass me?"

"Yes, I must."

"I wouldn't have to do this if my boss paid me halfway decent," Amy said.

"You shouldn't badmouth your boss. Give me some of that."

"'Shame on you,' my ass," Amy said, handing over a Reese's.

One hot afternoon, Amy went to the theater alone. She dropped into one of the worn velvet seats, and closed her eyes as the air conditioning cooled and dried her hot, sweaty skin. She sighed and settled in. As the projector began rolling, she heard a pop followed by a cranking sound. It was slightly squeaky. Then the strong smell of fish. She looked to her right.

"Is that tuna?" she whispered.

A young guy turned to her. "No," he shook his head. "Salmon."

"Canned salmon?"

He nodded. He ate it straight from the can with a spoon.

"I never thought of that as movie food," Amy said.

"It's really good for you. It has lots of calcium. From the bones—they grind them right in."

She nodded. *Who eats canned salmon at the movies?* she thought. She couldn't help but peek looks at him until the lights came on and she realized that as cute as he seemed in the light from the screen, he was even cuter in the bright light of day.

"He brought canned salmon to the movies?" Heather asked her later at work.

"Yes, but he's really cute. We're going out next weekend."

"I can't wait to meet this guy."

"You're going to love him."

At Amy and Matt's wedding, Heather fashioned a wedding cake from canned salmon, the pink labels and serious-looking fish on the can lined up perfectly, a little bride and groom perched on top, awash in pink light. She denied it was her doing, but Amy knew better.

Once Matt started working with Amy at Déguiser, they were usually home by five-thirty and some days earlier. They ate supper together, played with the kids and put them to bed. The timing of their events allowed them this togetherness, even if Amy had to leave later in the evening to strike a party or wedding. She would slip out and slip back in, the girls never the wiser, Matt caring for them in her absence. Déguiser had staff now, so gone were the days when Amy and Matt were doing everything on their own. Theirs was a version of the life Amy had always envisioned. She and Matt had made it a reality and sometimes she felt lucky and other times she felt a bit self-righteous, as though she had gotten it all just exactly right. She was slightly embarrassed to admit this even—and only—to herself.

Late afternoon. Summer breeze through her kitchen curtains.

She watched her babies play together out of the corner of her eye. She didn't want to intrude on them straight on.

"Okay. So I'm making the houses," Rachel said to Sage, and pointed to herself. Sage looked up at her from the middle of a large pile of blocks. She held one in each hand, tapped them together, put them down. She picked up two different blocks.

"You're the mommy of this baby." Rachel shoved a doll at Sage, swiped the blocks from her hands. Sage screamed.

"But I'm trying to make the houses," Rachel said loudly and slowly at Sage.

Amy sponged the counter, let them solve it. If it got too loud, she would intervene. Their mom had always jumped in when Amy and Heather bickered, just as they were in the midst of working things out. Amy clearly remembered wondering why Mom was aggravated with them. They were simply talking.

Amy heard the front door.

"Hello!" Matt called. Amy walked to him and hugged him hard. His bag fell to the floor with a thud.

"I thought we'd do a picnic supper at the beach," she said.

"Cool. You didn't go today?" It was one of her weekly days off.

"No. It was too late after the pediatrician." Annual visits for both.

"Oh, that's right. Everything fine?" Amy nodded. She watched as Matt tossed Sage into the air, kissed Rachel on the head. "Daddy!" she said. Sage said, "Dadadadadadada."

Whenever she remembered to take in the moment, she simply stood back and watched. She marveled at how she got here. Here. Here in this spot, in this kitchen with these people. Matt, tall and slim with his curly honey hair and two babies out of the blue. She stood there wondering how much she had to do with making all this, knowing everything, everything.

"I have hummus and veggie roll-ups for anyone who wants to go to Cattail with me," Amy said.

"And cookies?" Rachel said.

"Cookie!" exclaimed Sage with a huge tooth-baring grin.

"Maybe. Or maybe a different special treat later," Amy said mysteriously. She bent down and whispered close to their faces.

"Ice cream?" Rachel whispered.

"Maybe," Amy shrugged her shoulders. "Who knows? Should we go?"

At the beach, they fed the girls first, then stretched back in their beach chairs, rubbed their feet in the sand, ate their sandwiches.

"It was so hot in the city today. This feels so good," Matt said.

They fell into the sound of the ocean. The rhythm and whoosh, more soothing than any other sound. Amy gazed at him as he watched the water. She wished she could see it all through his eyes.

Matt grew up in Iowa, among endless farmland and green hills spread like butter over the Earth. Ten miles between towns, John Deere tractors inching along the edges of sweeping empty, rural US highway. When he moved to Massachusetts, the congestion of the coast, trees and people and houses covering the horizon, astonished him. From farmland to Boston—hot concrete, streams of people on the sidewalks and cars in the streets. Tall buildings hovering above. He could no longer see the edge of the world.

Once, when they were first dating, Amy told him about a trip she took to Colorado. How the wide open space made her feel dangerously untethered. Too much edge, too few trees holding the land and sky together.

"Yeah, all of it together was claustrophobic at first," he told Amy. "All those people and trees here—no horizon, no escape. I felt closed-in."

So Amy took him to the edge—her favorite piece of the horizon.

"Seven years in Massachusetts and never been to real beach," Amy said to him on the drive to Cattail. "And Revere Beach does not count." They had been dating all that summer. It was time for Amy's August family vacation and Matt was coming for the weekend. It was trial by fire—he'd only met her mom and dad once for dinner. They'd come into the city to eat in the North End with its Italian food and red wine, and Matt charmed them almost as thoroughly as he had Amy.

"I've heard about your ex-boyfriends, Amy. The bar was not set very high..." Matt smiled when Amy insisted he required no comparisons.

It was dark when they arrived at the cottage. After they got settled, they stood out in the grass under the pitch dark sky.

"This makes me think of home," he said, staring up at the sky, bright with a full moon and a mass of stars. "Open space, darkness."

"Nothing like the city and all its electric light," Amy sighed, contented. The ocean scent, a cool breeze carrying it. Warm, in a well-worn cotton sweater she found in a bureau drawer, bare feet soaking in the dewy grass, Matt's arms around her as they looked at the night sky together.

She got up early the next morning, before sunrise. It was just before dawn. She woke him from a deep sleep. She made him keep his eyes closed and led him from the tarred road and onto the sand. The sound of the ocean was loud and close.

"Keep your eyes closed," she said. "Seriously, I will blindfold you if I have to, Matt."

"Wouldn't be the first time." She swatted at him.

"Shut up!" she hissed, looking back over her shoulder toward the cottage.

He laughed at her. "Who's going to hear us?"

She turned his body toward the shore.

"Okay, open 'em."

The ocean spread far to the right. It curved up to the left, a perfect crescent. Dune grass swayed in the breeze coming off the water. Sun, pink and yellow butter rays, burst from the horizon into a fair blue sky. The sun seemed to spout from the ocean itself.

Amy looked at his face. He turned to her and smiled deeply. "It's amazing, babe."

They turned their faces back and watched the sun rise. He took her hand.

There was the edge. Again.

Now, years later, they sat and talked about his day and hers. They watched their children play.

"You have to get a shot. Don't be scared," Rachel said to Sage. "Here. You can have a lollipop." She hugged Sage. "All better?"

"Had shots today, huh?" he said.

"Yeah. It's terrible every time. For me. They're fine as soon as they get the lollipop. I think that makes it all worthwhile for them." Amy worried about the medicine shooting through them. She worried about bad reactions and illnesses, side effects. She worried about the alternative—not giving them the shots at all. She worried which was the bigger danger.

Rachel pantomimed a shot to Sage. Then, a big hug. "You're alright," she crooned. Sage wriggled away. "Shot," she said and poked Rachel.

"Well, that's one way to work through it," Amy said. Amy and Matt spoke their quiet language, secret from the children. The girls' own language being carved out and patterned every day in front of them into a language Amy did not understand. One that was all their own.

Matt's fingers wove through hers, his skin soft. Fine hair curled on his knuckles. She gazed at his sweet profile while he watched the girls.

Once, she found a picture of Matt. It fell out of one of his books. When she opened the book a small paper fluttered to the floor and she bent down and picked it up. A tiny infant, new and pink and smooth. He looked out, calm and wise and perfect. His baby expression caught her, held her eyes.

"Matt, where did this come from?" Amy asked.

He took it from her, squinted at it and handed it back. "Oh, this is the one they took in the hospital when I was born." Amy looked at him closely. She could see him—the grown-up him—in the edges of his bones, the angles, the very same expression. She could see the plushness, the fatty fullness of his baby face. The bones that would form. The eyes were the same. The baby who peered out of the faded photo with knowing eyes.

She held his beach hand in her own, a little sticky from the salty air, a little prickly with sand. She looked into his face and saw the softness, the memory of plump fleshiness superimposed over his bones. She sat trusting the wisdom in his eyes and felt at peace.

The sun was low and orange in the deep, deep blue sky and a sliver moon spoke sharply in one corner, night, night. The air was cool and the ocean loud. She sat, thinking she might never move and that would be good. Forever. She might never have another moment like this—never would there be another moment just like this. And at that thought she couldn't move; she simply soaked it in, her flesh wrinkling, saturated with the sound of the ocean, the color of the sky, Matt's skin, her babies' voices.

She gazed at him and he sensed it and turned to face her. She placed herself in his eyes for a moment.

"I suppose we should go?" he said. Amy nodded but took a moment to store it all inside herself, tucked it safely away.

At home she put away the leftover food, wiped out the cooler, left it open to air, its mouth wide-gaping into the soft darkness of the kitchen, reassuring in its familiarity. She peeked in on Rachel, splayed on her bed, her arms and legs tossed this way and that. Amy pulled a light blanket over Rachel's small body and watched her even breathing, her soft face. Funny how every single curl on her head, the gesture of each finger both haphazard and choreographed, were perfectly placed.

She walked soundlessly to the baby's room. Sage lay on her belly, her bottom up in the air, hands buried beneath the baby flesh of her neck. Her thick eyelashes, impossibly long, nested softly on her full cheeks. Her pink mouth gaped open, a tender pink O, an endearing gesture for a baby. Amy thought of the many forgivenesses easily doled out to babies. Why couldn't that generosity hold out for a person's whole life? Why did people get stingy? Amy ran her hand lightly over Sage's downy head.

In bed she curled against Matt. Blanket, darkness, breeze through the window, crickets. He undressed her and she him. Smooth palms over skin. His soft familiar mouth and touch and no need to speak. She opened and felt his body as a presence larger than matter. Their presence together. She curled into the space under his arm configured only for her. And they breathed—their bed, their bodies, their shared inhalations and exhalations an island. She never felt as though she were drowning there. Her sanctuary.

~ ~ ~

Amy wrote *awakening* on a sheet of paper in her sketch pad. She underlined it. She drank some coffee and doodled around the word. The sun just risen, Matt showering and the girls sleeping peacefully, she sat in her kitchen happily.

When the realtor had led them into the unit, she had known simply by standing in this kitchen that this was their home. Windows all around and appliances that looked like something she remembered from old black-and-white pictures of the house in which her father grew up. She painted the room a golden ochre, very pale. A drop-leaf round table was placed under the longest set of windows. That was where she drank coffee alone or with Matt or when Heather stopped by in the morning. All the best things happened in the kitchen. Food tasted fuller, talk was richer, laughter more abundant, time plumper, denser. The light made everything more beautiful—a face, an expression, a motion. The room seemed to rise and brighten along with the sun. Morning was the most hopeful time of the day. Those new-day hours made her feel as though anything were possible. The earlier it was, the broader the hope.

On her days to stay home with her girls, she got out of bed when Matt did, went to her kitchen and started a pot of decaf. She waited until she kissed him goodbye to take her first sip. At six-thirty, she had a treasured hour before the girls woke. It was her quiet time, her quiet habit, even on weekends like this when Matt liked to sleep in. She didn't find her routines boring—she looked forward to them and the order they brought to her life. She waited to take that sip of coffee. The waiting for it, the moment before the coffee met her lips, was almost better than the coffee itself. She felt a little let down once the pot was emptied and she was forced reluctantly to turn off the machine. She could have made more, but that was not the point—it was the first of the morning that was most savored and cherished.

On this Saturday in mid-July, the summer sun pushed through her kitchen windows as she looked down at Commonwealth Avenue, as the B Line trolley squealed noisily along its tracks. She was seldom consciously aware of its clamor anymore, even during summer with the windows wide open. She'd grown accustomed to it. The grass and trees in the medians between the carriage roads and the avenue provided a bit of nature amongst the long line of brick and stone apartment buildings that flanked the old street. The vista suited her. Since moving to the city for college, she had cultivated a dichotomy for sea and city. She loved them equally.

She thought, *awakening*. This was what they had titled the art show. She needed six pieces and felt as though nothing she had in her portfolio came together as a meaningful whole. She usually worked with mixed-texture fabrics, creating woven pieces from patchwork and disparate material, but she wanted to do something more delicate for this show. She wrote *egg, flowers, mermaid, tree of life.* She sketched out some images, trying not to form anything too concrete, trying to stay dreamy at this point in the process.

She felt Matt's scruffy Saturday face on the soft skin of her neck. He peered down at her sketches.

"The show?"

She nodded and felt his stubble scratch against her. "I was thinking embroidery on silk."

"I like it. It's ambitious."

"It's time-consuming and time is one thing that's pretty skimpy in my life right now..." She tilted her head back and he kissed her softly on the mouth. "Want to go to the beach?" she said.

"Didn't you just say you're short on time?"

"But it's summer!"

"We have the Herdman wedding tonight," he said.

"I know but it's a straightforward event. I think the crew can handle it with Sheila in charge. What do you think?"

He smiled at her. "Why don't you pack things up and I'll run out to the deli and get sandwiches for lunch. And I'll grab a movie for later." Amy smiled and nodded. A sweet and simple day ahead. Simplicity—such a pretty sentiment.

The sun rose fully and there was summer, full and rich, right there in her kitchen. She stood at the counter, putting their beach snacks together. The intercom buzzed and she clicked, "Hello?"

"It's me, Amy!" Heather's voice came through the old system as a familiar crackle.

Amy listened for Heather's feet on the worn marble stairs of the hall and the click of the door as she came in. Amy hugged her, inhaled her warm and spicy scent. "No kids?" she said.

"Nope, they're with Andy. I'm going to meet him at the beach. I needed to get some inventory done at work this morning."

"We're heading there, too. Matt is grabbing sandwiches. You got enough crew for the Herdman wedding?"

"Oh, yeah. This is an easy one," she said and swiped a couple of carrots off Amy's cutting board.

It was a rare summer Saturday with a light event and she and Heather would make it a good day.

Rachel came padding into the kitchen, the chubby bottoms of her feet slapping lightly on the tile floors. Amy picked her up.

"Hi, sweetie!" she said as Rachel slumped onto Amy's shoulder, sleepy and cuddly, not sure she wanted to be awake. Amy loved these morning cuddles with her little girl, who at three had less and less time for snuggling. Amy put her nose in Rachel's soft honey curls and inhaled. Soon Rachel began to wiggle. Amy placed her on the floor and got up. "Breakfast?"

"Yes, Mommy," she said, adding quickly, "please." Sage began to chirp from her bedroom.

"I'll get her," Heather said. Amy moved to the refrigerator, gathering ingredients for the girls' breakfast.

"Heather, want some yogurt or something?" Amy called.

"Sure." She came back to the kitchen with the sleepy baby, who grinned wildly at seeing Amy and catapulted herself into her arms. "Mama!" she exclaimed. Amy hugged Sage, moved her to her hip and began to prepare food with one hand as only mothers can do.

At the beach, they found Mom and Dad. Soon, Andy and the kids turned up. Unplanned and here they all were. Just like always.

~~~

"Want to watch that movie?" Matt asked Amy. They never got around to watching it the night before—they stayed on the beach until just before the gates were locked. Amy and Heather left to bring back pizza and beer for supper. Then a trip to the ice cream shack. Sleepy, sticky, salty children for the ride home.

It was Sunday night, and hot—they ate a light supper. There were early cool baths and bed for the girls. Amy and Matt settled in on the couch. She snuggled up close to him and tried to push away the terrible Sunday night gloom. Ever since childhood, Sunday meant melancholy. She'd never been able to shake it, even now. There was no school tomorrow, but the feeling remained.

When they were little, Amy would lie in bed close to Heather, clutching her hand, eyes wide in the dark. She thought about her desk at school, the long, long day ahead. The many long days she must endure before the solace of the next weekend. The Sunday despair persisted during school vacations, seeped into summers. Its remnants trailed into her adulthood. She hated Sunday nights almost as much as she had when she was a child.

"Why, sweetheart? What's so bad. It's just another day," her mom had asked her when she was little.

"It's just sad," Amy shrugged. It was the end of something good. Even as an adult, she stared at the clock on Sundays, overly aware of time passing. Three-twenty, four-forty-five, five-thirty. Every second was precious, and she worried she wasn't doing enough to fill it properly, to appreciate it suitably. Every time she looked up, another treasured hour had passed.

That sad Sunday night feeling started somewhere around four-thirty or five and sank into her, water in a pair of jeans, heavy and damp, sand in a pair of socks, dragging her down. Staying busy sometimes helped, but not enough, and the feeling stayed with her until later in the evening, long after the babies were put to bed, when she finally gave in and accepted Sunday and read herself to sleep cuddling close to the comfort of Matt.

So a few years earlier, she decided to put an end to it.

"We're going to do Sunday nights together," she told her mother and sister.

"You still have that thing, don't you?" Mom said.

"I totally know what you mean," Heather said.

Most Sunday nights they got together and played games or watched movies, ate potluck. During the cold months, they watched football. They carved pumpkins in the fall and made Christmas crafts in the weeks following Thanksgiving. The men drank beer and watched TV, while the women and kids amused themselves. They tried to do something special every week—freeze ice cubes in special trays in shapes like stars or snowmen. Or whoopie pies, a favorite, with colored frosting in blue or purple, whipped out at dessert time so the little ones could dig right in, no waiting. Mom always came up with great art projects that kept the older kids busy. The babies dozed and the women chatted, glass of wine in hand. In the summer, they'd leave Cattail together and Sunday night would be a cook-out. They took turns showering, the kids took baths together, as many as would fit in the tub. The fare on summer nights simple, cheeseburgers or linguica, salads, some fresh grilled veggies and always a big pot of corn on the cob bought from the old man on the way home.

The night wrapped up, the sun long since fallen behind the horizon, the stars shone and crickets sang. Sleeping babies were tucked into cars, kisses exchanged, cars pulled away, the door closed and locked. Amy went to bed tired and happy. It took the edge off Sunday night.

Some grooves were impossible to shake free.

Some Sunday nights she and Matt were on their own, like this one. She curled into him and lost herself in the movie. She breathed and allowed Sunday to fall away.

~~~

"Have you started making your vacation list yet?" Heather whispered to Amy.

"Vacation is not for three more weeks," Amy whispered back.

She cocked her head, raised one eyebrow and peered at Amy in the low-lit room. They sat on the carpeted floor of the mezzanine above the grand ballroom of the Copley Plaza Hotel as a wedding ceremony took place below them.

"Okay, yes I have," Amy admitted.

"I knew it! Can I borrow it? You never forget anything."

"I'll print a copy for you."

"Because, of course, you have it saved on your computer," she said and giggled at Amy.

"Shhh!" Amy said and then laughed because they weren't supposed to. They got up and stumbled to the bathroom where they laughed loudly.

"Oh, shit, we better hope that bride didn't hear us!" Amy said.

"No way. That chuppah is completely insulated with fifteen thousand dollars worth of hydrangeas."

They went back to the mezzanine and watched the groom break the cloth-wrapped glass. Kisses and *mazel tov!* and the guests were whisked to a different room for cocktails while hotel and event staff poured into the ballroom like ants to sugar. They worked quickly, transforming the room from formal ceremony to dining and dancing grandeur.

When the room was ready, Amy, Heather and the other event staff went to a bar around the corner for snacks and a beer or two to wait out the wedding, and later they'd head back over to clear it all away.

When she got home, before she crawled into bed to curl up next to Matt, and after she peeked in on her sleeping girls, she printed off a copy of her master vacation planning list for Heather.

"You can laugh at me all you want, but what would you do without me?" she'd asked her sister earlier.

Heather had put an arm around Amy's shoulder. "Honestly, I have no idea."

Without Heather

There will be one big bed in the room Amy reserved for them at the inn. It's a small room with one tiny bathroom. One armchair. No television, no radio, no kids, no distractions, no buffers. Just them. Heather is here and Amy is here. Heather is hardly real to Amy right now.

Amy's first experience of being without Heather was school.

First grade was terrifying. Kindergarten and preschool were easier because the days were shorter and she didn't have to go every day. And the teachers were young and kind. But first grade was scary. Amy was alone all day for the first time. Alone without Heather, which to her was the most alone she could imagine. Heather was her ally and protector. But at school Amy hardly saw her all day. She was alone in the school yard, classroom and worst of all, lunchtime.

Amy had a metal lunchbox with a picture on it of Holly Hobbie in her big soft bonnet. It was white and blue with a blue plastic handle. A thermos nested inside in which warmish milk sloshed around. Mom sent a sandwich, tiny boxes of raisins and crackers for snack time.

The cafeteria was huge to Amy's small eyes. Long tables stretched over the dingy linoleum floor, metal chairs lined up noisily along the edges. Weak light filtered into the basement. It smelled of old bread and over-ripe bananas. It was like a dungeon. And here, Amy was expected to chew and swallow.

All of this was terrible but not the worst of it. Their school was a small kindergarten through eighth grade. Lunch was organized on two shifts—

first through fourth grades on the first shift. Kids sat with their grade and when they were finished eating were shuffled off to the playground. There was no unnecessary hanging out. The second shift was the older grades. The Big Kids. There was little to Amy more scary than not finishing her lunch by the time the Big Kids headed down for theirs.

Amy was a slow eater.

The thunder. Down three flights of stairs she heard them growing louder and closer and louder and closer. The handful of smaller kids remaining in the cafeteria frantically packed up their lunch boxes, chewed and swallowed what was left in their mouths, dashed up the opposite staircase before the Big Kids burst through the swinging doors. Their large feet and hands, their height, their Big Kid clothes and loud voices.

Each day Amy waited for the last bell to ring and the time to come when she could meet Heather in the front yard of the school, slip her own hand in her sister's and wait for Mom to pick them up. They'd go home and play Barbies or one of the other familiar things.

They hated to be separated.

Giggling in bed.

"Do I need to come down there and separate you girls?" Mom called down the hall from the living room where she and Dad watched TV.

"No!" the girls cried in unison, giggles muffled into pillows.

They shared a room with matching pink gingham curtains and bedspreads and ruffled-edge pillows. The walls were covered with a creamy wallpaper dotted with tiny pink rosebuds and soft green climbing ivy. Everything girlish and gentle. All hand-picked by Mom. No thorns.

Although they shared a room, they slept together in one of the twin beds whenever Mom allowed it. When Amy was very little, she coiled at the foot of Heather's bed, to sleep by her feet. Somehow they did not view this as sleeping in the same bed, a treat their mother allowed only on non-school nights.

"You don't get enough sleep cramped in a twin bed together."

"But Mom! We sleep better when we're together."

She paused, looked at the girls. They tried to look pathetic. "How about Fridays and Saturdays?" she relented.

They squealed, hugged her. "Thanks, Mom!"

Later, Sundays were negotiated.

They stood in the living room in front of Mom. She put down her quilting. They were dressed for bed in lace-trimmed flannel nightgowns on a Sunday night. "But, Mom, Sundays are so sad. We have to go back to school tomorrow and we sleep better when we're together. Please?" Heather implored. She always litigated for them.

"Please. Sunday is sad," Amy echoed.

Mom knew that Amy especially, afraid of school, meant it.

"Okay. But no fooling around or I'll have to separate you. Get in and I'll come down and tuck you in in a minute." Her face softened into a smile.

They settled in, pulled the pink gingham to their chins and curled up into one small ball.

Summers were great because it was never a school night.

Since the accident, Amy has spent very little time with her sister. None alone. Worse, there is distance between them that has nothing to do with physical space. A black chasm, it is an insurmountable distance, Amy has thought more than once in the last year. Because now when she thinks of her sister, she thinks of Heather standing at the shoreline on that terrible day. This is the image that will not fade. The image that has seemingly replaced all the others. And there were so many others. Even when Amy finds herself longing for Heather, in creeps the image to sit heavily between them. She can't get back to her sister—she can't traverse the distance. She is with her, she is able to talk to her and touch her, but they are far apart.

She aches for her sister. Amy pushes her sister away yet wants her back, like twins at odds.

Amy asked her to go away this weekend. Amy suspects Heather probably wanted to suggest something like it, but Amy has made her sister fearful of asking anything of her. Most of all forgiveness.

Amy has been stingy.

She wants to forgive. This weekend is supposed to help her. She feels as though this is the farthest step out there. The final option. It is Amy's safety net—if nothing else has worked, this will have to. She has counted on this notion. Which is why she is so afraid. If it does not bring Heather back into her heart, she may have nowhere left to turn. But it is as though the Heather she knew has been replaced by the Heather in the image she cannot forget.

Amy knows she must let go of one or the other: the image or her sister. Her uncertainty of which scares her. Heather is perched on a ledge, the edge falls away sharply to a black chasm, and Amy can pull her sister back into her life, or not.

What they brought to the beach.

Crisscross mesh chairs, towels, tri-folded and bulky, shoved under an arm, thermos jug of powdered drink mix dangling from its white plastic strap, food cooler, beach bag full of tissues, comb, lip balm, Sea & Ski, books, Band-Aids, long-sleeve shirts.

Just in case.

Mom was primed for anything, which made her, as far as some people were concerned, peculiarly ready. Prepared for conditions that arose somewhere between every-once-in-a-while and never. But when a situation did arise, she had the tools necessary to diffuse any problem. People outside their family may have thought it was strange but seemed grateful, even relieved, to accept her help. In Amy and Heather's sight it was unerringly normal. What mom wasn't ready for unexpected falls into puddles? Getting hurt or wet or dirty was completely fixable. What mom didn't have the ouchy spray, the paper towels, the Band-Aids and the change of clothes, ever-prepared for sudden cold, heat, injuries, rain? Every mom carried extra panties, right?

Heaven

Dad's olive-toned skin rarely burned, but instead deepened all summer long to a burnished hue.

Both Amy's and Heather's skin possessed the same olive despite the milky skin of their mother. All the little girls had olive skin, too. They were their summer-brown babies. Pinky-peach bands buried beneath rolls of brown baby fat where the sun could not touch. Amy, Heather and Dad bore similar lines— bent fingers revealed white strokes at the knuckles. They tanned right through the sunscreen they slathered on before stepping onto the beach. Babies wore hats, T-shirts, were put in lightweight cotton long-sleeve, long-leg jumpsuits. Yet, they turned brown.

They still burned sometimes. Mostly the adults who were apt to ignore their own bodies while being diligent of the children's.

"Your shoulders are getting pink, honey," Mom might say to Amy. She'd turn her head and tip her right shoulder forward to look at it, then slip on the light, thin peasant shirt she'd bought on her honeymoon.

Later, like a visit to Amy's childhood, Mom gently rubbed cold lotion into the burned areas. It was the same brand she had always used and Amy would close her eyes and inhale its clean scent. Mom rubbed it between her hands first before touching the hot, pink skin so there would be no cold shock. It felt so good and cool on the heated, irritated skin of Amy's shoulders and back. It almost made a sunburn worth it.

~~~

In the early years when their businesses were still getting a foothold, Amy and Heather had difficulty going away for summer vacation. As Glimmer, Inc. and Déguiser expanded, their summer weekends became more and more filled with the white of weddings. In those days, they'd dash up and down the highways between the city and Cattail in an attempt to cobble together some likeness of a vacation. They scuttled from sand in between their toes to yards and yards of sheer white voile and blush-hued pin lights. And before the sleep-deprivation of motherhood, they still possessed the energy to manage it. Now, the businesses firmly established and in the black, they employed trained crews and could count on their two weeks at Cattail every August.

In her studio space early one morning, a week before vacation, Amy stood over her enormous work table, ran her hands along its smooth, cool surface and peered down at the length of cream-colored silk spread out like a river of milk. The studio was silent— no crew prepping for an event and Matt away at site meetings, working on promotion and marketing this summer day. She unblinkingly contemplated the flowing creaminess of the silk. She imagined the embroidery pieces expansive in size, color and texture mushrooming out softly. She almost hated to limit them to a finite size—hated to cut them off. She needed to think of some way to harmonize the dimensions of the fabric with the concepts of the designs. In the meantime, she gently stretched the areas she was hand stitching in small embroidery hoops. The fabric needed to be taut, but she must be careful not to stretch the fibers out of shape. And she was not entirely sure how the pieces would unfold. She wasn't concerned, though. She knew she would think of something—her creativity never failed her. It was one part of her life she never questioned. She may dwell overlong on results, but she trusted the process. It was always there for her; a constant on which she could depend.

What she loved most about creating was its lack of perfection. Or, she supposed, the absence of her striving for a singular ideal. When she initially created something, before she began to question or alter it, it was unadulterated energy, pure execution of idea. A spark and a flame.

There was nothing, yet, for which she needed to forgive herself.

Its discovery was less an overblown moment and more an unfolding.

Two in the morning and a cavernous coffee mug—her typical circumstance her last year of college. Her projects had grown in scope and detail and she quite often found herself in the middle of the night with a full pot of coffee, hot and sweet in her tiny kitchen, clip-on light blazing over her work table. She might have been tired, most probably should have been, but in those moments she was fully alive, and any fatigue fell by the wayside.

The project she was assigned in the first semester of her senior year captivated her.

"Your semester-long assignment is best summed up by the phrase: 'from idea to meaning,'" her professor announced on the first day of class in September. This project was the most in-depth and widest in scope Amy had yet been assigned. "Choose a larger concept, sketch a progression of ideas to be integrated into a larger piece to be created in the long term. This is deep work, people."

Amy chose *evolution* and by the bright light of her clip-on lamp and the heat of her endless cups of coffee, she stitched fine black lines on bleached-white linen. The fine black lines feathered into fuller texture, bled into color upon color, sparsity into saturation. She pricked her fingers to bleeding, so sharp was her needle. She bent over her work for months and seemed to lose minutes, hours, days of time that slipped away without her awareness but for the light of the sun creeping in around the window shade. She was joy-filled—a brimming happiness had expanded fully though her consciousness, her physical body.

This was the mood she stumbled into whenever her hands were busy making, her mind busy conceiving, the two working together in perfect accordance, the only perfection of which she cared to take note in these ample moments.

The sun had moved from the eastern windows and from its slant, Amy realized it must be after noon when she finally straightened from her stooped position over the table. As she stretched, reaching her hands high above her, she heard the creak of the door hinges.

"Amy?"

"Back here," she called.

"Good afternoon!" Sheila hugged her tightly. She was the lead events crew member. She held up a paper bag. Amy would have known the aroma anywhere.

"Noodles from Brown Sugar?" It was their favorite Thai in the Fens, where Sheila lived. She nodded. "You," Amy pointed at her, "are getting a raise!"

"Am I?" she narrowed her eyes at Amy.

"No. But, seriously, thank you. I have been slumped over this table since before the sun came up and I am in need of a break and sustenance. And this is some fine sustenance." Sheila exclaimed over the lustrous silk and Amy's sketches. Then they sat on the floor to eat their lunch. Amy opened the schedule book to review the events planned for the weeks she would be away. It was hardly necessary—Sheila knew these venues inside and out and she knew these kinds of events just as thoroughly. They'd done hundreds together. She was the first staff member Amy had hired at Déguiser.

"It goes without saying but you can call me if anything comes up."

Sheila waved her hand, dismissing Amy's concerns. "Yeah, yeah. If some bride has a full-on conniption I'll let you know."

"You say that as if it weren't a possibility..."

"Oh, I know it's more than a possibility."

"Remember that one on the Cape?" Amy didn't need to elaborate. They laughed at the memory. This bride had pushed her sister, the maid of honor, seat-first into a koi pond. The serene event planner quickly produced a blow dryer, gave the bride and maid of honor a flute of Dom Perignon and a muscle relaxant each and everyone was smiling by the time they walked down the aisle in the enchanted tent, sparkling with fairy lights and swathed in sheer white voile, pink-edged hydrangeas and blown-out ivory roses, the ocean crashing in the backdrop.

Noodles and an afternoon latté later, Amy and Sheila had everything smoothed out to their mutual satisfaction. Sheila left and Amy returned to her fabric. She prepared a length of the silk, stretched gently taut. She threaded colored floss through the eye of a fine, sharp needle. She twisted a knot, pulled the needle through, shaping the first stitch. Tentatively, then with greater surety. Eager to see what it would become.

~ ~ ~

Déguiser was ready for Amy's vacation. She was ready, too—all the to-dos done, all the packing organized and looked over once or twice more, just to be sure. The pile was expansive with two little ones to consider. Gone were the days of throwing a few things in a bag on her way out the door.

"Is this everything?" Matt stood over the wide and high pile in the entryway. "Not too bad."

Amy stepped up next to him, her hands on her hips, evaluating the pile. "You're kidding, right?"

"Yes, I most certainly am. What is all this?"

"I know...insane, right? I whittled it down, too, if you can believe it."

"How can two tiny people require this much stuff?" he asked.

She shook her head slowly, "I find it hard to fathom, too. But when I try to pare back there's nothing I can eliminate. Not a thing."

"How do you suppose the pioneers travelled light?"

"They didn't have pack-n-plays. Or more than two outfits, one of which they wore."

"Is that true?"

"I have no idea. But it seems like it could be true."

He pulled the car keys from his pocket and jingled them. "Okay, I'll get it all into the car."

"Approach it as you would a game of Tetris."

"That'll make it fun."

"Exactly."

They left for vacation as the sun moved across the early morning sky.

"We're going to the beach," Rachel sang her own made-up song.

"Beach," Sage said. "Beach, beach, beach! Go!"

"For two whole weeks!" Amy said, knowing they possessed a soft grasp on the concept of time. Matt took her hand. Amy concentrated on leaving behind everything but the people riding with her in the car. She closed her eyes as the sun warmed her face. There was Matt's hand and the chatter of her babies and everything else slipping away from her as the distance between real life and Cattail grew.

Amy knew she was lucky. Her life had evolved without sharp edges cutting into soft flesh. Any changes had been gentle, flowing in, making their mark, moving the sand, grinding the stone to dust. Bit by small and often unnoticed bit. She suspected most people experienced life similarly, but that just as many did not. Life had been gentle for her and she tried to remember that even in the difficult moments, hardship was relative.

Her family's adult rendering of Cattail, of their two weeks at the cottage, also came about gently. Change evolved slowly, comfortably from childhood to adulthood. It was slow and bobbing, unfolding itself out as it should, in a way she knew surely as right.

Vacation was always in August, ever since Amy and Heather were children. It was a part of them, so deeply ingrained and loved, that the cottage felt as though it were theirs even when they were still renters. August might not possess the blazing heat of July, the peak of the full ripening of summer, but the weather was consistently lovely. Seldom was there sticky humidity; rarely did discordant storms blow through. And the slant of the light in August was sweet and soft. Mornings, Mom started a pot of coffee; children awoke, Amy, Heather or their husbands stumbling after them. They ate breakfast together in the tiny kitchen. (Although, this year would be different—there was a much bigger kitchen now, Amy reflected.) Mid-morning was time to get the babies down for early naps, or there would be hell to pay for the remainder of the morning and through lunch until they collapsed from sheer exhaustion. Amy and Heather made sure they got their naps. Constant motion usually did the trick. They put them in their strollers and walked for as long as it took to help the babies drift off and keep them asleep. She knew everything would evolve, as the conditions of life are certain to do, yet at the same time she couldn't imagine it any differently. Amy loved the rituals.

Even though countless summer days had been spent at Cattail, the two weeks at the cottage felt far-away and glorious. Cattail seemed as if it were farther from home than it did on a simple beach day. The miles stretched somehow. To be able to stay and not have to drive home at the end of the day was decadent and fine.

The car bumped over the crushed-shell road and Amy peered out at the cottage.

"I don't think we can call this a cottage anymore," she said.

"Not accurately," Matt said. "It's huge!" He had only seen in-progress photos up until now; this was his first time seeing it close-up.

"Yeah," she said. Three stories, a deck protruded from the second floor, a Juliet balcony from the third. The cedar shingles that covered the house were still fresh and fragrant, buttery yellow, the trim clean white. Blue jeweled hydrangeas bordered the front porch, where several smooth, white rocking chairs moved backwards and forwards slightly in the breeze, waiting and inviting. The renovations on the house were nearly complete. The most necessary amenities were functional, with just some finish work left to do.

Mom and Dad weren't going to allow that to interfere with their family vacation.

"Wow!" Matt said as he dropped their bags in their new bedroom. "This is enormous." Amy and her family were staying on the third floor, an entirely open space that spanned the width and depth of the house. There was a bed for Matt and Amy to share, a twin bed for Rachel and the pack-n-play for Sage. A sitting area with a love seat and an easy chair took up space near sliding doors that overlooked the ocean. He stood in front of the door, pushed it open. Amy could smell and hear the water. "That's quite a view," he said.

She flopped into the depths of the pillowy love seat. "I liked our old bedroom."

"Are you serious? It was tiny! The walls didn't reach the ceiling!" Matt said.

"It was quaint. And," she pointed at him, "a lot of memories were made there."

He sat down next to her. "We'll just start over."

"I guess it's not awful," she muttered.

"Not so bad," he said as he lay across her and kissed her. She pressed into him and, kissing him more deeply, ran her hands under his T-shirt.

"Hello!" Mom called up the stairs. "I've got your towels!"

Matt pulled away from her, their faces still close. "She's got our towels," Amy said.

"Of course she does."

Mom held a stack of bath towels whose height in her arms exceeded her own.

"Every year I wonder why you think we might need this many towels," Amy teased. "How wet do you think we will get?"

"You never know. Better safe..."

"...than sorry," Amy chimed, mimicking her mother's tenor.

"Brat," she said. "How did I, a virtuous, nay, nearly sainted woman, raise a brat," Mom said, handing them over to Amy. "Blue for all of you." Each family was assigned a different color towel—Mom's idea. "To avoid confusion," she explained the first summer she started with the color-coded towels.

"Thank God, Mom," Heather had said. "Terrible things happen due to towel confusion. Everyone just using any old towel; no one knowing whose towel is whose. Mass chaos."

"I shudder," Amy had said.

"Brats."

They headed downstairs and as Amy, Heather and their mother packed food and changed their clothes, the men were given the task of changing the kids into bathing suits.

"And load them up with sunscreen," Amy called.

"That'll keep them busy for a while," Heather whispered.

"There is never not a good time to laugh at husbands," Amy whispered back.

"Where's the sunscreen?" Andy came into the kitchen to ask.

An assortment was kept in a basket on the table by the door. Heather pointed it out, gave Amy a look. They smirked and giggled. In no time, everyone would find where everything was always kept. They would remember.

~~~

The days moved languidly, Amy easily forgetting to mark the passage of time. "What day is it?"

"Who cares," Heather said, as she stretched out across Amy's bed. Amy sat in the love seat, feet tucked beneath her, a large piece of silk spread across her lap. She held the embroidery hoop lightly in her left hand while her right hand moved fluidly above and beneath the fabric. Above and beneath, over and over again. A murmuration of starlings in a sapphire morning sky on the fabric. Their pattern was an ash cloud seashell spiraling out, dense at the center, a strewing at its dissipating boundaries. The stitches fluid yet tight, and more than anything graceful.

Mom carefully sat down beside her. "Oh, Amy, it's exquisite."

Amy smiled at her mother. "And you are not the least bit biased."

"I wouldn't even try to deny it. But that fact does not negate the truth."

Heather got up to get a closer look. "It really is, Amy. Mom's right."

"You have always made such lovely things," Mom said. "I remember your preschool teacher telling me what a talent you were. She pointed to a pumpkin girl you made. Orange pumpkin head, triangle dress, accordion legs dangling down, brown shoes. Looked a holy mess to me—like all the others hanging on the wall! She must have seen it on my face. 'No, look closely,' she said. 'See the detail: shoelaces on her shoes and barrettes in her hair, buttons on her dress. It's all the detail—she has talent.' I thought she was just being nice! Maybe she knew what she was talking about after all."

Amy spent her childhood making things. Tiny paper and glue cut-outs, pencil drawings, feathery colored chalk. Her mother saved toilet paper rolls and egg cartons and aluminum cans for Amy's projects. Her fingers were perpetually stained with color. But Amy never thought of it as anything more than that which brought her pleasure and peace.

Mom winked at Amy. "Truly, sweetheart. It's beautiful."

"Thanks, Mom." She placed it in her lap and stretched. "These pieces are taking forever. Thank God I have a year to finish."

"You look so serene when you're working," Heather said.

"I sort of lose my sense of time. Oh crap, look at the clock!" She said. "We need to get lunch going!"

"Well, all good things must come to end," Heather said.

Amy laughed. "It is lunch time, right?" She laid her embroidery in a box and placed it on the top shelf of the closet.

"Taking no chances?" Mom said.

"Not a single one."

"Smart girl."

They spent the day at Cattail and returned to the house as the sun started its afternoon arc toward the end of another day. In the grass of the front lawn, Mom gently brushed sand from the children's feet and shins with a towel, sent them inside for their baths. They sat in the filled-up tub as salt and sand were washed from their slippery limbs, their round bellies. In the kitchen, Heather and Amy started supper.

"Can you turn on some music?" Amy said.

"Mellow or rockin'?"

"Hmmm... I think mellow."

"Mom-approved or Mom-opposed?" Heather asked.

"Enh, let's throw her a bone."

Sweet, warm strumming and Joni singing about all she wants.

"Ooooh!" A joyous shriek from the backyard. "I love this one!" called Mom.

"I think of Joni Mitchell as autumn music," said Amy. "All except this album. This one works all year."

Dad had run to the seafood market for some fish to grill. He would return to clean children and the boys out on the porch, bottles of beer in hand, a cold one waiting for him.

Amy leaned up against the counter. "I'm all done with the veggies. I'll go jump in the shower."

She grabbed a towel and went out back to the outdoor shower. They all loved this simple thing—a shower outdoors. The old cottage had one, too. Amy stepped inside, the door springs salt-air creaking as the door closed. She performed more beach rituals: brushed off the sand and seaweed stuck to her naked body, hung her towel and wet bathing suit from the wooden pegs secured to the wooden walls, turned the knobs and sighed as the warm water touched her chilled skin. All she could see was the sky, the tips of the trees, the gulls flying by. The times she waited until nightfall to shower she saw only the stars, the big white moon, heard the muted laughter of her family rolling in lazily from around the corner.

Amy dressed and walked into the kitchen as she rubbed her wet hair with a towel.

"You smell good," Heather said.

"You want to go next?" Amy asked.

"Okay, I'll just finish the salad first."

"Let me take over. Mom?" Amy called out the open window.

"Yes, honey?" She was still out back, hanging beach towels on the line.

"Should I start the corn?"

"Sure," she called back.

The hiss of the ocean was the constant backdrop.

"Mom, you want to shower next?" Heather called.

"No, you go ahead, sweetheart."

Once everyone was clean, they ate supper together. Amy had learned that eating was different when you were the mother of two small children. She stole a bite here, a bite there; she did not eat a plate of food straight through. She ate what she could in between spoonfuls to babies and orders to small children, *eat your peas, stop wiggling, drink your milk, please take two more bites of fish*. The men ate quickly and relieved the women of the children, who once set free, took off like birds into the twilight. Amy, Heather and their mother relaxed in their chairs and were able to finish their supper leisurely, spoke and laughed easily between bites. They stayed at the table after they finished eating, delaying the clean up just a few minutes longer.

Dad's face appeared in the screen of the dining room, Sage perched on his arm. She poked at his ear as he leaned in to peer at us. He playfully bit at her hand. She giggled and grabbed his nose.

"Hey, the ice cream place closes in forty-five minutes," he said.

"That a hint, dear?" Mom said. "I guess you're paying." In their family, the first person to suggest ice cream paid for the trip.

"You've got some money, don't you, hon? What's yours is mine." He walked off with a grin.

They loaded everyone up and drove the ten-minute ride to the ice cream shack.

When Amy and Heather were children, trips for ice cream belonged to summer almost as much as Cattail did.

"You girls want to go for a ride after supper?" Dad would say, pretext for a trip out for ice cream. They never went to a place close by. A summer night after supper, when there were still a couple hours of weak light, ice cream always meant a ride. The car windows let in just enough cool air to allow Amy to forget about the imposing heat of the day, the promise of the same the next. Summer songs played on the radio. Dad always got something heavily laden with chocolate, Mom always got coffee fudge and the girls usually chose something different every time. Or chocolate chip, the old standby.

Their summer vacation ice cream place was up on a hill, close enough to Cattail that they could almost hear the ocean moving, could smell the tide. The little girls were bouncing at the bounty—there were at least two dozen flavors. Sage and Tara had no idea where they were until they saw the huge dishes of ice cream and then they got excited, too.

Dad walked over with a huge cone of chocolate.

"Did you get a medium, Daddy?" Amy asked him. He wasn't supposed to, and if he didn't eat it fast enough for Mom not to notice the size, he'd catch hell.

"No, it's a big small," and he pulled his arm sharply away from her as if she wanted to steal from him.

"I'll tell Mom," Amy said.

"You little brat," he said, but then kissed her cheek.

Mom fed the babies little bites, and they chirped excitedly, little birds, their arms flapping with unadulterated joy. It was one of the few times they'd sit in one place as a captive audience. Captives of ice cream. She bought one small cup of vanilla and fed little melty tastes to the babies, grabbed a spoonful for herself quickly between baby protests.

"One for Sage. Okay, okay, wait your turn, Tara," she crooned.

"She's reasoning with them," Amy said to Heather as they watched the scene from several feet back, licking their ice cream.

"Let's just stand right here and let her feed the babies and let the men watch the kids and maybe no one will notice we're not doing anything." As she said this, Amber's scoop fell into the dirt with a plop. The stricken child looked up at her father.

"Daddy, it fell!" Her heart broken.

"Oh, no," Amy and Heather said at the same time and looked at each other.

"Jinx," they both said.

"Double jinx!" Amy said a second before Heather did. "Ha!" she said.

"I know, baby. You can finish mine." Andy handed his down to her.

"What a guy!" Heather said and walked over, pulling Amy's hand. She put her arm around her husband and kissed him. "You saved the day."

Ice cream kisses and they packed everyone back to the cottage and bed.

~~~

Amy didn't count the days, never really kept track, while they were on vacation. Time was honey pouring. It was morning it was afternoon it was evening. It was night and the stars were out. It was first morning light. Again, again.

"Good morning!" Heather said to Amy who sat on the deck in the increasingly warming sunshine. Amy had just shed the light sweater she'd put on when she first got up.

"Why do your kids always seem to sleep later than mine? I've been up with them for two hours already." Amy nodded her head at her girls playing in the grass.

Heather yawned. "I drug them."

"And you've never shared with me."

"They've actually been awake for a while. Andy took them out for a walk so I could sleep in a little."

"What? That's not fair! Obviously I need to have a talk with that husband of mine..." Amy sipped her coffee.

"Decaf?" Heather said and pointed to the cup.

"Yeah. There's more in the small pot."

"Lovely. Be right back."

She returned with a steaming cup. "Oh, how I long for caffeine. Won't it be nice when caffeine can make a comeback?"

"Yeah, but that'll mean our babies aren't babies anymore," Amy said.

She sometimes tried to remember what it was like to consume without thinking about its effect on another person. To eat and drink with no bearing on a child's well-being. She thought about it without annoyance, merely curiosity. She was happy her body was attached significantly to those of her children. She just could hardly remember what it was like before in the time when she didn't think about it or not think about it.

Heather took a luxurious sip. "You know, I know it does nothing without the caffeine, but I need it anyhow," she said.

Amy nodded. "The idea of it. It just feels good—a thing you do every day."

"Mmmm." She nodded her head a little. "Want to go for a swim before breakfast?"

"What time is it?"

"About nine-thirty."

"I can't right now. Sage will need to nurse and go down for a nap soon."

"Let Matt give her a bottle."

"I planned to read with Rachel while Sage is down. Anyway, I already had breakfast."

Heather sighed. "You know what I mean. Fine. A swim before breakfast for me and after breakfast for you."

"I can't."

"It wouldn't make you a bad mother." Her tone was light, as if she were joking, but Amy knew better. "I'm not a bad mother."

"I didn't say you were," Amy said.

"It's okay to leave them every now and then. Break their routines from time to time."

"I do leave them. I work at my studio three days a week. I work events on weekends. But I try to keep some semblance of consistency in their lives."

"Girls, knock it off," Mom said from the kitchen.

"We're not doing anything, Mom."

"Knock it off anyway."

"But we're not doing anything!" Heather called. "What are we, ten years old?" She slumped back in her chair. "Let's just go for a swim together at Cattail later."

"Okay," Amy said.

Heather got up and Amy heard the screen door creak and slam shut. Amy listened to her talk to her kids and husband for a moment. She stood, stretched and joined Matt and their girls playing in the grass.

"Hi, guys," She said. She knelt in the grass alongside Matt. "What are you playing?"

Sage came toddling toward her, threw herself into Amy's arms. It was a gesture of sweet and absolute trust. *I will always be caught.* "Hi!" Amy said and kissed the baby's face all over.

"We're finding things!" Rachel said and ran ahead. Sage disentangled herself from Amy and followed Rachel. Amy turned to Matt, "Things such as..."

"Rocks mostly. But it's more exciting than you might imagine. We're also laying them out in a very specific way. Please do not disturb any of it."

Rachel came back over. "See, Mommy!" She placed another rock in the line. There were a few sticks and some broken shells, too. Amy picked one up.

"No, Mama!" She took it from her. "Here." She placed it back precisely in the spot Amy had taken it from.

"Oh, sorry."

She ran off. "I warned you," Matt said.

"See rock," Sage said bringing one over. Rachel followed.

"Put it here," Rachel told her. Sage put the rock in line with the others. Amy watched Rachel's tender way with the baby, the way Sage imitated Rachel's every move. Amy was a silent observer of their secret language. She never grew tired of trying to decipher it.

Amy plucked at the grass, pulled out a handful and tossed it.

"What's wrong?" asked Matt.

"Oh, Heather just gave me shit because I wouldn't take a swim with her. She loves to make me feel like a martyr because of the way I want to take care of the kids."

He shrugged. "Well, she has her own ways."

"I wish she respected mine."

"She does. They do their thing and we do ours."

"She doesn't seem to know when to shut up."

"I know. But don't let it bother you." He kissed her. "As long as we're happy with how we're raising Rachel and Sage, nothing else really matters."

He was always able to let go; he never read more into the nuance of words. Amy wound up and up and Matt uncoiled her, helped her land safely.

"Okay," she said, standing up. "I have to get the little one down for a nap so she'll be rested for the beach."

Amy carried Sage into the cottage, small and sun-warm in her arms. She was already sleepy, as

Amy had known she would be, and rested her head on Amy's shoulder. Her baby breath was moist on Amy's neck. Even though it was hot, Amy didn't mind Sage's body against hers. They sank into the big, soft easy chair in the cool of the cottage. As she nursed, Sage's hand rested on Amy's cheek. She gazed up at Amy, her eyelids floating slowly, slowly to closing, her eyelashes cocoa brown. They were a color Amy could try to describe, a softness, a fineness she could try to articulate. But she couldn't, really. Words fell flat and there was only feeling.

Sage softened in her arms. Her hand fell gently from Amy's face. Amy stood, laid her in her pack-n-play and covered her with a light blanket; made a safe nest. She watched the baby's chest rise and fall. She watched her small pink mouth, a little circle. Her hand curled near her face. Time was irrelevant in those kinds of moments. It was difficult to walk away, but she did—there were things to do. She closed the door quietly.

Later at the beach, Amy smiled at Heather as she played with her children. Heather grabbed Amber and tussled with her. Laurel joined in and Tara toddled over. Heather rolled them around, sand flying. She tickled Amber, held Laurel upside down and allowed her to tumble into the sand. Laurel popped up and threw herself back at Heather. Heather and her kids were one large jumble of different-sized limbs and hands and feet and a blur of colored bathing suits. Amy's play with her children was softer, gentler.

"Enough, you monsters! Mama needs to breathe!" Heather disentangled herself and plopped down in a chair. "Who wants lunch?" Her three girls trotted over happily, giggles around the edges of their faces.

Everyone was wound up when they first arrived at the beach, but at some point it all seemed to float down. Mom flipped through a magazine, Dad quietly stared out at the surf. Matt dozed, a crashed-out Rachel on his lap. Andy played at the water's edge with his girls. Sage was in the sand at Amy's feet, a big spoon and a bucket, all she needed.

"Want to take that swim?" Amy said to Heather.

She smiled and nodded.

"Mom? Can you look after Sage while Heather and I go for a swim?"

She closed her magazine. "Sure, sweetheart."

The water felt cold to Amy's sun-warmed skin. "Brr," she said.

"Oh please." Heather rolled her eyes, but smiled. She knew what to expect from Amy.

"Don't rush me," Amy stated.

"Don't make me count."

The surf that day was made for body surfing. The swells were large and rolled in one at a time in orderly lines. The sky was clear and big. They could see straight to the horizon, a distinct watery line, as if carved out with a fine, sharp knife.

They could watch for the perfect wave and wait for it. They could jump on top and ride, ride, ride it together.

Amy and her sister could meet up at the shore.

~~~

"Why don't we take Sage and Tara for a walk so they'll nap," Amy said to Heather as they lingered over morning coffee. A week of vacation had passed. Time was slow, days falling away like sand through fingers.

They buckled the babies in their strollers and set out along the shore road, Sage and Tara peeping happily until heavy eyelids and heavier heads silenced them. They walked past the rocky stretch of shoreline, the summer trailers and RVs set on the beach. They crossed the long, narrow causeway that led to a tiny island, ocean lapping on both sides. They spoke quietly and, as always, constantly, as though there were an urgency to get it all out, everything, share everything, during their time alone. Hours and hours spent together and they never lacked for conversation. They couldn't account for the content later. Had they been asked, "What'd you talk about?" they would have looked at each other blankly, shrugged and said, "Nothing."

But really it was everything, everything.

Amy exhaled. "At this time next year, the kids will be older, and balancing work and little ones will be easier. At this time next year, everything won't feel chaotic, right? It will feel normal. Tell me I'm right."

"We'll survive it."

"I hope so," Amy said. "There are just always so many events and how can we decline any of them? Their weddings pay our bills."

"It's just people getting married, right?"

Amy made a dismissive motion with her hand. "Just people."

"They eat. They shit. They..."

"Got it. They're just like us."

"Exactly. Except with money to flush—oh!—with money to wipe their..."

Amy laughed. "Got it!"

"Everyone parties, Amy. You can't escape it."

"Some of us are better at it than others. You sure could never seem to escape."

"Escape a good party? Never!"

"I will never get back all the hours I sweated it out waiting for you to come home from sneaking out...You owe me!"

"I owe nothing but gratitude to the fates that you never cracked. I cringed with fear every time you opened your mouth in front of Mom and Dad. The only thing I could think of was 'how long are we going to be grounded?' You were awful."

"Ha ha," Amy said dryly. They walked along in silence.

When they were in high school, Heather used to sneak out after curfew for parties on the beach, joy rides thorough dark back roads, fogging up cars with boys. Amy regretted that she never climbed out her own bedroom window and ran to an idling car with darkened headlights; she simply did not possess the fearlessness that Heather had. Instead, she lay in her bed, ears perked for any sound to indicate Heather's return, when she'd get up and pull Heather in through her bedroom window.

"Shhh, Heather! You're too loud," Amy would have to say when Heather was too tipsy to regulate the volume of her own voice.

"I love you. Do you know I love you?" Heather would implore.

"Yes, I know. Now shut up and get into bed before you wake Mom."

"I love you so much."

"Yes, I know. I love you, too."

Then Amy would lie awake as Heather's breathing fell into a slow rhythm, thinking about how badly this might have gone.

"I didn't do that too often," Heather said. "And I never once got caught."

"Thanks to me!"

"I only needed you when there was Purple Passion involved. When I was sober, my Jedi powers were solid."

"Purple Passion!"

"You can laugh, but that shit was delicious."

Once they reached the island, they sat on one of the chiseled square stones that spread out from the causeway. Both Sage and Tara were still, peaceful and soft with sleep, smooshy faces pressed against the sides of their strollers. They were able to relax so deeply. Amy wished she could feel that way, even for a minute. She absently reached in and stroked Sage's silken leg.

"Heather, how did you always find the way out?"

"Luck. Don't be so quick to hand out any award for bullshit mastery."

Amy listened to the ocean crashing behind and in front of them. The sun was getting hot and warmed her back. She removed the light sweatshirt she'd needed an hour earlier when the air off the ocean eclipsed the struggling early morning sun. She looked out at the horizon and tried to fathom the great distance from where she was to that long curve of water, knowing it was farther than she could possibly imagine. "You were brave," she said.

Tara's head flipped from one side to the other, her eyes flew open, then slowly slid shut. Heather leapt up.

"Time to move again," she said.

They crossed the causeway and headed back to the cottage.

Amy left Sage sleeping in her stroller and walked to her room, slipped out of her clothes and tugged on her bathing suit. She looked out the window, watched their little girls at the neighbor's fence. Their little hands gripped the wooden boards. Two golden retrievers stood on their back legs, drooling happily at the kids. Their kids never tired of those dogs. The dogs never tired of them. It was like a brand new experience every time.

When it was time to go to the beach, they loaded up the cars and, just as when Amy and Heather were kids, the beach day flowed into its pattern. They flowed through it, it flowed through them. It was what home meant to Amy. That magical word—it was right, as in the opposite of wrong. They set up, talked about nothing all day, stared at the water, read, dozed. They went swimming, and when they could, went for a walk to the Point before supper as the sun slanted into early evening. Amy cherished the order. The grooves were her comfort. She slid her feet, her hands into the smoothed-out paths and patterns of everyday life.

They set up at lifeguard station eight and Amy watched the kids play in the sand at her feet, she felt her family around her and put her head back, to close her eyes for a moment. Just to rest them.

~ ~ ~

Amy awoke slowly, placidly unaware of her whereabouts, and realized with a start that she was at the beach and she was alone. Her heart pounded. She sat up quickly and struggled to gain her surroundings. She shrouded her eyes from the sun and located Heather at the edge of the water, sitting in the surf with the happily splashing babies. The little girls waded close by.

Amy walked down to the shore briskly. She was breathless when she reached her sister.

"Heather, you can't bring them all down here!" She didn't mean to sound angry, but her voice possessed an edge she had not consciously intended.

Heather's brow furrowed. "Why not?"

"Because how can you keep an eye on all of them?" Amy crouched down, placed her hand on Sage's back. She looked up and grinned big at Amy. "Mama!" she said.

"Amy, they're fine. I wouldn't endanger any of our kids," Heather reasoned.

Amy pressed her shoulders down. "How long was I sleeping? Where is everyone?" she asked and squinted her eyes in the sun.

"Mom and Dad went up to the bathrooms and Matt and Andy are swimming. Looks like Mom and Dad are back," Heather said, looking back at the sand. Amy turned her head sharply toward the water.

"Rachel! That's too deep, honey! Let's go see Grandma, guys!" Amy called. The three kids ran to Amy and they all made their way back to the sand.

"Anybody need a sandwich?" Mom asked.

"Me, me, me!" Dad said.

"Why doesn't that surprise me? Hey, ease off the chips, mister," Mom told him and slapped at his hand.

Amy fed Sage spoonfuls of yogurt, watched each bite Rachel took. "Chew it good, Rachel. You know how Mommy hates choking," Amy muttered the last part for Heather's amusement.

"We know how Mommy freaks out over large pieces of food," Heather said in sing-song to Amy. "Even the itty-bitty ones."

"Well, when my kids sustain unobstructed windpipes, we'll see who has the last laugh."

"Girls, girls. Let's all strive together to have a gag-free day," Andy said.

The afternoon passed lazily. Dad, Matt and Andy returned to the cottage to catch the end of the baseball game on TV.

"I think I'll head back, too," Heather said shortly after they left.

"I'm not ready to go yet," Amy whined. The sun slanted in its precise place, the air pleasant and temperate; everything right.

"I'm not ready to leave, either," Mom said.

"Stay. I'll take the kids back," Heather said.

"Should we go for a walk?" Mom said to Amy.

Amy and Mom helped Heather get the kids into her van and then they took off down the shore together. They moved in silence through ankle-deep water. They looked down at their feet, the sun straight ahead in their eyes on the way to the Point.

"Mom, do you think I worry too much about my kids?"

She paused a moment. "Sweetheart, you're a wonderful mother."

"And again, you're not the least bit biased." Amy smiled at her mother.

"I'm serious. Everyone has different comfort levels with their kids."

"But do you think I'm one of those overbearing ones; always hovering?"

"Did I ever tell you about Judy's friend, Ann?" Amy shook her head. "Ann was one of those who could look at any situation and envision the worst thing that could happen. It drove Judy crazy when all their kids were little because Judy is just the opposite—let them do what they're going to do, let them fall; it's how they sharpen their reflexes, y'know. She and Ann learned to disagree. Ann hovered, Judy let them run. Nothing bad ever happened to any of the kids. And if it did you could be sure that it wouldn't have been because one smothered and one didn't. Bad things happen sometimes and sometimes they don't. You won't know and it makes no difference to worry. All that being said," she took Amy's hand, "you are a wonderful mother."

The sky began to darken down the shore, the sunlight obliterated by dark clouds. They walked in silence.

"Thanks, Mom."

"You are, Amy. You do everything you can to keep them safe. It's the best any mother can do."

Amy loosened, breathed in the salted air, reveled in the ocean water over the tops of her feet. Her mother's words resonated as truth. Not token comfort, or salve, but what Amy knew in her bones to be true. What she cherished most about her mother were the small, unnamable things. She possessed soft, cool hands that always knew what Amy needed—a tissue, a snack, the gentle rubbing of an anxious belly. She never had to be told. When Amy was a child, it was a mystery. Amy wanted to untangle the mysteries for her own children—to instill in her babies an unwavering trust that she would know what they needed, without being asked or told.

Her pregnancy with Rachel was difficult; full of spotting and sporadic fetal heartbeats, then the infant's refusal to shift into the optimal birth position. She endured hours of back labor, yet Amy was weak with relief that her baby had grown to fullness, rolling around reassuringly in her belly. The stampeding heartbeat in the fetal monitor did not falter, but still Rachel was a tiny wonder to Amy. Miraculous because she'd fought her way through Amy's anxieties. She never showed any sign that they'd rubbed off on her. She was happy, robust, loud, emotional. She looked at Amy with large adoring eyes and when Amy walked into the room, she'd flash her one of her huge smiles. Amy didn't think it was possible to love another child equally, even another of her own. Then came Sage, who did not give Amy a breath-span of worry. The pregnancy was easy—enjoyable—and Amy was armed with the confidence of having done it before. Sage cooed at birth, looked out at the world through huge black eyes. She rarely cried, was a tiny fat Buddha. Amy found more depth to love.

She knew love was different from harping, from hovering. Or maybe it was a part of love. Her love.

"You should mellow out," Heather would tell her, trying to be gentle.

Amy understood her intentions, yet she bristled. "I'm just careful. You could be a little more careful."

"I just want them to know freedom. I want them to learn how to get up from their mistakes."

Amy could only imagine the big ones from which they would be unable to get up. "I'm just cautious," she'd say.

"Mom, did you feel as calm as you seemed?" Through Amy's child eyes, her mother's calm and soothing grace flowed from some pure and pristine place, into her and her sister. She feared she would not give her own children the peace she had known, that sense of safeness.

"No, sweetheart. I'm the original worrier. I always wanted to feel more free than I actually did. I liked the idea of it so much. I wanted it so much more than I could express it. I was a worrywart."

Amy looked at her mother. "No, you weren't."

Her mother tipped her head back and laughed. "Oh, sweetheart! Really?"

She simply didn't remember her mother that way.

They walked mindlessly through the water. A crack of thunder brought Amy back to her body.

"Looks like a storm," Mom said, as the first raindrops began to fall. The ocean danced with it. "Up there!" Amy pointed to the bathhouse.

Up on the deck, sheltered by the eaves of the bathhouse, they looked out at the storm, framed on the horizon. A staged show. Beachgoers and lifeguards ran off the beach, towels or hooded sweatshirts pulled over their heads. The sky was black, black. Lightning flashed. The surf growing angry. When the sun was shining that same water was tranquil, lulling. Wind whipped at them, the raindrops propelled, sharpened needles.

They watched silently. The rain began to slow and then the wind abated to its soft breeze, the black sky turned gray, turned blue. The sun sparkled on the water once more. They walked over the wet, pitted sand. Amy looked over her shoulder. Slowly, a few people were making their way back onto the beach.

"You'd think we'd be used to those storms by now, but they always catch you by surprise," Amy said.

"It's like they happen often enough that we know how they operate, but infrequently enough that we forget they can happen," Mom said.

The storms rolled in out of nowhere. Not often, twice maybe three times a summer. They were used to them; they were not afraid, even if surprised. Charcoal clouds rolled in, a smear of ominous black across a sky that had been blue moments before. Small children were gathered and people hurriedly bolted to their cars.

Amy, Heather and Mom never ran from the storms. They sat and weathered it out. Because most storms were all bark and no bite. They would pass and it would be beautiful again in ten minutes. The clouds grew heavy and the sky broke loose in torrential rain and the wind whipped up. As long as there was no lightning, they put the towels under a plastic bag and waited. Inevitably, the sun pushed the clouds out to sea and sparkled back down on the ocean and the wet wavy sand.

But now and again, a storm grew fierce. They sat, prepared to weather it out. They were tougher; they knew what this storm was all about. Then it roared a crack of thunder, streaked a bolt of lightning.

"Okay, girls, get to the car!" Mom said. "Now."

Amy reached for a beach chair. "No! Amy, it's metal. Leave it."

They ran to the car, laughing harder as the rain came down, fierce and sure. It turned to hail; small, hard, fast pellets.

"Ow!" They laughed in a kind of hysteria, could not get up the boardwalk quickly enough. In the parking lot, nearly empty of cars, Mom fumbled with the keys and the car door.

"Mom, hurry!"

It hurt, yet they laughed wildly. They collapsed into the car, slamming the doors hard. Then they caught their breath.

Through the car windows they watched the sun push the clouds out to sea, just as it always did. It shone through the raindrops on the windshield. They went back down to the beach.

It was the same now. Amy looked up toward the Point; they returned to the conversation they were having before the storm interrupted them.

"Heather's a great mother but maybe a little too...reckless. Sometimes," Amy stated.

"Oh, I don't know, Amy. You're both great, just different. You've always been more watchful. No, I don't think you're paranoid, if that's your next question. Different," Mom enunciated.

Amy was almost convinced.

"I trust her, though. Of course I do. Even though we're different, I know she knows how I like my girls to be looked after." She believed it without waver.

Quiet

Not a good, soft, welcome quiet.

It is an unsettling silence.

Two things occur to Amy. First, she and Heather have been alone together so infrequently since the accident that she had not realized what it is like to be alone with her now. And this kind of quiet has never happened to them before. She had not known it was possible.

On the ferry, they buy burgers and french fries which they dump into a brown paper bag, grease and grainy salt accumulating in the bottom. Their hands touch as they both reach in.

"Oh, sorry," Heather says, pulling back as if burned.

"It's okay," Amy says mildly. "Here." She hands her a few fries.

"Thanks," she says softly.

It is night when they dock on the Vineyard. The island is dark but for the lights inside the homes. By the time they make their way to the inn, it is the dark of night. The inn, weathered gray shingles, wrap-around porch, brick-red door, is lit by porch lamps, the beams refracted through cut glass. Rays of light point out at them in every direction. It is just as Amy remembers it. They check in and go to their room. There is still no television. The room is as lush as Amy once thought, but she's not as impressed. She has seen more in the last fifteen years—more nice hotels, more places. Her eyes slide coolly over the antique wood. The down and chenille are still inviting, the furniture still shiny and smooth with the oils of many hands. They get ready for bed. When the light is turned out they go to sleep.

Silence descends upon them heavily.

Silence takes the place of what used to be.

The next day, after lunch and a little shopping, Heather says, "What should we do now?"

"Is the pool any better?" Amy asks. They laugh.

On their first visit to the inn, they were excited to learn about the pool. The aqua-blue, sparkling pool on the cover of the brochure that caught the rays of the sun. Lounge chairs encircled the cement at the perimeter of the pristine water. They envisioned themselves parading around in their bikinis, suits they were only grudgingly allowed by their father since they were eighteen and he supposed he could do nothing about it. They arrived, tied up their tiny suits, grabbed towels and stopped dead at the rim of the murky water. It was a slimy, viscous green. Brown leaves and dead bugs floated in intricate patterns on the surface. The diving board was gone, rusty stubs protruded from the ground, bled red onto the cement. The two remaining lounge chairs were missing strips in crucial places. Its decrepit state was so out of line with the fineness of the place.

They went back to the room. No one was around to appreciate their little bathing suits anyhow. That quickly took the fun out of their bikinis.

Neither of them wears a bikini anymore. Too much trouble. Too much sucking in of stomachs (which didn't used to be a necessity). Too much worrying about keeping nipples covered. Their bodies have become utilitarian. Amy and her sister care more now for their usefulness, their strength and flexibility. Their bodies have become practical. They still take pride in their bodies, still take care, but more for their power and less for their sex appeal. Age and motherhood precipitated this perspective. In many ways, they find it freeing.

They walk out of the inn, unsure where to go. They wander the grounds slowly and come to the metal gate that closes off the pool. Amy pushes it open.

They stand side by side, scrutinizing the depths.

"If it's possible, it's even more gross," Amy says."Why don't they bulldoze it in?"

They peer into the murky water. Heather sits at the edge of the pool, kicks off her sandals. Amy moves to a semi-intact chair and watches her. Heather looks at the water. Amy feels as though Heather wants to speak. Or hear something from her. Amy shifts her gaze to the water.

She says nothing.

Part of her hatefulness is allowing these silences. They are unbearable to her, but she knows they are worse for Heather. In all the quiet lurks the unsaid pain, the insinuated blame. Ugliness covers what used to be.

Amy hears a small splash. Heather has dipped her foot into the water through the layer of murk. Amy almost cries out in disgust. Heather swirls her pointed foot in the water. The green layer separates, floats away. The water underneath is clear. Seemingly endless.

"Look at that," she says.

Feng Shui.

Once they arrived at the beach, they walked to their spot and set up. Not spot in a capricious sense. There was an architectural sensibility about the location, a Feng Shui awareness. Of course, they had never heard of Feng Shui—they just knew what they liked. Beach chairs lined up, three in a row, cooler between Mom's chair and theirs, towels set on top of the cooler to help it stay cold, little folding table placed in front, beach bag behind the cooler.

They knew what they liked. It was always the same, secure in their reliable rituals.

One Moment

"This day is perfect," said Amy.

They almost always had good weather for their vacation—August was predictably agreeable. But this particular day was even more lustrous, all grace. The kind of day that made Amy feel alive. More than alive, like anything was possible. She knew why she was alive and she was grateful for all of it.

On the deck of the cottage, Amy stood tall and stretched. She and Heather were alone with the kids. Mom and Dad were at a Red Sox game, the tickets Dad's birthday present. Andy and Matt were off on a bike ride.

"We'll join you at the beach later," their husbands said. Amy and Heather doubted it. "When those two get together they get lost. Time, space, you name it," Heather said. She smiled at Amy, linked her arm through hers. "It can be our day."

"Can't be our day when we have the kids."

"Quasi our day."

"It'll have to do," Amy nodded, stretched again. "But it's a shame that they're all missing this perfect day. It's so clear you can see the islands from here."

Cattail was nothing but pure blue sky, golden sun, light breeze off the water. Because it was a Tuesday, the sand was only sparsely freckled with people. Sailboats with taut white sails floated on the horizon. No noisy jet skis, no radios blasting pop music beside the oiled prone bodies of teenagers. Only seagulls, dulcet surf and the occasional tinny music from the ice cream truck rolling back and forth on the tar path in front of the boardwalk.

They fed the children lunch and then watched them play while they ate their own.

"Not in your mouth, Sage," Amy said. The baby held a rock the size of a walnut in her fist. She grinned at Amy and brought the rock inches from her mouth. She knew. It was a game they played. Amy slinked toward her. Sage laughed wildly.

"Not in your mouth, monster," Amy said, squatting down and tickling her. "Oh, geez." She jumped up, pulled a faded cigarette butt from Tara's hand, just before it went into her mouth.

"Gross," Amy said, tossing the butt into a bag of trash they'd started. "Why do people have to come here and litter? How challenging is it not to be a dirt-bag?"

Heather nodded, shook sandwich crumbs from her fingers and got up. "It's sickening," she said as she chased a stray kid, hauled her back.

"If you're going to defile our beach, you're not going to be allowed back," Amy muttered.

After lunch, they brought the kids down to the water to let them splash for a while. Amy ran after the babies at the shore, while Heather stood knee-deep with the little girls.

"They're so quick!" Amy called out as she pulled Sage back from an oncoming wave into which she was quickly toddling. The breakers came up fast on them, bowling them over if Amy and Heather weren't watchful. Every one of them had gotten a mouthful, a nose-full of salt water at some time or another. Amy could see that she would soon have to pull Tara back, too, if the little one made a go for it. Heather turned away from the little girls to look back at the babies.

"Heather, keep an eye on them!" Amy called.

"They're fine! Aren't you, girls? Should we go for a walk?" she said to Amy.

"Sure. Stay there, I'll get the wagon." Amy carried Sage and Tara back to their stuff and plopped them in the wagon. They sat facing one another, toys scattered in the bottom to hold their attention. Amy pulled the wagon back to the shore. Heather and the girls joined up and they headed up toward the Point. The kids would never make it all the way, but they were usually good for at least the short trip to the private beach and back. The little girls trotted ahead, running back and forth, picking up seashells, chasing sandpipers, poking at dead jellyfish.

"Dear God, what is that? Don't touch that, Rachel!"

Amy and Heather said, "Ooh!" wide-eyed at each rock they were shown.

"That's beautiful, Laurel!" Heather called out. "How can they get excited about rocks every time?" Heather said once the girls were out of earshot.

"I know. Every time!" Amy stared ahead, keeping her eyes on the girls, peripherally enjoying the ocean, the beach. She pulled the wagon behind her, the constant weight assuring her of the babies' safety.

They reached the private beach.

"Should we head back?" Heather asked. The babies were sleepy and quiet and would soon drift off. The little girls were still running back and forth together, but might lose steam at any time.

"We'd better."

They turned. "Come on, girls. This way. Get ahead of us!" The little girls twittered past, a blur of hot pink, aquamarine, trailing silky hair.

Amy stopped, "I have to pee."

"Go up to the private cabanas."

There was a private beach halfway between Cattail and the Point. People paid hundreds every summer for membership. It was a nice little stretch of shore but no nicer than any other part. It was, in essence, the same exact stretch of the Atlantic shore as Cattail. It was the only expanse that didn't belong to everyone.

"Snobs," Heather always declared. They all agreed that there was nothing better about the private beach. Except, they learned, the bathrooms.

There was a large bathhouse with individual cabanas, more like little changing rooms, and a place to leave your beach gear. These people didn't have to schlep their stuff from the parking lot, to the beach, then back to the parking lot.

And clean bathrooms. Spotless. The toilets at Cattail were always a mess of sand, seaweed, toilet paper clumped and sodden. Leaking, stopped-up sinks and toilets.

"State workers standing around doing nothing while those bathrooms remain an abomination," Mom said often. She filled out one of the little *How're we doing?* cards several times every summer. But it never changed.

One day, walking past that snobby bathhouse, they decided to see if things really were better at the private beach.

"We can't go up there," Amy said.

"But I have to pee. We're going up," Heather said. Mom followed.

"Mom!" Amy implored.

She turned to Amy. "I want to see what they're like," Mom said.

They walked casually across the sand. No one seemed to notice. They climbed up the weathered gray wooden steps. A cool breeze floated across the deck of the bathhouse. They found their way to a small single stall.

Mom went in first. "They're so clean! They must have someone clean them several times a day!"

When Amy was in kindergarten, she wet her pants one day at school. She'd never done that before.

"What happened, sweetheart?" Mom had asked, bending down so she was level with Amy. She held

Amy's shoulders lightly. Her thumbs stroked up and down.

"I was afraid the bathroom would be dirty," Amy had answered tearfully.

They all took a turn in the private bathroom and started back down the stairs. "That was a pleasure," Mom said.

"It even smells nice," said Amy.

No one took any notice when they headed back to the shore and up to the Point.

But Amy hesitated now. If she stopped moving, the babies might stir, get their second wind and that would be it for a nap.

"Nah. I'll go when we get back up to Cattail." Everyone would fall asleep and she could walk up to the bathrooms alone.

They moved on back down the beach.

No one was tired that day. Sage perked up and got Tara going, and despite their frantic running, the little girls showed no sign of stopping. Amy and Heather tried to settle them once they returned to their spot.

"Nope. Not going to happen," Heather said, pulling Tara from her breast, tugging her bathing suit back into place. "She's just messing around."

"Sage wouldn't even sit still on my lap to try to nurse. Look at them," Amy nodded her head toward the little girls who played happily in the sand with colorful buckets and shovels. Heather shook her head. "Maybe they'll go to bed early."

"No they won't. That's a pipe dream."

"Why did we have kids just to go on a perpetual drive to render them unconscious?" Heather said.

Amy laughed. "And I still have to pee," Amy said.

"Go ahead. I'll watch them. I'll take them down to the water, let them wear themselves out."

Amy hesitated. "Wait here, I'll be right back. That's a lot of kids for the water."

Heather grinned. "Amy, we'll be fine. Go. Stop worrying." Her back was turned as she gathered the children. "Come on, girls, let's go swimming."

Amy watched. "Okay. I'll be right back." She started to walk away, then turned back. Heather was heading down to the water with the kids. "Be careful!" she called. "Heather!"

"What?"

"Be careful!"

Heather nodded. "Go, would you!" She smiled at Amy.

Amy smiled, too. She turned her back on her sister and her children and the ocean she loved.

~~~

The sky darkened. In the cave-like bathroom, it grew even darker. A deepening, an engulfing. There was a rumble and then a loud crash of thunder.

Amy bolted from the stall and ran to the door.

She stepped out of the bathroom. The sky was ashen, blackening down by the water. As she walked away from the bathroom, hard cold rain hit her body. Lightning flashed over the ocean. People ran off the beach, clutching their belongings haphazardly. Lifeguards ran toward her to the refuge of the bathhouse. They ran past her, a tomato orange blur. The tar was beginning to cool as the rain freckled it an opaque black. The air smelled of ozone. Amy did not have her flip-flops; she had forgotten them. Lightning lit the sky. It looked like it was hitting the ocean and it seemed the water might shatter with the cloudburst as thunder cracked loudly. Her feet slapped painfully—they stung against the tar. Sand grated between the hard surface of the path and the soles of her feet. The pelting rain struck her face. Her hair, sodden now, stuck to her brow, her eyes. She scraped it away so she could see where she was going. But she still couldn't see. She kept running.

She kept running.

Then her feet hit the sand. She almost slipped, her feet almost came up from beneath her, but she caught herself hard. She hurt her ankle, but she kept going. Lightning struck. She kept going. She could see Heather at the shore. She was gathering the children. There was a baby in her arms. It was Tara. Amy got closer. The rain was an assault, the sky heavier. She wondered how that could be since the rain was coming down so hard.

She reached them. Heather screamed, "Sage!" Amy thought *Sage*. Heather held Tara screaming on her hip. Heather was at the shore, in the water, frantically moving her head up and down, over and over. Laurel held Rachel's hand that held Amber's hand. A chain. Amy thought of that game they played when they were kids. Whip. Crack-the-whip.

"Amy—Sage! Get Sage!"

Amy couldn't see her.

She turned and plowed into the surf. The baby should have been right there. Amy looked down at her feet. The water was jumping and white from the rain. Her eyes scanned frantically.

She saw her. Tiny bottoms of feet and bum.

She grabbed the baby. Her baby, Sage. Sage's thin hair was wet and dripping and stuck to her head. It was the color of dune grass. Her eyelashes, long and brown, dripped, wet stiff triangles. Two streams of water ran from her small nose. Tiny nostrils. They were so small. All Amy could do was run to the boardwalk, to the car. Heather struggled in front of her with the three children, her own baby in her arms.

Sage did not stir in Amy's arms.

Tara screamed. Amy could hear her from the side of the car. Amy shoved herself into the front seat, slammed the door. The rain drummed relentlessly on the metal roof. Whimpering children filled out the sound in the car.

Amy looked at her baby. Her baby was bluish. Her baby did not have breath. Amy put two fingers to Sage's nose. The baby's mouth. No warm breath. No milky toothy breath. Where was her breath?

She turned her head slowly, maybe quickly. Heather sobbed. Great and gasping breaths and gulps. She reached for Sage.

Amy wouldn't let go.

"Amy! Amy!" Some sharp thing in her tone penetrated. Amy inhaled coarsely—gravel air—and turned her head toward her sister.

"We have to help her! Do you remember CPR?" she said.

Amy's mouth was agape. Words were thick muck trapped in her throat.

"Give her to me. Amy! Now! Give her to me."

She handed Sage over to her sister. The backs of the baby's legs moved swiftly across Amy's palms. Her hands tingled from the smoothness.

She watched Heather breathing into Sage's mouth. She used two fingers to pump Sage's chest. Her tiny heart. It was all coming back to Amy now. It was different for babies than adults. Gentler. There was a rhythm to it. Heather created a steady rhythm.

Amy started to think Sage would be okay. She was okay. She started to think *she'll open her eyes cough a little and cry and I'll hold her I'll hold her and then we'll go back to the beach when the sun comes out and later tell everyone how scary this whole thing was.* She could almost feel the relief of it. She was looking forward so much to the relief that would flow over her like water. Then they would eat supper and put the kids to bed and she and Heather would each have a big—a big—glass of wine and laugh with weak relief that the day was over and everything turned out fine. Sage was fine. Amy could see her asleep in her pack-n-play, belly moving up down up down. Of this she had grown certain.

"Amy!" The index and middle fingers of Heather's right hand pumped pumped pumped over Sage's heart. She blew lightly into Sage's mouth. "It's not working!" She pumped, she breathed. "I have to keep doing this." *Of course!* Amy thought. *Heather knew what to do.* She breathed. She pumped. "Run up to the lifeguards and tell them to call the paramedics! Go!"

Amy hurtled from the car. Her hands arms legs did it all on their own. The rain had stopped. She chose this as a good sign.

She ran slap slap slap of her feet.

The lifeguards ran back with her.

Amy said words to them that may have been *help* and *my baby.* She was not sure, but they jumped up and ran to follow her.

She couldn't feel her feet. She couldn't feel her lungs. She heard a siren far off and thought, *No we won't need that.* She expected—she knew—Sage would be breathing when she got back to the van. Amy knew she would be fleshy and pink. Amy would hold her. And Sage would be fine. And it would all be fine.

~~~

The sun came out, pushed the black clouds up the beach, and *I knew it would*, Amy thought.

Amy found herself saying the words we believe we will never say. The words that were for other people to say.

There were words for police reports. Even if she had to say them a hundred times to get it right, the words might not have been just right and they must be. She said them and said them and she found herself embellishing the details. What was the baby's coloring? *The baby was blue* became *the baby had a blue-gray tinge, white around the mouth and nose.* Amy didn't know if these details were real. She thought maybe they were. Could possibly have been. They came out of her mouth, pushed out by her breath, formed by her lips, tongue, teeth.

They were in the emergency room of the hospital. Someone had placed a white blanket over Sage. Amy looked at the white cotton cloth lump on the rolling bed from the ambulance. The blanket had a basket weave. It pooled around Sage's body.

Amy sat on the floor, her back pressed against a pale green wall. An arm wrapped around her shoulders. It was warm.

"Matt's on his way, sweetheart." It was Mom. When did she get here? Didn't matter.

Matt was on his way. Amy had forgotten about him and now all she wanted, the only thing, was his familiar body and smell. His familiar face and voice. It became the only thing that might save her. Maybe she nodded at Mom or maybe she did not. Mom didn't insist on a response. She squeezed Amy's shoulders, kissed her cheek and pressed her face to Amy's. Her cheeks were wet.

The blanket moved. Amy's heart jumped, squeezed tight in her chest. She stared without blinking. Frigid air moved across her body. It was the air conditioning coming on. She was frozen in the spot she found herself.

Heather and Dad stood near a navy blue policeman. Amy heard Heather's hysterical voice climbing. "I tried to gather them all...there was lightning. The rain came so fast. A big wave toppled her...it all came so fast. The little girls couldn't hear me telling them to go to the sand...I couldn't get them all..." She choked out each phrase.

"Shhh," Dad said.

Amy was very still.

The sun slanted in through the emergency room windows. This was her favorite time of the day at the beach.

Heather's voice rose up again.

"And I didn't mean to...it was so fast...a big wave just knocked her..." She sobbed louder, hacking up the words.

"Sweetheart, calm down. Just tell them what happened." Dad's voice again.

Two policemen took notes, a doctor and several nurses milled around. Where were all the kids? They must have been taken somewhere.

Amy wished the air from the vent would stop rustling the blanket. She couldn't go over and do anything about it because she couldn't move. She had forgotten motion.

There was a light touch on her arm. Matt stood above her.

"Amy," he said. It was so quiet. She was not sure if she heard it—if he really said anything. He looked like a child. The same way he looked in pictures of him at two or three years old. His eyes looked like a child's. He pulled her up slowly and they crumpled into each other. She held him, stroked his back. Stood firm. She held him as he cried. She was dry. Dried up.

Might have floated away. She stared across the room to the other side.

MELISSA CORLISS DELORENZO

PART 2

Foggy days were different. A sure, cool breeze off the water and a hidden sun chased beachgoers away. They never knew it was foggy at Cattail until they arrived. It might be sunny, unbearably hot and heavy at home. The sun stayed with the car until they crossed over Old Pine Hill Road where they were met by a pale gray sky; chill on their arms resting on the open car window. It made them draw their cooled limbs inside.

"I think it's foggy today," Mom would say. Amy and Heather peered intently out the windows, as if their scrutiny could change anything.

The fog was visibly thick by the time they rounded the corner at East Beach Road. No view of the distant Elizabeth Islands. No view forty feet beyond their eyes. But they'd come too far to turn back. And besides, all there was at home was heat, heat, sticky heat.

Amy and Heather still went swimming on foggy days—it was never too cool to keep them out of the water. The lifeguards stood ankle-deep in the surf, wore their red-hooded sweatshirts, kept their eyes stiffly on the water. They whistled people in.

You had to be careful on foggy days.

Amy and Heather liked to play games in the fog.

"See how far you can go before I can't see you," Amy said.

Heather walked ten feet.

"Go more."

Turned. Walked ten feet. Turned.

"Go. I can still see you," Amy said.

Turned. Walked.

"Go more!"

Walked backwards.

Disappeared.

"Heather?" Amy called. There was a lengthy pause.

"Here I am." She walked back toward Amy, her body misting back into wholeness, solidity.

"I lost you for a minute!" Amy said, smiling.

They clasped hands and galloped down the beach.

What's Left

Amy unwillingly learned that there are many things one needs to do because of death. They were learned only when they must be done. She learned that no matter how well it is put, how nicely someone says the words, like almost everything death is a business.

There were things to purchase. There was shopping. There were details.

Amy made a checklist. There was:

choose coffin

choose funeral parlor (what was the criteria for the choosing?)

call newspaper about obituary

buy appropriate clothes for Rachel to wear to funeral (should she go?)

choose songs for service (there were no songs)

choose a menu for the after-funeral family gathering (your mother said you must).

The living must be fed.

There were many things to do when someone dies. There were all the public things, the things categorized as "Final Arrangements." Then there were the private things.

There was a room in their home still filled with Sage's belongings. Looking around, Amy realized how little time it took to acquire a collection of things. Things she touched. Things that smelled like her. Amy ran her fingers across an aqua blue sleeper, worn soft and thin. It was Amy's favorite. She remembered Sage's tiny body in that sleeper with details so real it was almost full in her hands. Amy nursed Sage to sleep in the yellow rocker by the window, her fleshy body filling out the aqua fabric. Amy told Sage about the stars, the moon, birds and trees. She sang her hushed songs. Sage looked up at Amy with her sleepy, heavy eyes and she reached out to touch Amy's mouth as she spoke. She looked beautiful with that aqua against her olive skin like Amy's and her fair wispy hair, the same color as Matt's. Her tiny ears like seashells. Amy would tuck the fringes of hair behind them. Like her skin, her hair was exquisitely soft. Amy could never touch either enough.

There were favorite things of hers in the room. She had favorite things. She had toys, many of them gifts from family and friends and a few left over from Rachel's infancy. She hadn't played with all of these things. But she loved a few of them. Some books, worn and torn, mostly about babies. "Baby!" she would exclaim at each picture. When she said "baby" while in the tub or the living room, she meant the book. Amy would say, "Do you want to read your book?" She would bare her six teeth with her face-stretching smile. "Baby!" She had a language Amy understood. She played with miniature pots and spoons. "Cook noodoos," she'd say. Noodles. She pursed her lips way out to say the word. Amy had to taste her cooking over and over. She said it was delicious every time. "'Mell." Smell. Amy took a big whiff. "Mmmmmmmm," they said together. "Hot," she said. Amy must then blow on it.

The aqua sleeper had been tossed across the changing table, still warm from Sage's body, the morning they left for the cottage. Amy picked it up and held it to her face. It was soft and droopy, stretched with the movements of Sage's body. Amy inhaled the scent and stood in the room timelessly. It was morning, afternoon, a year ago, ten minutes ahead. It was the last moment Sage wore the sleeper.

She needed to put these things away. Things no longer needed get put away.

Where was *away?*

There was a tube of baby lotion on the changing table. It smelled of lavender and rosemary. She removed the cap, closed her eyes and inhaled. The last time Amy touched the tube was to rub some on Sage's skin. She peered at it in her hand. She looked for some essence of Sage there; something left over. She couldn't move her eyes away—if she did, this feeling of being near Sage would fade, would slip away.

Amy laid the aqua sleeper in a bureau drawer and left the room. She closed the door quietly and gently behind her with the soft click of the doorknob catching.

She returned to the kitchen and sat at the table, pulling a lined pad of paper and pen to her hand. The paper held the details of Sage's service, the vicious to-do list. The words written on the paper in her hand repelled her. But Sage's service would be perfect.

There was no other way.

Amy told the funeral director Sage must wear these clothes, these shoes, this diaper. The clothing sat in a cloth bag Amy held tightly in her hands. The funeral director's face was lined and swampy, a knife through soft butter. He said, "Ma'am." His voice so very soft. "Of course you can have everything, anything, you want. Leave all the details to us."

But. No.

She must wear these things. I must know it will all be this way. All these words came as one big word too large to fit in her mouth at once. Yet they did.

"How will I know everything has been done as we ask?" Amy said.

He smiled, gouges sunk into flesh. "I assure you. They will be."

Sage must have the tiny pale green cloth shoes with the pink dress. The outfit Amy had been saving for Matt's birthday in late summer. He loved when Amy dressed them up like dolls. "My pretty dollies," he called them.

At the funeral parlor, Amy spent a long time choosing. Matt grew frustrated. Amy sensed it, yet still she persisted; she was powerless against her compulsions. Every detail must be laid out, ironed out, smoothed out. She kept thinking *there is only one perfect one specific one right choice and I'm not sure if I've pinpointed it.*

They left and she changed her mind. Back and forth. She could not stop talking.

"Enough!" Matt shouted in the car. "Babe, that's enough. It's settled. Leave it."

"But what if we made the wrong choices?" Her voice was hoarse. Words, air hurt as they pushed through her throat. Tears fell on her hands in her lap.

He took her hand. He drove the car.

"We didn't. What does it matter?" His voice broke. His face was wet, too.

"It just does," she whispered.

She called the funeral director the next morning while Matt was still in bed.

"Mr. Hayes?" she kept her voice low so Matt would not hear.

"Yes?" he said.

She changed a few things. A little later that morning, she'd changed her mind again. But Matt was up by then and she couldn't call Mr. Hayes.

By the time she went to bed that night, she'd come around to another decision anyway.

They planned a quiet service in the cemetery. There would be no wake—that was too gratuitous, too intrusive. Amy didn't know how to do it another way. She had attended funerals and everything seemed well-planned and smooth. But here it was she who had to make it happen and she had no idea where the first place was to begin it.

There must be a party afterward; a more appropriate word to use, "gathering." That's what Mom called it. But, Amy thought, what was really different? Nuance was lost when your baby had died.

"What will you serve everyone at the gathering?" Mom asked.

Amy looked at her blankly. She assumed she would be exempt in this case. Weren't mothers of dead babies given a pass on the party?

"I don't know. What do you serve?" Amy asked. Mom would know.

"Well, maybe some lasagna and salad. You know, big pans of things that go far to feed a crowd. We can get rolls from the Portuguese bakery."

Amy was alarmed. "How many are going to come?"

"Well, you have to kind of have an open invitation to anyone at the service who wants to," she answered softly.

"What if I just don't want to?"

"Sweetheart, you have to." Her tone was gentle but her message final. "Want to have it at my house? Let me take care of this for you."

Amy shook her head. Did it really matter where? "I can do it."

She made a list and stared and stared at it until it jumbled. How quickly words can come to mean nothing. It was like that game Amy remembered, when she repeated a word over and over until it became a meaningless sound.

Sage's death, all of this, was that. One deafening sound that made no sense. Ricotta, noodles, funeral for Sage. These sounds dug around in Amy's bones, clawing, grasping. At what? She couldn't get them to settle; couldn't make those words settle down. She couldn't form them into something she understood. Clawing, digging. The sound resonating, echoing, especially loud in the silences.

As the words on the list tangled on the paper, she recalled a night last spring when she and Matt went out to their favorite Indian restaurant. They parked a few blocks away and strolled hand in hand up the street.

"Where is it?" she said. They stood in front of the old brick building. "It was here, right?" She knew it had been. They'd been there so many times before.

"As far as I recall," Matt said.

What had been their favorite Indian restaurant was now a sub shop—a bright, garishly decorated, franchised national chain. It was sad to think of it, those kind Indian people being pushed out by tuna and cold-cut subs with nationally advertised prices. Nothing hot and fine made from scratch by elegant hands; no finesse, no grace.

Matt laughed at her. "How do you know they were pushed out? Maybe they made a ton of money, sold out and skipped town to Florida."

"What if they didn't? What if their dreams were broken?"

"You are so dramatic." He laughed at her some more.

It was sad because she and Matt had been there many times and now it was gone. As it was fading away she had been completely unaware. It was sad because it had been a part of their routines, which meant a part of their lives. She had just found the place closed and already she desperately missed the samosas and the chutneys and the chicken tikka masala, the best version she had tasted anywhere.

"I can't believe it," she moaned.

Matt shrugged. "There's another Indian place in Kenmore Square. We can just walk over there."

Amy was aghast. "But it's so sad that it's closed."

He pulled her away, steered her toward their new destination. "So we're never going to eat Indian again? You're so sentimental."

"But we used to come here all the time. On dates in the beginning and then for take-out later. I made you drive me here when I was super-pregnant just for the tikka masala cravings. Now do you feel sad?"

"No."

"What do you mean 'no'? What's it going to take to shake the stone mass that is your soul?"

"Oh, boy. What's it going to take to get you to adjust to the world revolving?"

"Har har. Such a funny young man." She poked him in the arm.

But she couldn't help but admire his adaptability. His ease in the face of change. She dug in and resisted; became nostalgic and sentimental. Her chest ached for what was never to be again. Matt was quick to recognize possibility. She believed he would always adjust and she would be able to follow along, faltering, stumbling maybe, in his footsteps. This she counted on.

Here, her feet on her kitchen floor, she watched the chaos of letters on the paper settle back into words. She gave the list to Matt.

"Can you go get these things?"

"Okay." He looked at the list. "This is a lot of stuff."

"It's for the gathering after the ceremony."

"Oh," he paused and stared at it. "Okay." He took his keys from the table. He stopped at the door and turned. "Why do we have to do it?" he said.

"I don't know. It's just what you do," she answered.

They held each other's eyes. She thought he was going to say something, but he didn't. Then he opened the door and left.

He brought the stuff back in large paper bags. Amy left them on the kitchen floor after she removed and refrigerated the cold items. The cheese took up too much space in the refrigerator drawers. It displaced their regular stuff.

She went to bed.

She woke from heavy sleep, her shirt wet and splotchy. She felt her milk let down; felt the tingle in her breasts, and there was no one to feed. Her body did not know. She cried quietly, her hand over her mouth. She looked at the clock. In the dark and quiet of two in the morning, she stared blindly at the ceiling. She soundlessly moved the light bedspread off her body and paused when Matt stirred, waited for his breathing to return to its steady sleeping stream.

In the kitchen, she turned on the weak light above the stove and shook with sobs. The kitchen was washed in soft yellow light that didn't reach the dark corners. She removed the pasta and tomatoes from the brown bag and folded it neatly. She placed it on the table, smoothed it out, reinforced the folds with her thumbnail.

She had not been up at that hour since Sage was tiny and not yet sleeping through the night. On those long nights, she had sat in the butter-yellow rocker Matt bought her while she was in the hospital recovering from Rachel's birth. She came home to find it by the window in the nursery. It was an overstuffed chair, soft yellow with white piping at the seams, perched upon half-moon wooden rockers. She had seen it in a catalog and he arranged to have it waiting for her when they brought baby Rachel home. When Sage still called out for middle-of-the-night feedings, Amy sat in the rocker and filled Sage's belly until she drifted off, a thin stream of milk trailing from the corner of her mouth. Amy often stayed in the rocker holding her for a while, watching her sleep; her face peaceful and undisturbed, her lips parted, her jaw soft. Amy forced herself to place Sage lightly into her crib and go back to bed. She knew she needed sleep, too.

She began to think about the funeral party. Would lasagna be good enough? Maybe she should call a caterer. Mom said they could do it themselves, but now she wondered. She rearranged the ingredients on the counter. She put the kettle on for tea and sat heavily into a chair in the dark kitchen to wait for the water to boil.

None of it mattered. None of it. None of this food. None of these worries. None of these people.

What she thought about, what mattered, was putting Sage back in the crib all those times. Amy couldn't believe she ever put her back in that crib before she was ready. She should have watched her for as long as she wanted. She should have looked for one more minute.

She slumped in the chair and cried, her shirt sticky and hot with milk. Her breasts full with no mouth to feed, no belly to fill.

~~~

Two days before the funeral, the heat ratcheted up. Amy was prickly and sweaty, like hot breath too close. The heat was ruthless, mean. She stared out the kitchen window at the train tracks. The green trolley squealed past every so often, stopping fifty feet from the entrance to her building. Its doors whisked open and people came and went to and from Commonwealth Avenue. She felt much farther away than where she was: a woman two floors up from the sidewalk, scrutinizing a world she no longer felt a part of.

"Amy?" her mom called from the foyer.

"In the kitchen." She was equally jarred at the intrusion and relieved for a distraction from her thoughts.

Her mother had come to help cook the food for the gathering. She had wanted to do the whole thing, but Amy said no. Sage was her baby; she would cook for her. She told herself that she would take these ingredients and make this food. She could turn on the oven and she could do this.

But the only thing that filled her head was the thought of her baby in the cold box at the funeral home. All she could contemplate was how she would manage to watch them lower Sage into the dark earth.

Mom hugged her. Amy's body was rigid; she could not make her body soft. "Hello, sweetheart." Amy could not speak.

Her mother held her for a few moments, then pulled away and, running her hands up and down Amy's arms, said, "Okay, where's the stuff?" She turned and opened the refrigerator. She moved to the cabinets, opened and closed them, looking. Her efficiency, single-mindedness and clarity unnerved, infuriated Amy.

Then there was a slipping inside her. It felt so real, Amy grasped at her abdomen. All at once, she was certain she could not make this food.

"I don't want to do this! Why are you making me do this?" she shrieked. Her breath was ragged and uneven; she was lightheaded and raging. This was not a tone she ever used, but all she could do in this moment was howl.

Mom's face turned soft with compassion. "Amy. I can do this for you. Please let me do this for you." She approached her with open arms. Amy jerked away and stepped back pointedly. She bumped harshly into the counter, the small of her back stung. It felt good and sharp and clean.

"No!" Amy shouted. "No, Mom. You always take over! Just stop taking over! I can make my own lasagna. I can make my own baby's funeral party!" She had to stop to breathe. "Go away!" she screamed.

Mom grew pink around the eyes, her lipsticked mouth puckered slightly. "If that's what you want, sweetheart." She picked up her bag and keys. She walked over and kissed Amy's cheek. She touched her arm with a softness, a gentleness that made Amy ache.

"If you need me, you just call, okay?" Her voice was kind and loving. Amy wanted her mother to hold her. She wanted her to stay. She wanted to sink into her mother's skin and familiar smell, feel the bones and soft places she knew so well. But she didn't. Amy watched her go, watched her car pull away as she stared down from her kitchen window. When she was gone, Amy sank to the floor and sobbed.

For her wedding bouquets, Amy wanted tiny nosegays of fat roses, the stems wound with creamy satin ribbon. And no bows. "No bows," she said to the florist more than once. She watched him note it next to all the other things he'd noted. The morning of the wedding, the flowers arrived in a big, white, cold box. Tiny nosegays of fat roses, stems wrapped in creamy satin ribbon. And bows. Big loopy bows with ribbon trailing down. Oh, bows, she thought, but it was too late to do anything about it and she realized she was too excited to care. Two years later, as she sat in rush hour traffic, she suddenly recalled the bows. *I could have just cut them off.* But the thought never occurred to her at the time.

The light in the kitchen shifted across the room from the windows near her table to the windows near her sink. The light reflected off the edge of the white porcelain. She heard the click of the door and footsteps coming toward her.

"Amy?" Matt said. "Babe, what are you doing on the floor?" He crouched down near her.

"I can't," she wept, her voice raw. "I can't."

He looked around the kitchen and stood up. He took the garbage can from under the sink. Slowly and with great care he placed the cartons and bags of cheese, the boxes of noodles, the jars of sauce into it. When it was all inside, he pulled out the bag, tied it up and placed it in the hall.

He sank to the floor and put his arms around Amy. "We'll call a caterer. We'll just...I don't know. We'll just get someone else to do this."

She leaned against him. *No one else can do this,* she thought.

~~~

There was a stain on the tablecloth. Curry from a long time ago. It was the turmeric in the curry that made the stain. Nothing removed that deep orange, almost crimson, out of the cloth. Nothing except maybe bleach, but the tablecloth was flax-colored stiff cotton decorated with paisleys and ornate colored borders and curlicues patterned all over in muted shades of turquoise and avocado green. Amy bought it in Cambridge at a very expensive textile shop. She hadn't been able to resist it and splurged when she and Matt were engaged. She thought of it as something beautiful for the home they were to make together.

"Did you try the Portuguese soap on it? And cold water?" Mom had asked when Amy consulted her about the stain. "Cold water?"

"Yes. Cold water."

"You line-dried it? Oh, you didn't put it in a hot dryer, did you?

"Nope."

"Hmmm. Let me think about it."

In the end, they didn't get the stain out.

Now the tablecloth draped, a soothing presence, and peered at Amy from the table. It sat beneath hot pads and paper plates and napkins. The things for later.

It was very early. Amy couldn't sleep and finally gave up and got out of bed. She stood in her kitchen, the room still and silent, on guard. Waiting to grit its teeth and withstand the noise and heavy footfalls and stuffy heat of the bodies it would enclose later. It would hold it all for Amy. It would press in and keep it all intact—prevent some rupturing. *Thank you.* Her prayer. But now, in this early hour, its gift was silence and fortitude.

There was the garbage can standing straight-spined in the corner. There was her shiny stove, her spotless counters. In the cabinets, she knew, boxes and cans lined up in neat rows. Waiting for her. The pans, the Tupperware, the lids for all of it. Spoons and ladles and muffin tins. All in their places. Their shininess, their cleanliness, their being in the place they were supposed to be. This was their language, their manner of speaking. They said in their profound silence, their slow way of saying, *We are here, we are solid, we are mass, we are heaviness. You know—we will sustain.* It was the deep calm that comes before the thing you don't think you can endure. The thing you don't think you can survive. *We are here.* And they were solid.

Amy moved a hot pad over the curry stain. *There*, the tablecloth breathed.

She made herself a cup of tea, sank to the floor, her back against a solid cabinet, and waited.

Matt woke up. Amy heard his feet in the creaks of the wooden floors. She imagined each part of him before he was in front of her eyes.

"Hi," she said. He bent down in front of her, cupped her face. His thumbs lightly wiped tears from under her eyes.

"I can't do this." She choked on each word. The words bit at her throat and mouth and lips. He said nothing as he pulled her up from the floor and they held each other.

"Mama?"

She dried her eyes quickly. "Morning, baby."

"Up please." Amy picked Rachel up and placed her on her hip. "I want to cuddle with Mama." She shifted the child so their bodies were flush in a hug. Amy concentrated on Rachel's small soft arms on the skin of her collarbone and neck. Her face on Amy's cheek. She closed her eyes, held Rachel and swayed.

Matt touched Amy's shoulder lightly. "Babe, we'd better get things going." He meant showers, breakfast, black clothes.

Amy resented all of it. It tore her insides raw, but she nodded.

"Here, Rachel. Daddy'll get you some yogurt and fruit."

"And granola?" she grinned. She settled into her chair and he began to pour granola over the yogurt. "No! I need the blue bowl!"

"Matt, she pours the granola in herself." Amy moved to the cabinet. "From this." She placed the blue bowl on the table.

Amy watched Rachel, secure in her habits. What she knew, the blue bowl, all good and right.

"What you did to the table? Why it's wearing a dress?" Rachel asked. She cocked her head, looked at the tablecloth-draped table against the wall.

"Oh." Amy looked at it with a blank mind and didn't know what else to say. "Daddy will get you dressed. Mommy has to take a shower. Okay?" Amy kissed her temple, felt Rachel's soft curls on her face.

She wandered to the bathroom. Did the getting-ready things. The sitter arrived and Amy asked her to take Rachel to the park for a while. The young woman nodded at Amy, her brow twisted in sympathy.

Then it was time to go.

There was a tent over the open grave. It was white but dirty at the seams and in the corners. It was a sunny day, extremely hot. The sun moved up the back of Amy's legs as the minister spoke over Sage's grave. She wasn't paying attention to him. It didn't seem to matter what he said. Mom and Dad stood to her left. She was relieved Rachel wasn't there. She wouldn't understand and Amy didn't know how to explain it to her.

"Mommy, where's Sage?" She asked Amy every day.

"She's in Heaven, sweetheart," Amy said. She kept her voice light.

"Oh," she looked at Amy quizzically. "When will she be back?" Amy should have known it wouldn't be as simple as a single question. She wished she had been prepared.

"Well, never, sweetheart. Her body is gone. Her soul is in Heaven."

"Oh." She paused, looked back up at Amy. "But where is she?"

"Gone, baby. Sage is just gone."

"But why?"

"I don't know, sweetie." *Give up, walk away.* Another prayer she recited silently. She didn't know the right things to say.

"Maybe she'll come back tomorrow." Rachel skipped away. Amy exhaled and bit back more tears, the endlessness of this new existence bearing down.

Five days. It had been only five days. Amy took great comfort in Rachel's soft, plush flesh; her warmth and smell. She held her to herself as often as she could and watched her sleep. She would never again assume anything. Such as the certainty of her high school graduation, her wedding. Such as tomorrow. She would not take for granted the measure of time when Rachel's hands were still small, her voice still high, the time when she still allowed Amy to be her mommy. She would never again stop herself or think there was something more important that needed to be done than whatever it was she wanted to do with her daughter at any given moment.

Heather and Andy stood a short distance from Amy and Matt. Their kids weren't there. Amy didn't know where they were. She hadn't spoken to Heather since the accident. Heather had called and driven over numerous times, but Amy screened the calls and had Matt put her off. She couldn't speak to her sister; could think of no words for her that strung together in some order. Only a lot of words running around barreling into each other.

Heather was crying audibly, wetly. Amy heard, but didn't look at her.

The only sadness Amy was able to internalize aside from her own was Matt's. His face was strained. She wanted so much to reach out and smooth the lines, but she could do nothing but hold his hand. His pressed firmly back in hers.

She had become aware of two distinct states: acute pain and acute numbness. She couldn't figure out which she preferred: feeling or not feeling. Being or absence.

Then the ceremony was over.

People at the edges, friends and extended family, began to break off, a big black dissipating pool, and got into their brightly-colored cars. The colors were all wrong—they were gratuitous. They hurt Amy's eyes.

"Sweetheart, we'll head over to the brownstone, make sure everything is set," Mom said. She put her soft arms around Amy, who remained stiff. It seemed she had forgotten how to be soft. Mom gave Amy a quick tight squeeze, ran her cool hands over Amy's hot cheeks. Her eyes were filled with tears, her lips quivered.

"Okay?" she said and tried to smile. Amy nodded. She wanted to curl up in her mother, be carried and held inside where she might be safe. Where all she would hear was a soft whooshing white noise; be engulfed in a warm, blind cavern. Dad pulled her to him and she inhaled his scent—his shaving cream, the same spicy cologne. He kissed each of Amy's cheeks and cleared his throat. He took Mom's arm and they moved toward the car where Heather's and Andy's shadowy shapes took up the backseat.

Matt gripped Amy as the last car drove away. She opened her arms to him. She strained to hold him, he was so heavy, but she tried. Would keep trying. His tears were in her hair. He pulled away from her a little, his breathing coming in gasps and bursts. Amy had never seen him like this. It tore at her. They said nothing, simply descended one into the other. Their eyes held for a long timeless moment. He buried his face in her neck once more, his head on her neck and the shoulder of her black dress that absorbed the sun and the intense heat of his sadness. She held him as tightly as she was able.

"How can we leave her here?" His body collapsed slightly and he sniffed, his breathing growing more even. He pulled away and looked her in the face, waiting for some answer.

"I don't know." She was only capable of leaving Sage there because in some dreamlike way it didn't feel final. As though there would be other times they would be here, doing this again. As though there would be other times she and Matt would stand at the edge of this hole wherein lay a box that held their baby. If they didn't close the hole then Amy could believe this was not some unbearable end. The open hole was somehow less definite. She glanced at the mound of soft, moist earth piled at the side of the grave.

They stood silently, hands clasped.

"Should we go?" he said.

"I guess so."

She wanted to break apart and allow the pieces to float off where nothing was known.

He pulled her to him again as they stood on the soil.

"I know." She rubbed his back in little circles, started to create a pattern. "I know."

She didn't know. But she said it anyway.

~~~

The lasagna was half gone. A giant bowl of salad was, too. The caterers replenished some of it, served it out. Amy walked through her kitchen and looked around. People stood and people sat with plates of food, full or half full. Maybe second helpings. It was hard for her to determine. They shoveled the red gooey pasta into their mouths with clear plastic forks. Disposable. Mom's idea. Less to clean up later. Later. More later. Always, later. People walked past Amy with red stained paper plates, back to the buffet. They stopped to hug her, say *sorry*, make *I'm sorry* faces at her. She poured herself another glass of wine and leaned against the counter, facing the table.

People sympathized, but they did not really want to face the reality of a dead baby. They did not want to think it could happen to them. They didn't want this to be too real. Like cancer, it only happened to other people. Amy glared at them—her family, her friends, especially people she did not recognize.

She flagged Mom over.

"Who is he?" Amy stared at the back of a large, wide man.

"Oh, Ted Fernandes. He works with your dad."

Amy watched as more food was piled on Ted's stained plate. She had never seen this man.

"He eats a lot."

"Amy! Shhh," Mom whispered as she gently touched her arm.

Amy gulped the wine, turned and refilled her glass.

"You should eat something. I'll get you some food, sweetheart," Mom said, already heading for the buffet.

"No. I'm fine. I don't want anything." She turned and walked into the living room. People were in small, serene clumps. Some laughed quietly.

Heather stood in the corner with a couple of cousins. Amy stared at her—her eyes bore into the curve of her sister's back and shoulder blades, swathed in deep navy blue. She turned and looked right into Amy's eyes. Heather was so afraid; Amy knew every thought, every emotion beating through her. A wave of satisfaction shot through her. Heather moved slowly toward Amy. She walked as though she were barefoot and the floor were broken glass. She couldn't hold Amy's eyes, but Amy didn't blink.

"Amy," she said softly. She took a deep breath. It shook as she exhaled. She tried to hide it by coughing, but Amy knew.

Amy remained silent.

Heather began to cry. She reached for Amy, who pulled back so slightly she wasn't sure her sister had noticed. Amy wanted her to notice but she was afraid, too, that she had.

She had.

Heather's face collapsed. "Please, Amy," she pleaded. She held her arms out like a child, sobbing, inconsolable. "I've been trying to see you all week. Why won't you talk to me?" she wailed.

Amy didn't know what to say. There was what she wanted to say that she couldn't say.

"Amy, please! Say something!"

"What do you want me to say?"

"I want to be here for you." She stood arms' length from Amy. She'd stopped trying to embrace her. Her hands lay limp and helpless by her thighs. One hand began to roll the seam of her skirt. Amy brought her eyes to Heather's face again. Too much welled up; she stood there waiting for the love to rise over the rage.

"No you don't. You want to feel better."

"What?" She took Amy's arm and pulled her into the bathroom. She closed the door and turned on the fan.

"What." It was a statement now.

"I can't help you with this, Heather."

"I didn't do this on purpose, Amy. I would give you anything to make up for it." Her voice caught, tears flowed down her face, collected as they fell.

Amy's instinct was to wipe them away; to catch the pool at her chin.

She didn't.

Cruelty rose up over compassion, over love. Cruelty and hardness. Amy felt hard—her heart, her face, her hands, in her bones.

"One of your own, Heather? Would you give that?" Amy spat. She didn't cry. Heather breathed. Amy could see her chest moving. The motion was fast and rhythmic. She tried to keep it under control, but Amy had seen her like this before, just never under her own thumb.

At the time, as her sister stood twitching before her, it felt good. Burning and cleansing.

Later it felt worse than almost anything.

Dispensing Pain

Sage is in the water. She is in the water. She is slipping out of Amy's hands. Amy tries to pick her up. She grasps a foot but it is slick and slides right through her hand. Amy locates an arm and it slips away. Then a wave takes her out of Amy's reach. Heather screams in the background. Amy pounds through the surf. Sage's bathing suit is hot pink. There is a ruffle on the bum, white with hot pink polka dots. Amy remembers where she bought the suit.

Where is she? Where is she?

A foot. Amy grabs it. It slips. A wave comes. She searches. She searches. It happens over and over. Every time she has her, she loses her almost instantly.

Amy wakes with a start, her heart pounding sporadically. She realizes she's sitting up. Where is she? Where is Matt? Then she remembers. This is Heather's prone body. They are on Martha's Vineyard. She lies down, her limbs limp as the adrenaline seeps away.

It is very dark. Shafts of angled moonlight cross the room. It is deathly quiet. Even the crickets are soundless.

Heather sleeps on. She does not stir.

Amy's breathing is jagged and rough. In her mind, she chants slowly: inhale, exhale. Inhale, exhale.

She rolls over and faces Heather. Heather's breathing is deep and regular. Her lips slightly parted. She sleeps on.

Amy is wide awake. She relives death.

Heather does not stir.

Amy can't sleep and is awake when the sun begins to illuminate the room. When the light falls on the pillows, Heather awakens.

"Morning," she says quietly. "How long have you been awake?"

When she speaks, it is an extension of Amy's own voice. She can hear herself in Heather's inflections, in the words she chooses. The manner by which words form in her mouth and are pushed through her teeth and lips, is as Amy's own words form, moving up and through and out her body.

When she hears Heather's voice, she wants to listen. She yearns to hear, to absorb the sound waves into her skin. It is basic comfort. Amy has never tired of it.

But lately it has become a heavy, dark wave, a burden. At first she thought it was simply a matter of not wanting to talk to her sister, as Amy harbored and clung to her dense, black, soundless anger. But she has come to realize that the problem is the inverse, because the burden is her deep longing for the sound. Amy longs for the feeling the sound once bestowed, a comfort that seems lost to her. As though she can never go back to that place where Heather's voice resonated in the deepest part of her soul, her bones, her blood.

But, tentatively, her thoughts are turning. She thinks—cautiously—you can always go back if you want to. Or find your way back if you choose.

These ifs are another great burden.

"How are you feeling, Amy?" she asks.

Amy and her sister: always conscious of each other's feelings. There have been few times when one is responsible for the pain the other is experiencing. They are careful. They care too much not to be.

There was a boy, Alex Porter. He was in Heather's class. The autumn he and Heather were seniors and Amy a sophomore, he went from being a fringe friend to a part of the regular crowd. Heather really liked him.

"*We should all go to the dance this weekend,*" *someone said at lunch one day. Amy had noticed the signs around school. Brightly handmade with tempera paint, newsprint wrinkled under these words:* Party All Night! Music! 7-11 pm Saturday! West Side Gym!

"*Oh, come on, we haven't gone to one of those since freshman year,*" *Heather said, a sandwich in her hand. She took a bite. "It's so dorky."*

"*I know, but we can dance, be the cool ones and leave early."*

"*Sounds kind of fun,*" *Amy said.*

"*Yeah, and none of us can ever get enough of the current Top Forty,*" *one of the girls said, rolling her eyes.*

"*I love Duran Duran,*" *Alex said.*

"*Of course you do,*" *Heather said, motioning to his black Dead Kennedys T-shirt.*

"*I'm into it if you guys are,*" *Amy said. She'd never been to a school dance, a consequence of being embraced by Heather's friends, older kids, right from the start. She never had to manage the gauche reality of high school dances, largely attended by freshmen, a dash of sophomores and the least popular juniors and seniors.*

"*I'll go,*" *Alex said, looking at Amy.*

"*Okay,*" *Heather shrugged nonchalantly, but agreed with him quickly.*

The kids on the dance committee had decorated the gym with the usual materials—streamers, crepe paper, huge hand-lettered banners. The dimmed lights helped them to forget this place was a center of humiliation, dodge ball and PE calisthenics. Amy and Heather and their friends walked in together, stopped in the doorway and surveyed the scene. There was a smattering of kids in the middle of the dance floor, a peppering of kids at the perimeter with cups of punch in hand. The room vibrated with the artificial beat of some pop song Amy vaguely recognized. They moved in, stood off to the side.

Heather and some of the other girls went to the bathroom.

"Wanna come, Amy?" Heather asked.

"No, I'm good."

The pop song ended and "Dancing with Myself" started up loud, booming off the concrete walls, barely absorbed by the shiny wood floor.

"Now this is cool," Alex said and grabbed Amy's arm. She laughed.

"Alex, what are you doing?"

"Dancing. We're at a dance. It's right in the name of the thing what you're supposed to do." He pulled her onto the dance floor. A small crowd jumped around. Alex was a really good dancer. He smiled and spun her around. He was so good looking. Why hadn't she noticed before?

Heather had noticed. The night before, Heather came into Amy's room late, their parents already in bed. She quietly opened Amy's door a crack and peered in.

"You up?"

Amy put the novel she was reading upside down on the bed beside her. "Yup."

Heather closed the door behind her, crossed the room and flopped down on the bed. She tossed a bag of Skittles to Amy, who tore open the package and dumped the contents on her quilt. They began to sort them by color. Heather split the colors in half. It was the way they had been eating Skittles forever.

"There's one extra orange and an extra purple," she said. "Which do you want?"

"Which do you think?"

She lightly tossed the purple to Amy.

They ate one color at a time, taking turns choosing.

"Yellow," Amy said. And they ate them.

"Green," Heather said.

Purple and red were always last because they were the favorites.

Amy's clock radio played softly, a Van Halen song they both liked. The room was lit only by the small clip-on lamp on her headboard.

Halfway through the greens, Heather groaned quietly and with closed eyes leaned back into the pillows.

"What?" Amy said and leaned back with her.

"Alex."

"Alex what?"

"Alex. He's so cute. He doesn't even know I'm alive," she moaned.

"Maybe he does, you don't know."

"He just thinks I'm one of the gang," she shook her head.

"Orange," Amy said. "When did you start liking him?"

She shrugged, drew her eyebrows together a little. "Maybe a month ago?"

"A month! Why didn't you tell me?"

"I kind of didn't know until, like, this week. You know how that happens?"

Amy nodded, thinking of her own crushes. How one day a boy was a boy and the next all you could think about. He practically glowed when he walked past you in the halls.

"Want me to talk to him?" Amy asked. "Red."

"No! God, no! He doesn't like me and I'd die. I have to eat lunch with him, and hang out. His locker is near mine. I'd be so mortified." Amy nodded.

"Purple," Heather said. "Now I can't wait for the dance, though. Maybe something will happen."

At the dance, as Amy and Alex pranced around the gym floor, she realized Heather was right about how cute he was. How cool he was. The song ended and she started to walk over to the group, but he pulled her back. She laughed at him. The others joined them on the dance floor. They danced to every song; the dance floor was theirs.

The opening notes of a really popular love song blared. Lots of kids moved to the edges. Alex pulled Amy to him. He waltzed her around, as though he knew what he were doing. Amy was loving it. About halfway through the song, he stopped goofing around and they swayed to the music. She had never felt such a strong awareness of her body or another's body near hers. His hand was so soft; she had never really known the skin of anyone outside her family.

Heather started to hurl dirty looks at Amy which she pretended she didn't notice.

They drove home with a cold and brittle silence between them. A solid, icy mass. When they stopped in their driveway, Heather slammed the car door and blew past Amy into the house. Amy went to her room and hid, crept out to brush her teeth when she heard Heather's bedroom door close. Amy washed up quickly, slinked back to her room, shut the light and rolled over. She did all this quietly, deliberately. She was wide awake for a long time.

They didn't speak on Sunday.

Amy avoided her on Monday morning as much as was possible in a small house with one bathroom. She deferred everything to Heather—the bathroom, *the cereal, any room she chose to be in. Amy hid without actually concealing her body.*

They executed all the usual motions at school, but they neither spoke nor made eye contact. At the lunch table, Amy could tell the others noticed, but they didn't ask. Alex was the only oblivious one, sitting near her, flirting. She shifted away from him. Then she could feel Heather's eyes on her. They slid away when Amy looked up.

"I need to talk to my chem teacher...about lab," Amy announced as she stood. "See you all later." She hid in the girls' room until the bell rang.

When she got home, she closed herself in her room after supper and slid into bed early.

Amy tried to read. It was late when Heather came in. She let the door hit the closet, not loudly enough to wake their parents, but enough so Amy would know it was intentional. "You are such a bitch."

Amy bristled. "It's not my fault, Heather." For an instant she had considered pretending not to know what Heather was talking about, but knew just as quickly she couldn't get away with such evasion.

"You knew I liked him. I told you." She looked so sad under the anger. Amy saw the sadness flickering like a candle over Heather's face, in the movements of her body, sharp and so unlike her—unlike all the pieces of her Amy had seen. She had assumed she'd seen them all.

"He was dancing with me. He paid attention to me. Not the other way around." Amy said, as if this could absolve her. But she didn't know what else to say.

"You didn't have to dance with him. Especially all freakin' night." Her voice and body were tight. She breathed through her slightly opened mouth.

173

Amy could see her chest moving up and down under her pajama top. Heather stared at her. Amy could think of nothing to say.

Heather began to cry. "How could you do that to me?" And Amy knew suddenly without a doubt why her sister was crying, why she was angry.

Amy began to sob. "I don't know why I did it," she choked. "I'm so sorry, Heather."

She sat down heavily next to Amy on the bed. "You knew," she whispered. They cried quietly together. They said nothing. Amy's digital clock kept changing, the red numbers glowing in the dark.

"I'm sorry," Amy said.

"Do you like him?" she asked Amy.

Amy said quietly, "I don't know." She hadn't liked him before the dance, but everything felt different now.

"I think he likes you."

"Maybe," Amy said.

They both knew he did.

They sat quietly in the dark as the radio played softly. Amy didn't listen to the music but instead to Heather's breathing. She waited as she held her own breath for Heather to speak, but she didn't.

"I won't do it ever again," Amy said. "Not Alex or any other guy." Amy cried softly.

Heather let out a big shaky breath. "Let's never fight over a boy again," she said.

Amy thought a lot about the two days of silence. They were terrible, but worse was knowing she had been the cause of her sister's pain.

"Never again," Amy said.

"Never," Heather said.

They moved under the covers and Amy handed Heather a pillow. They curved together under the covers, talked and giggled. Everything was right again.

"Little people, little problems," Mom always said about Amy and Heather's children. It's all relative, Amy knows.

On the Vineyard, the day moves forward and in the afternoon they decide to get a bottle of wine and take a walk on the beach. They walk to a small grocery, find a bottle with a screw cap and a couple of paper coffee cups. They make their way down to the shore. It is the same water that laps on Cattail's shore. The surf is placid, a quiet hiss, no roar.

"Let's sit," Amy says. They sit in the sand a few feet from the tide line. The surf almost reaches their toes. The sand here is coarse, not the sugar-soft sand of Cattail. Millions of tiny stones. Amy supposes the sand at Cattail is also millions of tiny stones, but individually they are finer.

They sit, not speaking, and sip their wine. The sound of the water fills their large silence.

Amy wants what used to be again. She doesn't know how to resurrect it. She longs achingly for what has been lost—her baby, her sister. She finds herself wishing so hard that black spots cover her eyes. Why can't I have this? Her body screams. She feels like a child who cannot have her way and will not accept it. She refuses to accept it. It is a hard thing running down her middle.

The late afternoon sun shines weakly on the rippling water. The tide is coming in and they scoot back in the sand. The sound and movement of the water are mesmerizing.

"It's so pretty here," Heather says. "So peaceful." Amy agrees.

Silence. But it is weighty as though something is coming. Amy steels herself.

"So, how are you feeling?" she asks. "About everything?"

Amy shrugs. Her gut reaction is to say nothing. Hasn't it been long enough? Hasn't the silence persisted long enough? A voice whispers this to Amy. Who is that? Who said that? She looks at Heather. She is so undeniably recognizable to Amy; every curve, every gesture.

And Amy still does not know what to say.

She watches the water flowing toward them and away again. Its pattern remains the same but the nuances shift. She watches one spot for a few moments and notices the rippling undulations. Simultaneously static and mutable, even though this does not seem possible.

"Remember Alex Porter?" Amy says.

Heather nods, smiles. "Yeah. I was so hot for him. What made you think of that?"

Amy shrugs. "I don't know. I was just thinking about stuff that seemed so important once. We laugh about it now, but, God, you were mad at me. I was terrified of it."

"Of what?" she says.

"I'm not sure. Of that feeling. Of being distant from you. Mostly for being the source of that pain beneath your anger."

Amy is still looking at the water. She hears that her sister has begun to cry softly.

"I felt like the smallest person. I'd never felt that small, that...low. Like the worst person. We fought and bickered sometimes. Remember how it irritated the shit out of Mom?" She pauses and they laugh a little at that. "But that wasn't real. There was no real threat there. Alex wasn't a big deal, either. I can't even really remember what he looked like. I mean I can, vaguely, in this general cute-boy way. You know?"

"Yeah, I can't remember, either," Heather says. "He wasn't a big deal. Sorry I made it into such a big deal. It was stupid." She speaks in a rush.

"No," Amy says. "It was a big deal. It was really big. And terrible." She stops. Amy knows Heather is confused—Amy is not making sense to her. She asks Amy how she feels.

"You want to know how I'm feeling?" Amy says and touches Heather's shoulder. She looks at Amy, sadness plain and unadorned on her face.

MELISSA CORLISS DELORENZO

Amy remembered times—so many times—being compared to Heather, by relatives and friends. The ways in which they were alike, the ways in which they were different. At times it was flattering and at times she wanted to be anything but a copy of her older sister. Then sometimes Amy intentionally emulated her. Mostly she noticed that the line where Heather began and she ended was blurry. (The line was grayed and muted, smudging away any sharpness.)

It was not strange that Amy knew her sister's body so well. So often people shy away from each other, from touching. Everyone clothed, a gauzy film of woven fibers taking the form of leg, arm, neck. The clothing a barrier, not only thinly physical, but symbolic—everyone feels safely separated. But touch a person, hug them, and you feel flesh and you press into bones.

There are bodies we know.

It took time to know a body. Amy knew Heather's body in a way she didn't think about. Contact with her was so natural as not to impress her consciousness.

There were years when their bodies were different—Heather ahead of Amy with hands a little larger, legs slightly longer. Then suddenly they stood together, looked in the mirror at equal height. Amy's baby fat smoothed and thinned over her cheekbones, both of them with slim faces, shoulders meeting, breasts falling softly, hips pushing out to the same slender width, recovered from the widening of pregnancy. When they hugged, it was like embracing their own self. Everything lined up as they faced one another, laced fingers, pressed foreheads, shared breath. Sister bodies.

No Surface

There was a silence like being underwater; very still water. Amy was engulfed but could see the hazy surface, pale yellow-green light, rippling gently. She felt cradled. Her senses dulled, vision softened, ears packed with cotton, throat milky. She felt almost safe.

But there always came the time when she had to emerge.

The silence stayed with her as she made attempts to move. It was a white noise slowly punctured by the sounds of her home. *Poke.* Birds. *Poke.* Trolley car. *Poke.* Coffeemaker. *Poke.* Rachel's small voice. That sound made her wish she wanted to get up. It made her get up in spite of not wanting to.

Her eyes quivered, bobbed back and forth, as though moving through viscous water. She could not focus them when she stood. The simple act of breathing felt off. When she took a deep breath, it was as though small deposits of water pooled in the bottoms of her lungs; those tiniest of air sacs drowned. What were they called? She could not remember.

A yearning more powerful than deep thirst burned in her throat, made more desperate for the knowledge that the thing for which she yearned could never be brought back. She ached to touch soft limbs, delicate fingers, small round downy head; run her hands, her forehead over the exquisitely smooth skin. Feel the tug at her breasts, now slack and dry. Her body still responded at the baby's imagined cry which sounded so real. She heard it in her head like a signal. Sometimes sharp, sometimes cooing softly. Amy could almost feel Sage, her small density on her

179

chest, pressing into her lungs, her rib bones. She longed painfully to run the backs of her fingers over the plump elbows, encircle the tiny soft ribcage with her hands to see if the tips of her fingers met.

She recalled, with cruel and relentless clarity, the sensation of losing. She could not stop reliving the sensations of loss—her body memory, her heart memory. She wished she could stop her mind from forming those same images; piecing history together, moment by moment, with vicious accuracy. It seemed to happen without her conscious aid; certainly without her consent. Why wouldn't her mind allow forgetfulness of the thing she never wanted to remember again? There were entire years gone from her memory. Sometimes she forgot the three items supposed to be purchased at the supermarket on the way home. And yet her mind recalled with miserable clarity every body sensation, every scent, sound, color of the moments she wished to obliterate from her consciousness.

She could feel Sage's slack body, the smoothness of her baby limbs slick with salt water. The grotesque unliving way her head fell back from the soft rolls of baby flesh at her neck. The neck muscles that had gained strength enough to hold that head only a few short months. The blue lips, the foam coming from the corners of her tiny nose. The coldness of her body. Amy could not forget. She could not forget her own screams, her feeling of helplessness.

But she could never say "no" to the little ghost that haunted. Little ghost, not flesh, but real in its own way.

She would take the pain if it were the only way. She would take what she could get.

And then sometimes the horror would float past and the sweet memories swell and she lay on the pillows, relived the sentient moments projected on the white walls of her bedroom and fell deeply into remembering until she reached that moment, blessed and floating, when she forgot that the images on the wall were not real. Sage was safely back and Amy placed her at her breast.

Alveoli. That's what they were called.

~~~

Amy pushed herself up and out of bed. She pushed out of heavy, groggy sleep and up onto the floor, put her feet onto the floor and up. She pushed to walk to the kitchen. She pushed to be cheerful for Rachel. She knew Rachel needed her.

A month went by. Maybe a little more.

There was a hard steel rod where Amy's spine used to be, holding the doily that had been her ribcage, her lungs. They dangled and flickered in the breeze, with the slightest movement of air.

Every day when Matt came home, Amy left. She went to the grave. She didn't make supper, merely threw food together. She didn't eat. Then she left and sat in the grass near her baby's headstone. Over Sage's body, where she was now, was a pile of brown dirt, still slightly damp. Tiny grass tender green poking out of the fecund soil. Amy pulled them out one by one as she spoke to Sage. She could never recall what she said. She went back home and put Rachel to bed. Sometimes she ate a little and sometimes she forgot to eat.

After Rachel was asleep safe in her bed, Amy found Matt in the kitchen. He opened and closed cabinets.

"Amy, there's no food. Rachel wanted a snack and there's no food. We can't keep eating sandwiches! We can't keep eating hummus for supper! That's all we have anymore. It's not good for Rachel."

Amy stared at him, her eyes wide. Her mouth was open and she tried to say the right words. *I'm afraid to go to the grocery store.* But she said. "What's good for her? How would you know? I'm the one who gets up and up and up and pretends I'm okay. All damn day! You're the one who gets to escape." She hadn't gone back to Déguiser yet. She conferenced with Sheila over the phone when she must. She claimed Rachel needed her, which she believed was true. What she left unsaid was that she couldn't face it. She was too exhausted and sad to be grateful even for Sheila's experience and willingness to take it all on. She was oblivious to anything but her pain. But Matt went in and made sure their company kept running. Amy wasn't grateful for that, either. Relieved, but that was as far as her generosity stretched. And yet here she flung it at him.

He stared at her with stone in his eyes. "I don't want to rank who has a harder time every day. But since you never ask me, I'll tell you about my days. I go in and take calls and answer emails and pretend to give a shit about meetings and all the 'crises' that arise. No one asks about our daughter. No one asks me how I'm doing anymore. All the condolences were already doled out. Now it's status quo. You try that and I'll do the fucking groceries." They stared at each other, neither blinking. The house was silent, as though it were afraid to breathe.

Amy covered her mouth. She didn't want to cry, but her eyes stung. "That was mean." It was a whisper when she hadn't meant to speak.

He came over and he curled into her and she coiled into him. "I'm sorry," she said.

"I'm sorry," he said. She felt his hot breath, his mouth, wetness through her thin shirt. She couldn't buy her family food, she couldn't cook it. She couldn't remember the last time she showered.

"I'm scared to go to the grocery store," she blurted.

His shoulders sank and he sighed. "Oh, babe. Tomorrow I'll stay home. We'll go to the store together. The three of us," he said. Amy nodded.

"I'm going to go wash up," she said.

She stood in the shower and pretended the water possessed the power to wash anything away.

~~~

Amy took Rachel to children's story time at the library. Rachel loved it and Amy wanted her life to flow in some normal patterns. Nothing felt right to Amy, but there were some grooves she could try to make do.

Rachel complained of aches and pains since Sage died. She cried out in the night.

"What, baby? What is it?" Amy asked her in the dark, pulling her close. Her small heart beating like a bird's.

"My leg hurts! My leg hurts!" Her voice sleepy and hoarse.

"Which one?" She pointed and Amy rubbed it gently as Rachel cried. As Amy rubbed, Rachel's crying slowed. Amy rubbed and felt Rachel's heart slow down near her own. She rubbed until the windows behind Rachel's pulled shades grew pink. Then she lay down near her daughter and fell asleep.

The doctor checked. "It's nothing but growing pains," she said. *No. The pain of missing*, Amy thought. Phantom pains.

Amy and Rachel walked to the library. Labor Day had passed, but a dead summer heat returned to mid-September. Amy yearned for the cool of fall, but she dressed Rachel in shorts and sandals and they set off for story time.

Amy recognized the other moms and their children by sight, a familiarity bred from shared motherhood. Story time was a loved thing. All Amy ever needed to say to her girls was "library" and all joy broke loose. Even in Sage, as little as she had been. Today, Rachel hopped around when Amy told her they were going. All the regular things, the good things, must be kept up for her. Amy knew she had to. This she told herself. *You must.* She was split—grieving mother and cherishing mother, nurturing. Grateful yet shattered. *You must.* A new prayer she recited. The reciting itself a chore, never mind accomplishing all it dictated. All the things that must be done, and done again.

The air in the library was cool on their sidewalk-heated skin. Amy breathed it in, stale and recycled, but cold. The children's room was already tightly packed when Amy settled Rachel into a small seat, powder blue and smooth. The kind she remembered from grade school. She stood at the back with the other parents. She looked up and eyes darted off her. A few lingered and smiled sadly. Amy's breath seized up, floated away on the stagnant, frigid air. She had not thought of this, or perhaps had forgotten, about others. Somehow she thought she would be anonymous. She breathed and straightened up. She made her way over to one of the mothers she knew. "Can you keep an eye on Rachel while I go look for a few books? I'll be back before this is over."

"Of course," she said.

Amy hesitated. She glanced at Rachel, who was engrossed in the story. "She'll be okay, right? You'll watch her?"

"She won't even notice you're gone. Don't worry." She touched Amy's arm. She stared at the woman's hand. Amy felt spongy inside, her organs slipping. "It's okay," the woman said. Finally Amy walked away.

She sat at a computer. She needed to find books about grieving children. How to help them because Amy had no idea and she didn't want to make mistakes with this.

She wandered through the shelves and pulled out books. She flipped through them—pages and pages of words. She couldn't be sure which were the best ones—the ones that would help her. In the stacks she recalled college and the hours she'd spent happily searching for the books that would unravel a topic she needed to understand. The books and all they promised to impart excited her. Now as she lay her hands along the spines, she was only tired.

As she made her way back to the children's room, she heard the screaming of a child. There was terror in the child's voice. *That is my child*, Amy thought without conjuring up the actual words. She slapped the books on the nearest table and ran toward the noise.

Rachel screamed, "Mommy! Where's Mommy?" Her voice was hysterical and tears tracked her cheeks.

"I'm here, baby," Amy called.

"Mama!" She ran to Amy who lifted her, cradling her. Rachel placed her wet hands on Amy's face. "I lost you. I couldn't find you."

"I'm here. I'd never leave you. Mama's sorry. I just went to find some books." Amy hugged her close. "Mama's so sorry."

"I was scared."

"Oh, no. I'm sorry." Amy held her until she began to wiggle, calm again. "Should we go home?"

"Can I pick out a book?"

"Of course. You can pick out a bunch."

"I can?"

"Yup!"

"But I want Mama to stay with me."

"Okay." When Amy looked up, some of the other women looked away. She was almost sure they did.

Rachel had never grown upset like that before. She was always independent. These were the quiet apologies she muttered to the librarians once Rachel had calmed down. Mostly she said these things to assure herself.

They checked out their books and walked home. Rachel chattered away as if nothing had happened. They held hands and Amy smiled for Rachel the entire time.

Later, she read the books about grieving children. The symptoms she and Matt might expect were printed on the page, bulleted and bold. Irritability, sadness, bodily discomfort, sleeplessness, loss of appetite, worrying, nightmares, loneliness. The books said that in small doses these symptoms were normal. They were to watch for *persistent patterned changes in the child's behavior.*

She thought of the leg pains, Rachel's terror when she couldn't find her in the library. What did a pattern look like? What qualified as persistent?

Matt sat down with Amy at the kitchen table. He handed her a beer and peered at the books in the pool of light. The day had cooled down at last and the evening air through the open windows was a relief.

"These any help?" he asked.

"Yes. No. It's all kind of general and vague." She shrugged and took a sip of the cold beer. "Piaget says children Rachel's age are egocentric. They believe everyone sees the world just as they do."

"Don't we all?" He smiled. She touched his hand.

"Are you okay, Matt?"

He paused. "I'm really busy at work. I think it helps." She sensed something weighty in his silence. "I've been calling a friend. From college. He's a therapist. In Cambridge." His words came out in little chunks. "It's not really therapy. Just someone to talk to."

"You have?"

"Just sometimes." It was an apology.

"I think that's great." They were quiet. They both looked out on the train track lit by the streetlamps.

"He can suggest someone. For you. If you want."

"Nah. I couldn't. Not now. I have to worry about Rachel." She didn't meet his eyes.

"I worry about you."

Softly, "I can't talk about this with a stranger. Not now. I have you." She moved her mouth into a smile for him. She couldn't bear to turn in on herself, to peer in too closely.

"Okay. If you change your mind..." They were quiet for a long time. Only tiny house noises breached the hush.

"Matt?"

"Yeah?"

"This is so awful," She choked. They grasped hands and cried together.

Amy immersed herself in the library books; for a week nothing but the books. Parents were to offer comfort and consolation. They were to share feelings and allow the child to talk about it. Rachel didn't talk about it. She was three—should they encourage her to talk? Amy looked through a dozen books, but there was so little to say about children her age.

"We have to make sure Rachel doesn't feel neglected since we're dealing with...everything," Amy parroted from one of the books. It was early morning and Rachel was still asleep. Matt stood, travel mug of coffee and work bag in hand.

He looked at her intently. "Okay." He kissed her and started toward the door. "Maybe do something fun today. Put the books down and relax."

"I have to make sure we're doing this right, Matt. We can't just half-ass this." Her heart bumped around uncomfortably.

"Babe, I know. But—just don't get too wrapped up in worrying about how we're handling this. I think we're doing okay. Do something fun."

Amy inhaled. "Fun? I don't even know what that means anymore."

His face hardened. "I don't know. It was just a thought."

"Fun...You think it's easy for me here. I have to make sure Rachel is okay and clearly I'm tackling that on my own." She closed the book noisily, stood and walked to the sink. She faced the window and stared down into the back garden.

"We've already established that's not what I think, Amy. Sage is gone. She's gone and nothing we do is going to change that. No matter how *perfectly* we do it."

"You don't understand anything." Her back was still to him.

"I'll call you later. 'Bye."

Bye. Three little spit-out letters.

Once he left, she made more coffee and sat down with her books. *Fun*, she thought with vitriol. There would be no more fun. Her child was dead. Her extended family was nothing but wreckage.

Heather called and Amy could not answer. She had stopped answering the phone altogether. The phone rang, rang, rang. Amy kept sweeping, doing dishes, staring out the window. The machine clicked on, her recorded voice politely requesting a message. She stopped whatever she was doing, broom stilled, soapy hands dripping, eyes frozen on the window glass.

"Amy?" Heather's voice. "Are you home?" Silence; sigh. "Okay, you're not there. Please call me back if you can. I really want to talk to you. I miss you. I hope you're okay. I love you." Click.

Amy leaned her broom against the wall, dried her wet hands, drew her eyes from the T tracks, walked over to the machine and pressed the erase button. The machine responded to her action with a satisfying beep.

Sweep, wash, stare.

It was all rubble. And she could never go back to Cattail. There was no more refuge for her. It was ruined—all of it. Everything that made any sense to her. Everything she had always loved and counted on. Gone. An ugly shell only hinting at what used to be. Matt didn't understand. Heather would, but she was ruined, too. Amy cried for the nothing she had left. She cried because of course she had something left— Matt, Rachel. How could she think *nothing*?

One of the books said young children couldn't comprehend the finality of death. Their belief that the dead person would return made it easier for them. They simply waited patiently, always in the back of their minds knowing the person would come back. Someday. Come in and the screen door would slam shut. "I'm ho-o-o-ome!" the dead kid would call out. "Finally!" the other kid would say. "Where ya' been?" The prodigal kid would shrug, raise her eyebrows *who knows*? And that would be answer enough.

~ ~ ~

Amy returned to work just as the leaves were beginning their autumn change. A smear of color here and there, the world still mostly green. The summer heat passed and the air turned cool and dry. Amy had been away from Déguiser for nearly two months. Matt and Sheila needed her and she hoped that if she put her hands back to work and turned her attention to something outside the bleak reality of loss, she might begin to feel again some part of the life she once loved. She wasn't convinced it was possible, but she couldn't stay home forever—might as well grasp on to some small fragment of hope. She wondered, in a detached manner, whether she would find it all irrelevant—brides' whims and mania, mothers' anxieties over every minute detail of their children's parties, the importance of hanging fabric just so. Looked at from a certain angle, it all seemed absurd.

But she got into her car and drove to the coffee shop on the way to her studio where she always bought her morning coffee.

"Good morning! Latté with one sugar?" Previously, this guy had made her coffee every day.

"Good morning—yes, thank you," Amy said.

"I haven't seen you in a while. How are you?"

She froze and could only imagine the look on her face because she was filled with horror. He looked a little startled.

"I'm okay. How are you?" she said finally.

"Good, good," he handed her the cup. "Have a great day!"

"You, too," she said as she handed him money.

She walked out quickly. It occurred to her with alarm that he was only the first person today that she would have to face from her work life since Sage's death. There would be many more. She stood outside and tried to calm her breath. How would she do this? She wasn't sure she could make it through this day.

But really, there were so many days ahead of her—a lifetime of days. This was simply the first one.

She had cloistered herself at home for weeks after Sage died, going out only when it was utterly unavoidable.

"Come to the mall with me." Mom called. "We can window shop new clothes for fall."

"I have a lot to do around the house, Mom."

"Put it off. Come on—I'll even treat you to one of those fancy expensive coffees you like."

"You are advising me not to clean?"

"Yes! Exactly! Don't clean—ever again for that matter!" The kindness of her effort brought tears to Amy's eyes.

"I can't go out, Mom. When I do, it goes wrong. It's too hard."

She paused. It was a soft thick pause, like an embrace. "Okay, sweetheart. Want some company?"

"No, it's okay. But thanks."

"Alright. I'll call you later. See how your day went."

"Thanks, Mom."

In public there were reminders—a baby Sage's size, a little girl with soft curls. She saw happy people, and both longed for and fiercely envied their ignorance. Their joyful obliviousness—the way she used to be.

Once, Mom convinced her to meet for a pedicure. They sat with their feet in the warm, bubbly water and Amy actually felt a loosening. She closed her eyes. A woman sat in the chair next to Mom.

"What are you knitting there?" the woman asked Amy's mother.

"Oh, a scarf for one of my grandchildren. Her daughter," she nodded toward Amy.

The woman leaned over to speak to Amy. "How many children do you have?"

Amy heard a loud whoosh. More so, she felt it. Her chest locked tight, her tongue a sponge. There was a grin splitting the skin of her mouth, although she did not feel as though she willed it.

"A little girl," Mom said. "Her name is Rachel. She's beautiful."

"Oh, how sweet," the woman said. "Maybe you'll have more."

In the car, Mom tearfully apologized. "I'm so sorry, sweetheart. That stupid, stupid woman! I should never have spoken with her."

Amy shrugged, pulled concrete shoulder to floating ear. "It's okay, Mom."

"People just don't know. They say the most stupid things."

They didn't know but Amy did; it was a knowledge she never could have imagined. Just as they couldn't because it wasn't theirs to know. Yet there would always be people. Always more and more people to collide against. There was no end. She would always need to go to the store for clothes and groceries. So she stayed away from any places but those she must, because avoiding the reminders was nearly impossible and concealing her reactions was exhausting.

Just like the man who made her coffee, there would always be people.

She walked through the pitted and cracked parking lot and stood in front of her building. She stared up, some static swimming on the surface of her vision. She walked in and stepped into the big old elevator and stared into the dirty corners as it ascended to her floor. It stopped and she pulled open the slatted doors. She stood in front of Déguiser's door, traced the ornate letters with her eyes. She had pored over font after font in choosing the perfect typeface. It had to have the right combined measure of whimsy and elegance, she thought at the time. Its importance had been fundamental. She touched them with one finger before pushing open the door.

"You're here!" said Sheila.

"I'm here," Amy said and they hugged.

"I'm not going to ask how you are. I suspect there is no phrase you have ever heard more and wanted to answer less. I'll just say I am so glad to see you." She held both of Amy's hands.

"You're right—I can't stand it anymore," she admitted to Sheila.

"They mean well," her mother said when Amy complained.

People called and sent cards and some dropped by with casseroles. They had softened features, eyebrows drawn in, and spoke gentle soothing words in low tones. Amy gave them drinks of iced tea or water in return. She went through tray after tray of ice cubes. It occurred to her that they had never gone through ice this quickly. She filled the freezer with Pyrex dishes full of soupy layers of noodles and meat. Strips of masking tape on the bottoms, permanent marker bearing the name of the owner of the dish. She knew they would never eat this food.

And the inevitable, "How are you?"

She could not pretend to be okay, but she could deflect their attention. The trick, she discovered, was to ask a lot of questions. She planned for the necessity to ask them—people could always be counted on to be distracted by their own answers. When they realized they should be asking her how she was doing, she smiled and said, "Okay," then she asked another question to push them back into themselves. If she talked too much, she knew they'd figure out she was not okay. She was held together by very loose stuff—too much talking and she would come undone, and coming apart belonged to her alone. It was not theirs to witness. It was an effort that exhausted her but she turned her chest, her heart, her lungs into a cinder block. She hated their presence. Her grief was hers. It was intimate. She did not want to share the pain, raw and throbbing. They had earned no access to the pain. She smiled and said politely, "Thank you," and seethed quietly for their intrusion. In solitude she could invoke the memories. In the profound silence of aloneness she called to Sage, *Come to Mama.* She could feel all of it and sob and drain herself. She could share this with no one but the ghost. It was theirs alone.

One Saturday afternoon, the buzzer sounded. Amy blatantly ignored it, but Matt dutifully clicked the button. It was Andy. Matt buzzed him in. Amy scuttled to the kitchen. To hide. But she stood near the door jamb to listen.

"Hey, man," Andy said to Matt. She heard the unmistakable thump of two men embracing. "How're you doing?"

"Oh, you know..." Matt said.

"I'm so..." Andy trailed and when he spoke again, his voice was choked. "I'm so sorry, Matt. I'm just so sorry." They were quiet for a moment. Amy listened to them sniffle and swallow hard. "How's Amy?" Andy finally said.

"She's...okay, I guess. You know."

"Heather made this casserole for you guys."

"Oh, yeah, thanks. That was nice of her."

"Yeah. Hey, listen. She's a wreck. You think maybe Amy might call her soon? I don't know what to do, Matt. She's hurting so badly. I just don't know what to do."

"I don't know. It's hard for Amy right now," Matt said.

"I know, I understand. Well, maybe soon. You give her a hug from me, okay? Tell her I'm thinking about her."

"Thanks, I will."

"If you need anything, man..."

"Thanks, Andy."

Amy stood at the kitchen door, her back plastered to the wall, her fist to her mouth.

Matt walked through the door and placed the casserole on the counter. He moved into her arms. They stood a long time in the silence of the kitchen, the only sound the ticking of the clock above them.

"What are you going to do about your sister?" he said quietly.

She only shook her head slowly back and forth.

~~~

"You are," Amy told Sheila, "my hero."

"I know," Sheila said softly, eyes lowered demurely.

"And so unassuming about it," Amy said. "Okay, where's the book."

Déguiser was fully booked for weddings in October and November and double-booked for half of those weekends with parties.

"December is starting to fill in for the holidays and New Year's Eve has been booked for months already. We've got two parties that night," Sheila said.

Amy placed her hands on her cheeks. "Wow." Before, seeing Déguiser's book this full would have energized her.

Sheila placed her hand on Amy's arm. "It's okay. We have the staff—this is not impossible or even worrisome."

Amy took a big breath. "Was the panic obvious?"

"All over your face. Like even your neck. And hair."

Amy laughed. "My hair is feeling the burden of this schedule."

They both giggled. "Amy," Sheila put her hand on Amy's arm again. "It's good to have you back. I promise to never ask you how you are," she said, and tears filled her eyes, "but know that I'm here for you. Whatever that means."

Amy hugged her tightly. "Thank you. You've already done so much." She pulled away and wiped her eyes, took a deep breath and said, "Okay, looks like we have some bar mitzvah centerpieces to make today. What in the world is this theme? 'Jon Appetit'?"

"It's a Julia Child thing."

"A what?" Amy asked.

"Yeah, apparently he's really into cooking. And Julia in particular. They're having a Julia look-alike do a cooking demonstration and Jonathan will be her assistant."

"This might be the weirdest one we've ever done." She looked at Sheila. "Is what I just said sexist?"

"Probably. Maybe?" Sheila teased. "But look at this." She handed the invitation to Amy.

There was Jonathan in a Julia costume, wig and all, grinning, dangling a raw chicken from one hand and wielding an impressively large cleaver from the other. Sheila and Amy laughed wickedly.

"Mazel-tov-etit?" asked Sheila.

"Something like that...okay, let's give them their 'Jon Appetit.'"

After spending the morning working on the centerpieces with Sheila, Amy settled in behind her desk and let out a sigh. Maybe it was relief at the familiarity, and even if it only lasted a moment, the firm ground of Déguiser beneath her was a small comfort. She might still break at any time, but in the moment she felt contained enough.

~~~

Amy woke alone in the middle of the night. When Matt didn't return, she moved soundlessly down the hall. She carefully stepped over the creaky places. She checked the dark rooms and looked in on Rachel. The kitchen was dim and empty. There was no prone body on the couch. She found him in Sage's room. He was looking out the window. He held a soft, worn giraffe in his hands. It had once been lavender and yellow, but had grown dingy from dirty little hands.

"Hey," she whispered.

He turned to her. "Did I wake you?"

"Not really," she said. "I just woke up and you were gone. Want me to leave?"

"No. I was just thinking. Not thinking. Just being in here." Then she noticed his face, his wet eyes. She wanted to ask him if he did this often, but she knew everyone needed their private rituals.

Amy went to Sage's room whenever she really wanted to remember her. All the unnamable things; the kinds of things you simply knew because you knew a person intimately. The concrete and the sublime. The way her hands moved, her smell. Her expressions—the ones she repeated, the ones she only expressed once. The different ways she cried when she was tired or sad, angry or hurt. The way she loved a bath. The way she craned her head around when she heard Rachel's voice. The way she settled into Amy's body exactly the same way every time she nursed. Amy could have weaned her—the pediatrician said Sage was old enough. But Amy kept telling herself just one more week, one more week. Because she loved being with Sage like that in that same way every time. What did the doctor know? What did anyone know? Just Sage and her mama—they knew. And what they knew was good.

"I've been meaning to say sorry for jumping down your throat the other day when you suggested I try to have some fun," said Amy.

He shrugged. "It's okay. I'd forgotten about it."

"Well, I am sorry."

They were quiet.

"Tonight at bedtime Rachel asked me if Sage would be back tomorrow," he said. "She made a drawing for her in preschool today."

"Oh," Amy sighed.

"Does she ask you about Sage?"

"Every now and then she'll say, 'Where's Sage again?' When I try to explain, she still thinks she'll be back. But she can go for days, weeks, not even seeming to notice. She sometimes wants me to buy a cookie or an ice cream for Sage when I get one for her." Amy paused. "Nice to see we succeeded in driving in the concept of sharing."

"It wasn't always so good when she was actually with Sage." They laughed a little, then she settled quickly back into her pain. She sensed he did, too.

"Do you think Rachel's okay, Matt?"

"I don't know. I think so."

"She cries when I drop her off at school," Amy said.

"Not often," he said.

"No," she agreed.

It didn't happen every time, but when it did, Amy was left weak and shaky. She never saw it coming. She kept her eyes open for signs but there were none, only tears at the time Rachel usually said, "'Bye

Mommy," and ran off to play. It made Amy worry. The books said to look for a pattern. Was this the pattern, the books warned. She thought maybe she should call the pediatrician. Or maybe just ask Mom. She thought she remembered her mother saying Amy used to cry sometimes when she was left at school. Oh, what constituted a pattern? There was only ambiguity and cloudiness. There was so much to be unsure of.

"I can take her, if that's easier for you," said Matt.

Now that Sage was gone, Amy insisted on taking Rachel to school.

"No, I can do it."

"Well, if you need me to..." Matt said.

She placed her hand on his arm, "Thank you." She looked out the window where Matt stared. She wondered what he saw. "Will we ever be okay again?"

He put his arms around her. "I hope so."

They went back to bed together, in the darkest part of night.

"Amy?" he whispered. "Amy?"

"Yeah?" She had grown sleepy.

He said nothing at first, but she could tell he was searching for words—the space between them heavy with thoughts of words.

"When do you think you'll stop going to her grave?"

She tensed. He reached out, rubbed her arm and found her hand under the blanket.

She said nothing, only pushed silence toward him.

"I don't think it's good for you, babe. You go every day."

But she must still go; think of her daily, never forget her.

"I don't know," Amy said.

"Maybe you could skip it tomorrow. See how you feel?"

"Maybe." Fury seethed, slithered inside her. "Don't you do anything to remember her?" Her tone was a knife cutting.

"Of course."

"What?"

He hesitated. "I walk through the Public Garden sometimes. I watch the kids play and talk to her in my head. I tell her what I see. The things I wish she could be doing."

Tears ran rivers behind her ears.

"You think I should stop going?" she whispered.

"Maybe just not every day. Maybe going is making it harder."

Harder than what?

She never told him about her fantasies. How she pretended Sage was sleeping in her crib. Not dead— sleeping. She went about her work and at the time Sage used to wake up from her nap, Amy set aside whatever she was doing, slowly walked to the baby's room and pretended she was there. When she opened the door, Sage would be there. Amy stood outside her room for a long, long time imagining what it would be like to find her there. Amy could just about hear her. She was almost convinced. But she never opened the door. To do so would be to lose Sage all over again.

"Besides, Rachel needs you here. I need you," Matt said.

Sage needed her. Amy couldn't leave her there alone.

"Okay," she told him. She would stop going before supper.

She did not have to tell him everything.

~~~

Autumn settled in firmly—in the color-strewn trees and the brisk air. The summer slipped into the past, all the while she kept thinking she might break. But she never did break. She realized again and again that the things she thought were certain, were real, often were nothing of the sort and the real certainties were things like her own beating heart and the blood flowing through her veins carrying on, ignorant of everything she thought would surely undo her. But those things did not. She said to herself, *You will not stop breathing, your heart will not burst in your chest. You will not go crazy. You will simply carry on. Your body will do everything it is meant to do in spite of what you think.* It did, so she simply kept going.

The cool of autumn was something of a relief. Minor relief, small comforts were the best she could hope for right now. There was no real hope—that was too much. She walked along the sidewalks where the brownstones lined up like gingerbread. The sky was blue, blue, and the foliage almost peak, which had always been her favorite time—the moment just before.

She stopped in front of her own brownstone and looked up to the very top of the tallest tree, the colors a wash of shades, smudgy and perfect. And she felt so small. She wanted to be absorbed into it—into all the red and yellow and orange bleeding into the summer green. Then she might be alright. She would not have to will her heart to carry on or do the hard work of taking one breath after another.

She had been startled to discover that the body carried on whether she believed it would or not. She was proof of that.

Stones

She feels.

What are the words?

People string shapes of sounds together and hope they begin to touch upon what they feel. Amy thinks that sometimes, what we feel are shapes for which there are no words. There are words, but they are too simple and they fall short. Because they have no shades, no gradations, no nuance. No grace.

Amy calmly tells Heather the words she is able to form. "I have an empty place that will never be filled. I ache in that place. I will never see her get married, write a book, become a doctor. I will never hold her babies. She will never cook me dinner. I am so sad. I wish there were a bigger word for sad. There should be. And I feel angry, Heather. As furious as it's possible to be."

She is crying. "I know, I know. Amy, I'm so sorry..."

"No!" Amy screams. "No! There is no fucking 'sorry,' Heather. There is no 'I'm sorry.'" She breathes heavily through sobs. "Not for this."

"I know, I know." Heather sobs, too.

"How could you have been so careless?"

All the things that have been resting heavily like stones in her belly come rolling out.

"How many times did I tell you not to bring them all to the water? Five of them, Heather! Five. Two toddlers. Why would you do that?" Amy is yelling. She doesn't say that she watched them go to the water. She doesn't say she walked away. Heather doesn't, either. At some point she doesn't recall, she tossed her paper cup of wine into the surf. She watches it bob, move forward and back with the

movement of the water. She thinks, I don't litter *and the thought makes her grieve somehow.*

Heather is silent. "I don't know what to say," she says after a while.

"There is nothing to say. You have your children. All your children." The words are caustic in her mouth. "I know you had to make a choice. Maybe I would have made the same one. I don't know." She says this softly.

"It wasn't a choice, Amy. It just...happened. It was so fast. I would never have chosen—not like that," she pauses, sobs, catches her breath. "It was not a choice."

"What would you call it then?" Amy's voice pierces, cleaves the rage, penetrates into her skin. "All your children are alive. One of mine is dead."

"I would call it an accident. A terrible, heartbreaking accident. One I would take back if there was any way I could," she cries. "I'm hurting too, Amy. When you hurt, I hurt. And I loved Sage. I loved her. For the last year I've felt I haven't had a right to say that to you. But while we're laying it all out, there it is. I hate that this happened. That I caused you this pain. That Sage is gone. But I'm hurting, too." She stops and looks at the water. Then up at Amy. "What do you want me to do?"

She wants to have an answer for Heather.

But Amy doesn't know.

"Girls! Let's go!" Mom called to Amy and Heather from the shore.

"Just wave to her. Pretend you don't know what she wants!" They giggled and waved to Mom, who motioned for them to get out of the water.

But they couldn't pretend for very long that they didn't understand. So began the negotiations.

"Three more jumps, Mom! Three!" They held up three fingers.

She held up two fingers. Amy and Heather agreed to the terms. They dived into or over waves. They turned back to Mom.

"No, no! That one didn't count, Mom! That wasn't a good one!" Mom nodded assent.

Finally, after many more than the negotiated amount of jumps, they dragged themselves dripping from the ocean, met Mom who held open dry towels she wrapped around them.

Amy never knew until she was an adult that Mom started rounding them up half an hour before she actually wanted to leave.

She always let them have one last jump.

Drift

Amy sat in her kitchen in the early morning just before sunrise. If she could sleep she would. If she could manage her memories better, she would stay in bed and try to get back to sleep. Instead, she got up and sat in her kitchen. This morning in the moments before she gave up on sleep, an image flew before her eyes—not those moments on Cattail, not the sweet soft limbs she could no longer touch. She tossed aside the covers and soundlessly moved to the linen closet. She sorted through the stack of pillow cases until she found the one she was seeking. Unbleached cotton with a pale fawn-colored pattern of cabbage roses blown out across the fabric. She took her basket of thread and needles and carried them to the kitchen. Flipping on the light over the stove, she sat down and sought out a deep cocoa skein of thread. She threaded the needle with a single long strand, knotted the end, pressed an embroidery hoop into place and began to stitch.

The sun rose and she didn't mark it until the trolley screeched to a stop on the curve in front of their brownstone and Amy moved her eyes from her stitching. She stood and stretched and pressed her forehead to the cold glass of the kitchen window where outside the trees were well on their way to shedding their leaves.

It was almost Halloween.

Matt took Rachel out to look for the materials for her Halloween costume. He spent hours searching to find everything they would need. He always devised great and elaborate costumes. Then ice cream sundaes, of course.

Mom came over and Amy made tuna melts and homemade soup—fall food.

She had begun cooking again and the things felt good in her hands. The wooden spoons and her pots, peppers and carrots and garlic and ginger. They felt good—taking care of Matt and Rachel felt good.

"When is this going to change with Heather, Amy?" The words were hard, but Mom's voice was soft.

Amy would not admit aloud that she needed Heather—that she wanted her back and missed her. But Heather as the sister she loved had changed irrevocably the day Sage died. All that she knew of Heather was gone, replaced by this other thing, this other Heather, the Heather inextricably tied to the death of her baby. She didn't know how to separate the two things or recover the Heather she knew. The one she desperately ached to have back.

"I don't know," she whispered.

"Sweetheart, I know it hasn't been ages yet, but you and Heather need to talk."

"Why? Why do we *need* to talk, Mom?"

"Because you are sisters. Because you love one another." Amy watched her mother's face grow pink—the way she looked before she cried. She put her hand over her eyes and tears dripped through her fingers. "I feel so helpless, Amy. You're hurting, she's hurting, I can't do a thing about it. And I can see you could help each other. Like you always have."

"I know." Amy took her mother's hand and tried not to cry.

"I'm hurting, too." These words squeaked out. "I miss that little baby so much. I can't stand to see you torn apart."

Amy pulled her chair over and put her head on her mother's shoulder. She closed her eyes and inhaled her unmistakable scent. She wept into her mom's sweater. This well of water and pain.

"You've always been there for each other. I know Heather wants to be there for you. I don't say this to hurt you, but she needs you, too."

Amy could not scale the stone-hard wall between herself and her sister. Forgiveness tasted bitter in her mouth. There was no room for generosity.

"Do you want to know what she's been up to?'

Amy sat up. She said, "Sure." The words emerged on their own. Something small dislodged. Acquiescing had loosened the question for which she hadn't known the words, only the feeling.

Mom smiled a little. "The usual. Weddings and parties. The big girls are in school."

"Who's watching the baby?"

"Her sister-in-law. Only three days a week. She's got a good crew over at Glimmer."

"She does. We used to babysit for each other." There seemed no end to the losing.

"I know," Mom said softly.

Amy looked out the window at what remained of the foliage. She looked forward to it every year, but this year it brought her mood low. The leaves browned, fell off, curled up crisp on the ground. She had always loved their fragrance. It seemed now to reveal itself to her only as the smell of death.

She wanted to love the smell of leaves crumbling beneath her feet again. She wanted to look forward to the fall holidays and Christmas and love her life as she had always known it. But nothing felt the same. She wanted simply to love Heather, laugh with her, be with her like always. But it was all wrong now. There was no returning to that time before; she knew yet stubbornly clung back.

When Amy was three, she fell off their swing set. She and Heather were on the teeter-totter and Amy wanted to get off, but instead of telling Heather, she let go. She catapulted backwards and cracked her head against the bar that rooted the swing set into the ground. Instantly, she was wailing.

Mom wrapped her in her sweater on the way to the emergency room. The sweater was an attempt to soothe Amy; a salve to end the tears. It worked. She felt special, wearing Mommy's sweater.

They sewed up the gash with twelve ugly black stitches climbing across her head like a big bug. Her soft honey curls were stiff with dried blood. The nurse gave her a lollipop, any color she wanted.

"Can I have one for my sister?" Amy asked.

Heather remembered being really scared and believing it was her fault. Years later, she told Amy of the bloody images that still plagued her—Amy wailing, holding her head. She said she was almost ashamed of the lollipop, but mostly she was relieved Amy still loved her.

Today, Mom gave her a warm hug and left for home. Amy waited for the sounds of Matt and Rachel and watched the sunlight go dim in the kitchen. She needed to turn on the lights but couldn't seem to move.

Perhaps she should embrace Heather, try to go back. But Amy wasn't who she used to be and neither was Heather. Amy hated her; she loved her. What was the middle of that? Nothing. But Heather wasn't nothing. She was Amy's own history. She could not be wiped away, as if Amy could rub her sister to dust and let the fragments fall from her palms. If that were possible would Amy then fall to her knees and scrape her fingers raw with the need to retrieve every grain? But in saving Heather, was she betraying Sage?

She grappled with her suspect emotions. She was furious with Heather. Her ethos, her rationality advised against that fury. Heather might have been the witness to Sage's death, but she was not the blame. There was no culpability but a senseless storm; an unconscious body of water; an unknowing rain. And yet, still, there was anger. It soothed Amy to place it, burning hot, on Heather. She could have draped at least a corner of the anger, the blame, on herself.

But it didn't want her; it wanted Heather.

Heather kept calling. The phone rang and rang. Matt walked past Amy and answered it. He spoke lowly.

"Heather again, Amy."

"Hmm." She didn't look up from the sewing in her lap. He knelt in front of her, took it gently from her hands.

"When will you talk to her?"

"I don't know." Every time she called, Amy unraveled a bit. Her sudden presence, the knowing that her voice whooshed through the lines to Amy's telephone. She began to cry. "I'm hurting so much, Matt." The word 'hurting' a sharp thing sunken into something soft and tender. "I don't know what to do. No one gets this!" she cried, her voice loud and high.

He was quiet, waiting patiently for her crying to slow, to subside.

Heather called every few days.

"Just call her back," Mom begged. "Even just to say hello. She wants to talk to you so badly, sweetheart. She's going crazy. I'm not saying either of you is wrong..."

Amy listened to her mother, the peacemaker. They drank the coffee she brewed. All the caffeine Amy wanted.

She hadn't spoken to her sister in three months. It seemed much longer and as the days accumulated, she couldn't figure out what she might say if she did call her. Should they begin with small talk or jump right in? This was too big and unwieldy and their natural way of being was lost. Amy had always believed without doubt that Heather would never do anything to hurt her. She'd had no capacity to conceive of it. If she had counted on one thing, that was it. Heather was it. Amy didn't know how she could ever reclaim her sister.

So she settled for anger. It was clean and easy.

"Aren't you mad at her?" she asked Matt.

"I don't know. Yes and no. I know it wasn't her fault—she didn't do anything on purpose. I wish she'd used better judgment. I keep thinking she could have got them to the sand sooner, before the rain started."

"It was fast," Amy said softly. They both stared at her hands.

"What do you want from her?"

"I want her to get this—to understand!" Amy said, her voice shrill. Then, in a whisper, "I don't know." Amy wanted her to hurt as much as she did. It was a mean and low thought. She knew it was small and it made her feel small. And yet somehow it made her feel powerful.

"No one can get this but us. No one else can possibly understand. It's just us in this. They can only imagine. They can only love us."

She knew his words were truth.

She still craved the unnamable.

~~~

They race to the car, between the piercing rain. Then everyone is in the car. Safe.

"Where's Sage?" Heather screams.

Oh, God.

Amy runs down to the beach. She looks everywhere. It seems hours pass. She keeps getting distracted, then remembers with a sudden cold panic that she needs to look for Sage.

"Is she yours?" a lifeguard says. It's her. Thank God.

"Yes!" He hands her to Amy.

But it's a doll. It's not Sage. Just an old doll with blank glass eyes.

Amy woke with a gasp.

It was three-thirty in the morning. There would be no more sleep now. She crept to the kitchen and put the kettle on to boil. She clicked on the lamp that sat on the kitchen table. Insomnia had prompted its placement. She could embroider when she couldn't sleep. It was better than sifting through everything again. But this night, she didn't pick up her silk; she instead took a piece of paper from behind the cookbooks.

Soon after Sage died, Amy woke one morning with a start. Not groggy, not forced, but filled with purpose. She dressed Rachel and drove to the police station. She asked for a copy of the police report; the detailed events. They gave her a copy on crisp white paper. She folded it and put it in her purse. Later, alone, she read it over and over. Each word dissected. She rearranged the sentences in her head to see if some reorder made more sense. She returned and returned to the piece of paper.

Surely something would be revealed.

She waited for the water to boil and reached behind the cookbooks neatly lined up on their shelf and pulled out the paper. It was creased and soft. She spread it out on the table. Same words. Same black ink.

She wondered until her mind went numb. She wondered what they could have done so that her child would be alive right now? Pink and breathing and asleep in her room and Amy would never know this horror. She, too, would sleep peacefully never having known.

She covered her face with her hands. She cringed at her uselessness that day at Cattail. What was the thing she could have done that would have changed everything? It was like searching for that small lost thing. She'd think she remembered where she saw it last, but it was never there when she checked. *It's got to be somewhere*, she'd think. Then she'd never find it. But everything is somewhere. The answer had to be that simple. There must be something and then it would make sense.

The water began to boil. She steeped her tea, dunking her teabag in and out of the water. She tried to think of nothing, hoped the answer would come through the silence. She drank the tea and peered into the cup. She looked for the dark specks of tea leaves. She moved the cup into the light.

Why had she gone to the bathroom—she could have waited. She knew better than to leave them on the shore. Her regret was heavy and drenching; soaking her in *why*? And why hadn't she done more when she pulled Sage from the water, when she lay still on Amy's lap? It should have been Amy's air pushed into her lungs. Her mother's air. Why had she done nothing?

She peered into the cup and looked for tea leaves, divining. She looked hard, her eyes ached.

She leaned away from the light. Hers was not loose tea—it was the kind in a bag. Of course there were no leaves left in the bottom of the cup. And she didn't know anything about reading tea leaves. She wouldn't know what they were saying. She didn't know their language.

~~~

Déguiser was a reprieve. At work she had purpose outside herself and its pace ravaged time, the hours blistering past, her mind entirely occupied with the tasks at hand.

In her sunny studio, she and Sheila unwound yard upon yard of shimmering pale salmon chiffon.

"Look how it catches the light," said Sheila, moving it through her hands.

"It's outrageously pretty." The hue of the sheer fabric changed from orange to pink with a turn of light. Amy gently twisted a segment this way and that, watching the folds shift color. "This is going to look amazing." It was specially ordered for a tent wedding in the suburbs.

"I still can't get over the idea of a tent wedding in November," Sheila said. "You would think we'd all freeze."

Amy shook her head. "I know. I'm always amazed how warm they can get those tents. Have you seen the color scheme for the flowers?"

"No—tell me!"

"Matt?" she called. "Do you have that printout of the flowers for the Clarkson-Smith wedding?"

He came out of the office and handed a sheet of paper to Amy. Tiger lilies, blown-out salmon and cream roses, bittersweet, Queen Anne's Lace and black-eyed Susans.

"Where do they get these at this time of year? Imagine the cost," breathed Sheila.

"Even if I *could* drop thirty grand on flowers, I'm not sure that I would," said Amy. "It seems wasteful. There's so much good that could be done with all that money for people who really need it."

"Don't bite the hand that feeds," said Matt.

"Can't we mock a little? I would say that's only a mild nibble," said Amy.

"Just don't break the skin," said Matt. "Wow, look at that," he said, touching the fabric.

"Isn't it pretty? Imagine it draping, the twinkle lights peeking through." She held the delicate fabric to the light coming through the window. "It's going to take us all day to trim and serge the lengths we need," she said.

As she and Sheila cut and sewed, Amy asked, "Can you remember which vendors are doing this event?"

"A lot of the usuals: Tim and his crew on linens and furniture, Chef Fitzpatrick on catering..."

"Oh, I love her! It will be a treat to see her. And she usually saves me a little taste—I'll share with you."

"...and Glimmer."

Amy saw peripherally that Sheila watched her face carefully, a look of hesitance on her own.

"Well, that's to be expected. They have the best reputation in Boston—they've earned it." She focused on the needles of her serger locking threads to the fabric to keep the raw edges from unraveling. "It won't be the first event we've shared since..." she trailed softly.

Amy and Heather's work overlapped with intention—from the time when being together was not mere preference but their dearest wish. Their work could not be untangled without harming their businesses. But Amy could evade her and move around whichever circle in which Heather happened to be. She created her own circles and avoided her sister—she didn't wave hello, didn't chat or meet her eyes. At the first event after the accident, Heather attempted to catch her eye and waved tentatively. Amy watched from the corner of her eye as Heather smiled cautiously. Amy moved away quickly and Heather hadn't tried anything overt since, but Amy felt her sister's eyes on her whenever they worked the same venue.

On the day of the Clarkson-Smith wedding, the crew from Déguiser piled into the company van and drove away from the city and out to the green of the suburbs. An enormous white tent sat stiffly and squarely in the back yard of an even more enormous stone house. Large fans blew heated air into the expanse of white canvas. Amy placed a ladder at the base of one of the posts and climbed to the top. Sheila stood at the foot and handed the salmon pink chiffon up to her. Carefully, Amy wrapped the post and secured the fabric with a long plastic zip-tie. Once the poles were swathed, they would drape swags of the fabric around the horizontal seams of the tent. Her crew worked in tandem around the perimeter. There were six of them today and still a space this large would take at least eight to ten hours.

In spite of the heaters, it was cold in the tent. Amy finished a swag and climbed down and walked up to the blowing air. She stretched her hands close, rubbing them together.

"A little chilly, isn't it?" asked Heather.

Amy turned. "Yeah, it is." She began to walk away.

"Amy..."

Amy stopped but did not face her sister. "What, Heather?"

"Can't we just..."

"Just what."

"Talk." She came around and stood in front of Amy.

"We're at work. This is not the place."

"Where then? You won't answer my calls or meet with me. Where?"

Amy tried to look anywhere but her sister's face. "I don't know. Please just let me work." She began to walk away.

"Amy...please..." Heather reached out and touched Amy's arm. She flinched away.

"You please," she whispered, angry. "Let me work."

She walked away quickly and beckoned to Sheila, who followed her to the van.

"I just need to..." she started to say before tears began. Sheila hugged her until Amy's crying subsided.

"I just need to breathe for a minute," said Amy.

"You okay?"

"I will be. I just want to finish the job."

Sheila nodded. "Want me to talk to her?"

Amy shook her head. "I think she knows I just want to work right now."

"Okay. Let's go." She hooked her arm though Amy's.

By the end of the day, most of the fabric and lights were in place and in the darkness of dusk, they tested out the lighting. Amy stood at one end of the tent with Sheila. The work floodlights were turned off and the party lights that Heather and her crew had installed were turned on. Muted tangerine gels and sparkling twinkle lights glowed softly. The chiffon softened the ungiving lines and edges of the tent, its color warmed the cold of November.

"It's beautiful," Amy breathed.

"Lovely," said Sheila. "It's almost not real."

Amy gazed into the apex of the tent. She forgot where she was for a few moments, lost in the twinkle.

She moved her eyes away and across the room met her sister's, sad and imploring. She turned away.

"Time to go," she said.

~~~

"Remember Auntie Heather? And Amber and Laurel and baby Tara?" Rachel said to Amy. She looked up from the floor where she played with her babies and stuffed animals. Amy froze, needle hovered over her pillowcase embroidery. Two closed eyes of feathered cocoa brown stitches of differing lengths, long lashes resting on smoky smudged under-eyes, as if this person she stitched never slept. Rachel looked over her shoulder at Amy.

"Do you remember them? Where did they go?" *She must miss them.* The thought came to Amy as if from nowhere. Why hadn't this occurred to her before?

"Yes." She swallowed a mouthful of sand. "They're at their house."

"Can I go play with them?"

Amy asked Mom if she would set up a play date at Heather's and be there to help with Rachel. "Can you? Are you too busy?"

"Of course not."

"I know it's a ride for you..."

"I don't mind, sweetheart. Truly."

It was a cold November Saturday. There was a biting wind and it was gray and drizzly. The leaves were brown and only a few clung to the trees. Most of them were already on the ground and they stuck to everyone's feet in the wet and got tracked inside.

Amy hurried Rachel into Heather's house. She stopped in the entryway to help Rachel with her coat and rain boots. She heard Heather's voice.

"She's not staying?" she said to Mom.

"No. She's dropping Rachel off. I'll stay and bring Rachel home later."

"I thought we'd all be together!" Her voice expanded with palpable sadness. "She doesn't trust me with Rachel!" Anguish.

"No. That's not it."

"Of course it is. I didn't mean to hurt Sage! I would never hurt Rachel!" She was crying now. "I can't believe she would think that. What can I do, Mom? I don't know what to do!" It was a wail as from a child. *Mommy, help.*

Amy stood in the wave of her sister's voice unable to move.

"Why is Auntie Heather sad?"

"Here, baby. Let's get your coat off." Amy sent her into the living room to everyone.

"Rachel!" Joy. In Heather's voice joy.

Mom came out to the entryway. "Amy." Her face was pink, her lips thin. "We didn't know you were here." She paused. "Please stay. Just try."

Amy shook her head. "Not yet. I couldn't even talk to her at work the other day. It was just...too hard."

"Soon?"

"Maybe."

Amy got into her car, turned off the radio and cried tears to the memory of the sound of Heather's words. She rode the wave of her sister's voice as she drove aimlessly through the gloom.

She couldn't bear the idea of returning home to an empty house. Matt was at the studio helping the crew load up for a wedding downtown. When Amy got to Déguiser, Sheila and a couple of the guys were stepping off the elevator with some of the tri-folding partitions they used when they decorated weddings at one of the hotels. Sheila pushed a rolling rack of champagne-colored voile, each hanger wrapped in thin plastic.

"Oh, that's one of my favorite colors. Are you ready?" Amy asked the crew.

"This is our last load." This would be an easy event; compared to the big tent weddings, the ballroom weddings were smooth and straightforward.

"Have fun," Amy said.

"You know we will! I'll try to swipe some cake for you!"

She watched the van drive off. "Hey, you," Matt said. "What are you doing here?"

She turned toward him. She shrugged, "Didn't feel like going home. Are you leaving?"

"Yeah, I helped the crew load-in. I guess I'll drive over and help them set up."

"You don't have to—Sheila's got it under control."

He looked down, "Gives me something to do."

She didn't ask, but suspected he wasn't any more fond of an empty house than she was.

"Okay. I'll see you at home later this afternoon."

She rode the old elevator up to the studio. Even though the sky was gray, light flowed through the windows. She looked out at the milky sky, leaned in and sat against the low window sill. The sky was opaque white; there seemed to be no boundaries. A couple of crows, inky against the white expanse, flew high in the sky, small soaring flecks. She felt lost in the sea of sky; the pale wilderness.

Amy dragged herself from the window and the spell of the sky and spread her embroidery work across the smooth surface of the big work table. Her work had been a half-hearted effort since Sage died. She kept dragging herself back to it, but it rarely spoke to her anymore. *Here I am*, she implored. But it was only silent. She smoothed out the pillowcase on which she had stitched the closed eyes—her only inspired work since the loss of her child. She didn't understand the meaning of the piece. It suggested to her the inverse of awakening.

The rushing flicker of creativity seemed to have slipped away from her, more sand between her fingers.

She turned to the window once more and contemplated the sky, still smooth and white as chalk. She didn't know when she might awaken. She wasn't sure it was possible.

She hoped to work on her embroidery that day, but no ideas arrived; no inspiration flared. She thought she might lose herself in thread and needle, stitches and knots. Thought she might get into that space where time neither moved forward nor back, was neither still nor in motion. But the day passed slowly, time sluggish. The show didn't even matter to her anymore.

Time was a funny thing since Amy had lost Sage; her experience of it had been altered. Before, there was never enough time—there was only a constant struggle to get everything done. It was difficult to simply enjoy time passing. Those moments when she was able to became the stuff of memories, the kinds of moments she wished she could have more of. But time moved quickly, slipped away. It was the measure of breathing, of the movement of bodies, of seasons. Monday always came too fast, summer was over too soon. Her wedding day passed in minutes.

But it moved differently once Amy lost Sage. It simply slowed down. She now waited for the clock to turn. Often, she could not believe how early it was. The best part of her day was when she needed to get things done—dinner or picking up groceries, making foolish centerpieces at Déguiser—when she could slip into busyness or the comfort of ritual. She waited mostly for bed.

She folded up her silk and thread and put it away. She turned off the lights in the studio and drove home through the haze.

~~~

She ate, she slept, she worked and then it was another Saturday evening.

"Babe?" Matt called quietly from the living room.

Amy was cleaning counters. It was getting close to Thanksgiving and she hadn't decorated the house yet. No pumpkins, no turkeys, no fall leaf bunting she'd made of embroidered wool felt.

"Yeah, hon?" Amy spoke quietly, too, Rachel asleep in her bed. Amy glanced at the clock. It was only quarter past eight and she was exhausted.

"Come here. I rented a movie." He grinned.

The air in the room was warm. She fell heavily onto the couch near him, rested her head on his chest and held his hand. He pushed his body closer to hers. As the movie started, she sank deeper into him, into his breath. It had become so hard to be still. Her entire body buzzed. She was attempting to feel herself in her body again. To inhabit, to balance. She breathed into Matt and tried to bring her attention to the moment, the television screen, but her mind cast forward to the next day—Sunday.

"I was thinking," Mom said over tea in Amy's kitchen the previous week. Mom paused broadly.

"What?" Amy said and narrowed her eyes a little.

"I thought maybe next week we could do Sunday again." The last Sunday gathering they shared was the Sunday before vacation.

"Wouldn't it be nice, honey?" Mom's voice was light and bright, but something that sounded like desperation tinged her tone.

"I don't know if I'm ready, Mom." She looked at the trees lining Commonwealth Avenue.

Mom spoke softly. Her eyes rested gently on Amy's face, a caress or a kiss. "Ready for what?"

"For Heather." Amy's voice dissolved, tears rolled down her face. Mom reached across the table and wiped Amy's cheeks with a tissue she had stashed up her sleeve; one of her tricks.

Avoiding Heather had seemed the natural thing to do. Amy could drop Rachel at the door for play dates, she could sidestep her sister when their work merged. She wasn't forgiving her or not forgiving her. She wasn't figuring it out or not. She was floating in the middle space where nothing definitive needed to be done. This way wasn't easy or painless, but it was less crushing.

"Can I tell you what I think?" Mom asked. Amy nodded. "I think you need to decide if you want to mend things with your sister. And if you do, you start small."

Mend or not. She wasn't sure she knew how to mend, but she could not say with a sure finality that she did not want to mend. She took a small breath. "Okay, I'll try. But if I change my mind, even at the last minute, is that alright?"

"Yes, yes! Of course." Mom's smile a joy-filled curve.

"I'm not ready to..."

"What, sweetheart?"

"Come down to your...house."

She rushed to say, "I'm sure that Heather will be happy to host. And think of how little traveling you'll have to do?"

Now watching the movie and breathing into Matt, tomorrow weighed heavy; a soggy, fleshy feeling she couldn't shake.

Mom had called earlier in the week to plan the details. "Heather's making a big soup on Sunday. Can you bring a nice salad and maybe a dip for chips before dinner?"

"Sure."

"Okay. Any time after three."

"Fine." As she agreed, Amy's muscles tightened and a buzzing roiled through her. She kept in motion to tolerate the sensation.

On Sunday afternoon, Amy saw Mom and Dad's car parked outside Heather and Andy's building when they pulled up. Amy chewed at her cuticles. Matt gently took her hand in his own, held it lightly.

"We don't have to do this yet," he said.

Amy nodded stiffly. "I know." She was stuck—wanting her sister's comfort, yet knowing Heather was inseparably entangled in her pain. Wanting Heather's friendship while she nurtured a rage more powerful than she was. Needing Heather's love, knowing she could have it, while some beast stood in the way.

"I'm alright," she said.

She took Rachel out of her seat and watched her sprint to the door. She carried the salad, walked slowly with shallow breath. She felt herself inhale deeply when Matt's hand touched the small of her back. She was aware of each step, her every breath, her stance, the places her eyes fell.

Heather's kitchen was warm and sunny, the cold persistent November chill held at bay. There was a small pumpkin on the table and some tiny gourds in a pale ochre ceramic bowl she had been putting out at Thanksgiving for as long as Amy could remember.

Mom rushed over and kissed Amy. "Hello!" she said, the way she always did when she was excited.

Amy smiled as much as she was able and returned her embrace. "Hello." Rachel was already in the other room with her cousins and Mom followed her, calling for a hug.

And then Amy turned and Heather was in the doorway. She took a few steps closer to Amy. Amy stopped her body from sliding back away from her. Amy waited.

It seemed there was no sound in the world.

"Hi, Amy," she said.

"Hey," Amy said slowly. Her eyes had not fully met Heather's. She looked instead at the center of Heather's chest at the logo on her salmon-colored shirt. *Pura Vida* it read. *It's all good* is what it meant. Amy had bought it for her while on her honeymoon. *Pure Life*, translated literally.

"Dip?" she asked, nodding at the bowl in Amy's hands.

Amy raised her eyes to Heather's chin, saw the honey blond tips of her hair sticking out from under her ears. Those honey crescents.

Amy shook her head no. "Dip's on the counter." She lifted the bowl in her hands a couple of inches. "A nice salad."

"Cool. I made a nice soup."

"I heard."

Amy shifted her eyes to Heather's. Something in Amy rose up, nearly consumed her.

"Amy..." Heather said, reaching out.

Amy cut her off. "I better get the dip out with the chips. Here," she hastily shoved the salad at Heather and looked away. "Can you please refrigerate this? It'll start getting warm." Amy spun away. She breathed around the tight belt that encircled her chest. She poured chips into a bowl, her back to her sister. After a moment she heard Heather rustling in the refrigerator, then waited as she walked out of the room, her sock feet padding nearly soundlessly on the hard tile floor.

She took one more breath and moved through her trembling into the living room, chips and dip in hand.

They watched a football game and then a movie. They ate the nice salad and soup and had ice cream for dessert. They talked and even laughed. She and

Heather talked around each other. Amy saw Heather try to catch her eye a few times, but she lacked the courage or generosity to make contact. It got late, but not as late as usual, and Amy said, "Matt, we better get going. Rachel has school tomorrow."

"You started her in preschool?" Heather asked. Her voice was sad and Amy felt knocked back suddenly.

"Oh, yeah—we did," Amy said, finally looking at her in the eye. There was a long quiet. Rachel had been in preschool for months. "Well, good night— drive safely," Heather said, gave a little awkward wave and blew a kiss. Amy gathered their bags and shuffled Rachel out. She heard Matt behind her saying goodbye.

She buckled in Rachel then sat in the front seat, crying quietly. She didn't want Rachel to hear but she did.

"Why are you sad, Mommy?"

Amy sniffled hard, pushed the tears back, turned to her and smiled. "Oh, nothing, baby. Mommy's just tired."

Matt looked at her when he got into the driver's seat.

"You okay?" he mouthed.

Amy nodded tersely. "We can talk later."

"Okay," he said.

Later she sobbed, shrouded in the darkness of their bedroom. "It was so awful! She didn't know Rachel started school!" She lay in his arms, her tears wetting the front of his T-shirt.

"Maybe your Mom just forgot to tell her."

"No! Heather always knows. I always tell her everything. Mom shouldn't have to tell her."

"You were the one who didn't tell her," he said gently.

She allowed the words to settle around and seep into her. "I know," she whispered. "But how can I?"

The house was nearly noiseless around them, the windows closed tightly against the chill of coming winter. As the quiet nestled into them, she was grateful for the onset of winter, the coldness and the dark of it. She yearned for the nesting of winter— bulky sweaters, heavy blankets, warm food. Comfort.

She thought of the absence of comfort. How much had she counted on things of comfort? What did her rituals amount to? The things, the people she relied upon to define her? She began to have the sense that none of it was real; that they might have been anything, could have been any number of things. She felt a sliding inside of her, her footing lost on slick ice.

How things changed without will or agreement. The change which was at the center spiraled out touching everything, until life was no longer recognizable. And yet it was her life. She was still there. What was its essence? The rituals? That which remained the same? No. That got pulled out from under her. No—it must be something else.

~~~

Always.

Amy thought, though not in fully-articulated words: *Sometimes, say if the dry cleaning needs to be picked up and it's not on your normal route, you might drive a different way to the grocery store or to your mom's or the pediatrician or anywhere. You might notice the way your hands feel different on the steering wheel, the feeling in the body different, the mind fresh. Some kind of new start even though the destination remains the same. Habits are a story told again and again while other stories play in tracks around us. What stories do you miss immersed in the white noise of your own story? What if you took yourself out of your life? How would you feel, think, act? Could it be different? Could you be different?*

What if she took the different turns on purpose. What if she were open. What would happen if she pulled her feet out of the grooves.

Swimming before supper.

Sometimes they ate supper on the beach and when they did, it felt like a holiday. Dad would head up to Cattail after work and meet them. Mom would bring a bathing suit for him, and Amy and Heather and Dad would go for a swim before supper, only them and the ocean. The water felt warmer because the air was evening-cool. They body surfed and tried to see who could catch a wave farthest to the shore. Dad usually won, but he had been doing it a lot longer, Amy and Heather reasoned. When they pulled themselves from the water, dripping and goose-bumped, Mom wrapped them in towels. She spread out a blanket for their wet behinds and handed them their supper. It was usually something extra good, like ground linguica fried with green peppers, onions and tomatoes on chewy Portuguese rolls. Their fingers were salty, and it seemed to make the sandwiches taste better.

The sun bobbed on the line of the horizon. The seagulls swooped down to the sand, scavenging for scraps.

Amy and Heather huddled in the towels draped around their shoulders, their hair still dripping, and held their sandwiches in both hands. Mom and Dad talked about their day. Dad settled back in his beach chair. He released the tension in his shoulders and looked warmly at Mom. Amy watched them as she rested her leg on Heather's. Heather crossed her leg over Amy's. Amy moved her other leg to the top of the pile. They fit together—a sister puzzle.

Rime

Quiet.

Windows closed tight. Layers of blankets.

Amy wore heavy socks to bed and padded around the house collecting dust balls. She picked them off and let them fall to the floor. She collected them again.

Cold is quiet, she thought.

Before the sun fully rose, frost gathered on the edges of the car, against the house, in the back garden, along the windows. The frost bloomed like yeast on whatever green remained. All the still things. The winter sunlight streamed in at a different angle through her kitchen window. It was thin, clear like water. It melted the frost, slowly, a sublime happening. She never saw any liquid, only the absence of the frost.

She woke one morning to blood in her underpants. It had reappeared soon after Sage died. The abrupt ending of Sage's need for milk precipitated the return of her cycle. Amy's body knew only that Sage stopped needing milk. Amy knew everything.

She had always been proud of her strong, sure body; her solid womanhood. Her cycle like clockwork every month, easy and uncomplicated. Now her blood was a betrayal. The same way hunger was. Her body craved food, her hunger never abated; every month her body told her it was ready to create new life, her uterus ripe and rich.

She wept as she ran her underwear through cold water in the sink. She balled it up and threw it into the laundry hamper. She looked herself in the eye in the mirror. It was she—the reflection that always appeared in the glass. Yet the image seemed vaguely unrecognizable. As though she were outside of herself; no longer a participant in her life. Everything swirled around her as always in the familiar patterns and she was caught up in the current, going along, not resisting. But she was not really a part of it. The shell of her carried on while some essence floated above helplessly observing, knowing everything was all wrong and utterly unable to do anything about it.

She mourned her baby. She mourned the loss of her sister. She mourned the loss of herself, a recognizable life. She knew she couldn't go back and she was lost.

She gathered more dirty laundry in the basket with her damp balled-up underpants and trudged down to the washer. All the mundane tasks that comprised so many of her hours had merged into one endless battle. One task to the next with nothing to break it up. She used to notice the good so much more readily.

Sometimes she fantasized an entirely new life. An external change—they could move away. They could run away from the reminders that made her long for the way things used to be. South Carolina. California. Somewhere warm. They could move the business—people got married everywhere. They would have a new house and new things to fill it. She could carve out new paths and rituals. She could leave behind suitcases filled with pain.

But I'll only carry it all with me.

She knew this on the inhale following the exhale of the thought that she would never escape this. She couldn't abandon anything; it would only follow. And then there was all she would lose; all the things she would never be able to try to get back. She wasn't ready to reclaim everything, she was not entirely sure it was possible, but she couldn't turn her back on the possibility of trying.

The phone jingled away her thoughts. She pressed the starter on the washing machine and ran up to answer the phone. She stood by the machine waiting to hear who was calling.

"Amy? It's Mom. Are you there?"

She picked it up. "Hey, Mom. What's up?"

"Hi, sweetheart! Not too much. How about you?"

She wanted to spill it all to her but couldn't think of the words. The words to say *What do I do? How do I change?* But she didn't know the questions. The word *change*, the idea *change* had not yet come to her.

"It's Heather's birthday next week." She stated and paused as though she waited for something from Amy.

"Yeah?" Amy offered.

"Well," she breathed with a cheerfulness Amy knew she forced. "I thought we could have dinner Friday night. Something simple: pizza, antipasto, I'll bake a cake." She stopped. Amy supposed she was expected to respond. She sensed she waited too long but took a bad-tempered pleasure in it.

"Yeah, fine." What had she thought—that it would be different than this? That these family gatherings wouldn't go on and on? As if she had gotten something over with that Sunday night a few weeks ago, or on Thanksgiving when she brought three sides and pie to dinner and floated around her family. This would always be.

They would always be and she would always be.

Her decision was to be a part or not.

~ ~ ~

Amy and Sheila decorated Déguiser for Christmas from the couple of boxes of decorations they had been using since the company was established. Swags

231

of greenery, shiny red glass ornaments, strings of tangled lights.

"I swear I wound these up at the end of the holiday season last year," Sheila said as she attempted to unwind the mess of lights.

"Yeah, I can see you did," teased Amy. She hung the greens in swooping swags from the tops of the high, wide windows. "I think it might already be dark enough to light them up." It was not yet four-thirty and the sun was already setting.

"There," Sheila said, triumphant in besting the snarl of lights. She strung them through the window greenery. "Okay, ready? Someone hit the lights," she called, and the studio plunged into darkness. She plugged the cord into the wall and the lights twinkled to life.

"Pretty," Sheila said as she came to stand by Amy.

"Yes," she said.

It was already mid-December and Amy had just decorated her own house. She usually started the day after Thanksgiving, but this year she couldn't face it. Finally, she did it for Rachel.

"You okay?" Sheila asked her.

"I just wish it weren't Christmas this year. I wish I could skip it. I want to fall asleep now and wake up in January."

Déguiser's books were loaded for the holiday season. Amy was setting up crews and absenting herself as much as possible. She had even hired another employee.

"I'm abandoning you to all these events and I feel awful about it. But I just..." her voice broke and her eyes filled.

"I know. It's okay. I swear—we can do this. You just take care of yourself and your family."

Amy hugged Sheila. "Everything I seem to be doing with you lately breaks all the employee/employer rules of appropriate behavior."

"I'll sue you later."

Amy laughed in spite of her tears. "Something to look forward to!"

At home, she stared at the Christmas tree, its tiny lights and its history of ornaments, and resented its intrusion. She couldn't hang the stockings; the absence of Sage's so expansive it pushed into all corners of the house. She would fill Rachel's on Christmas Eve; that was the best she could muster.

Another preschool morning and she scraped the frost from the car windows while Rachel sat inside, the heat blasting. She had forgotten her gloves and her hands ached and bloomed to a terrible red by the time she jumped into the car and slammed the door hard against the cold.

"Too loud, Mama!"

"Sorry."

Rachel had stopped the occasional tearful farewells at school. Now she had friends. She called every kid her friend. She played with Heather's kids at least once a week; Amy still made the arrangements through Mom.

"Maybe you'll stay today?" Mom asked each week.

"Not yet," Amy always said. The occasional Sunday night, birthday parties and holidays she could manage. But this, this thought of just her and Heather and the kids, it was too much.

Heather still called once a week. Amy still didn't answer. It was almost a joke now. She left messages.

"Hi, it's me. Calling to not talk to you. Ha ha. I miss you. I hope we can talk soon. I love you. 'Bye." She knew Amy wouldn't answer. That she would stand by the machine listening and then not call back.

But Heather kept trying. It stirred some little flutter inside Amy.

Christmas lights were up all around the city; the corners of lots taken over by Christmas trees for sale. One of the radio stations was playing Christmas music. The songs made Amy cry. Not because they provoked a sentimentality. Normally, the music roused her deep nostalgia for all things Christmas, but this year she cried because the songs made her sad. They didn't bring back her childhood—the smell of vanilla, balsam from the tree, the same small nativity with Mary praying over her baby. Amy knew goodness—the little things of a happy childhood, of a happy life. Most of the good little things that formed her life now felt distinctly of the past. The songs no longer reminded her of being small and safe and loved. The songs made her miss these things. The songs made her miss the songs.

She changed the radio station. Maybe this year there would be no Christmas music. Maybe there never would be again.

She dropped Rachel off at school and steered the car toward the brownstone.

Amy put on her best cheer for Rachel. But alone, now, in the quiet of home, the house belonged to her. Hers alone with only the furnace kicking on and off. Amy slouched back on the sofa, her feet up on the coffee table. The boxes of Christmas cards sat squarely near her uplifted feet. She told herself she should get them done. It was already mid-December—in past years she mailed them right after Thanksgiving. She pulled herself to the coffee table, picked up a pen and opened her address book.

This is absurd.

She couldn't understand why she had bought them. The very idea of Christmas cards suddenly made no sense. So little did when she stepped back and took a good look. Things she always did as a matter of course; that which she once enjoyed. She used to understand all of it.

There was a simple snowman drawing on the front of the cards. *May you know peace and love this Holiday Season* inside. Amy opened one and wrote *Love,* then stopped. She could not write only three names. She began to shake.

The phone rang. Amy sat, waiting to hear who it was. "Hi, Amy. It's me." Heather's voice.

"It's Tuesday, and here's my weekly message. I hope..."

Amy snatched up the receiver.

"Heather?"

"Amy? Amy!"

"Heather," Amy sobbed. Oh, her voice. "I don't know what to write in the Christmas cards." Amy's voice was barely audible.

"Amy...Amy, Breathe. It's okay."

"But I don't know what to write. The names."

"Oh." It was a sigh. It was so many things. It was her understanding without Amy having to articulate it.

Amy waited. "Write 'The Sanders Family'," said Heather.

"Right," Amy said. Of course.

"Or better yet, toss them out. Fuck it," she said.

Amy smiled a little, her tears blurring the Christmas tree, its lights spreading out in tiny bursts.

They shared silence for a few moments.

"You better now?"

Amy's breath was shaky but she was calmer.

"So, how are you?" Heather said.

Amy stiffened. She wanted Sage's name on those cards. She wanted back the flesh that bore the name. Inside her head was the frozen image of the shoreline where her sister stood, somewhere at her feet Amy's baby breathing salt water into her pink lungs. Out loud Amy said she wanted to dispel it. But now she embraced it, gave it color, fed it blood so it would live.

"I have to go. Thanks for the help," she said in a rush.

"Oh, okay. I love you."

"Thanks again. 'Bye." Amy hung up the phone.

She picked up the cards and tossed them in the trash. She shoved them down with the coffee grounds and apple cores and wet garbage. This year no cards.

She stood in front of the kitchen window and touched the cold, smooth glass. She watched the few people outside navigating the sidewalks. There was a thin layer of ice in the cracks between the square blocks. Amy thought about that which can be saved and that which is lost.

~~~

"Heather told me you talked to her the other day," Mom said. It was Friday night and she and Dad had come to Amy's for supper. She and Mom sat alone in the kitchen, tea between them.

"I was upset. I just grabbed the phone."

"I think it's wonderful. It's a step."

"Mom, it wasn't planned. It just happened."

"Sweetheart, listen to your heart."

Amy sighed at her mother tossing out that old cliché. In a college poetry class, Amy's professor told the students that it was no longer stylish to think of the heart as the center of love in the body. He said that to do so was *precious*. *Precious*, Amy realized later, a euphemism for *cheesy*.

"Mom, please."

"No, you *'please,'* Amy. You have to find a way to forgive her."

"Why?" Teeth biting metal.

"Because it is unacceptable not to. She did not do this on purpose. I have tried for months to be gentle with you. I understand what you're feeling but I know you love her."

"It's not that simple." Amy said. She crossed her arms around her ribcage. "So I guess she's right and I'm just wrong. Why are you taking her side?" Amy got up and began mopping the counter to have something to do. To displace the tension coiling and uncoiling in her chest.

"I'm not. And I didn't say you're wrong."

"You implied it." She threw the sponge in the sink. "Don't tell me how to feel or what I should do. You can just go off and be with happy Heather and her intact little family. That's fine with me." Some of the words felt cleansing and some felt spiteful and some felt simply untrue, but she could not stop them.

"She's not very happy, Amy."

"Well, good. Neither am I."

Mom got up and stood in front of Amy. "Sweetheart, all I mean is this anger is eating you. And it's eating Heather. It's not your fault. It's natural. But stop feeding it. Just let go. There is good left here. We can never replace Sage and we will never fill the loss or stop missing her. There will always be a hole. But see the good." She touched Amy who softened into her Mother's arms.

"I don't know how," she whispered. "I don't."

"A little at a time," she said. "Take small steps."

Small steps. Small breaths.

~~~

Amy stared out at the winter sky from the studio windows. A bare tree stood sharply against it, stark and leafless. The sky a color out of a tube of paint. Cerulean, or some other beautiful word. She stared out at the blue and waited for an answer. She did not know the question, but she waited. It seemed there must be an answer there in the vast expanse. Maybe some understanding would emerge if she looked long enough.

Amy wanted it all back in one giant lungful. Not only Sage—her whole life. Everything. But it was too big, too much air and she could not expand her chest wide enough to gather it all back. Small steps, Mom said. But Amy wanted it all back at once. She wanted the suffering to stop.

Her longing was a bottomless fathom and her pain was always present. It was a shroud—sometimes it was thin and she could almost see her own self through the translucence, and other times it was a dark and thick blindness.

Give it all back. Give back at least what's left.

She gave this prayer to the cerulean sky. As winter set in deeper, her body chilled, her bones, her blood running quiet and warm beneath her cold flesh, she gave it to the blue of the sky.

It Is

Amy is caught off guard. The thought that Heather would have pain about this had never formed in Amy's mind, but of course she would. Of course. Somehow Amy had not conceived it.

She is stung. How dare Heather. Amy is not sure if the basis of her anger is Heather's gall to believe she has a right to feelings or the fact that Amy never gave her sister's feelings a thought. Not for a singular moment.

Amy is ashamed. She flares in disgrace and then in anger. Heather possesses no right to make Amy feel shame.

"Did you think I didn't have feelings about this?" Heather asks softly. "You must know I loved her." The statement bears the lilt of a question. Amy knows she is wounded.

Shame floods her once more.

Again Heather asks, "What do you want me to do, Amy?"

"I don't know," Amy whispers.

But she does know. There is nothing Heather can do. This is not hers. Everything, every moment grieving, has brought Amy here and she has known for too long now. This is a matter of accepting.

The water continues rushing to and from the shore. They don't speak. There are no words. They keep proving to be too little. There is no answer—it comes to Amy. There is no answer for this. It simply is. It's not yesterday or five years ago or one minute before Sage's lungs filled with salt water. It is now.

It is.

Amy walks forward or stays stuck. Free or mired. She stares down the polarity of her choices.

She looks at her sister, her profile dark in the fading sunlight, like one of those delicate black cut-out silhouettes.

This is Saturday. They leave tomorrow. What did she think would happen this weekend? That Heather would provide some answer? That Amy herself would experience an epiphany? That they would leave here changed?

No, she didn't expect change. She fears change. Change is what she has been avoiding, grasping onto a past from which she has been alienated. No—change is exactly what she did not expect. Because she doesn't want it—what she wants is to go back; for everything to be the way it used to be. Even though she cannot and has known this all along, she has not been willing to accept it.

Is this the only answer?

Amy can never again be who she was. Who she used to be was destroyed as Sage lost breath.

She wants her sister back. But now that she is certain what she must do to have that, she is not certain she can.

Will you try?

A whisper.

"Let's head back," Amy says.

Heather nods, follows Amy back up the beach away from the tumbling ocean.

PART 3

In the path of sunshine.

When the sun flowed through the window, across the kitchen floor, across her cheek and lap and out through the opposite window, she got the feeling that nothing could ever be wrong in the world. Immersed completely in the moment with no regrets of past or worries of future, she was—simply. It was what she thought enlightenment must be.

It was the same when the sun washed up on the surface of the water. It washed right up to the shore. It did it perfectly, without effort. The sunshine was not a part of the water, it merged with the water perfectly—as if it were supposed to be this way; had always been this way.

Communion.

Spring Cleaning

Winter was like sleep; it could feel almost close to death. Sleeping Beauty and her castle full of servants and citizens slept for a hundred years. Waiting. Waiting like death. But life was there. Waiting. Waiting to come back. And it did slowly open, quietly unfold.

All that winter Amy carried grief for Sage, a heavy weight; an anchor. Like rocks in a pocket pulling her down to the bottom of icy water. Her knuckles, her kneecaps were left raw and bleeding, exposed to cold for too long. Her legs grew numb and stinging with cold as she sat on the frozen earth of her child's grave. As she read Sage's name over and over in the stone, looked into the granite, the speckled colors of the cold hard stone, she waited for it to tell her something she needed to know. She hoped for some meaning; some clear thing. It never spoke.

Amy said goodbye to Sage again and again. *See you again soon.*

Week after week, day after day—so many times to say goodbye.

Christmas arrived and passed by. She took it all down, boxes to the basement.

The oyster skies and obstinate wet of a New England March and April. Dampened to the core. Waited for the sun.

Then one morning, birdsong and blue sky, puffed white clouds and buds on the trees.

Amy felt a stirring that might have been hope.

Spring was about possibility; it was the season that felt like an early morning that rolled on for months. It rushed in every year, as if arriving late to the ball, excited and breathless and pink-cheeked.

This year the good played at the edges; a shy, small tapping *May I come in?* Amy said, *Maybe for a little while. We'll see how we do.*

During the frozen months of winter, Amy took small steps on the ice. One foot, another, forward slowly toward her sister. Slowly toward feeling. She wasn't explicitly avoiding feeling—she simply did not feel much of anything beyond sadness but a flat plane of nothingness. But she understood what she was supposed to feel and could pretend—happy, amused, excited, placid. Most of the time this is how she moved through her life. Then moments crept in quietly, stealthily, from some unknown place, and her muscles unclenched until she realized and tightened them up, closed once more. It happened slowly, but she remembered to feel again.

There had been this enormous change in her life and yet nothing really changed. The motions did not change—there was still work and taking care of her home and Rachel, there were still the family get-togethers, weddings, events they all attended. As the fingers loosened their grip on Amy's flesh, disentangled in her ribs, it became easier by small degrees.

Amy let Heather into her home. She answered the phone when she called. She went places with her and stayed together while their kids played.

Mom stopped asking her when she was going to talk to Heather again. Amy silently allowed life to progress. She supposed her mother took it as forgiveness.

It wasn't.

On a pretty Saturday morning, Amy, Matt and Rachel drove to a greenhouse out in the suburbs. They chose flats of flowers for the planters that lined the brownstone steps and for the bit of shared green in the back courtyard. Rachel loved the really bright flowers, the sticky petunias, in their audacious array of colors.

Life went along; Amy had not been able to stop it. Elation, tragedy, it stopped for none of it. It was Amy's arduous lesson and she was left amazed—amazed she still breathed, that spring arrived, amazed that nothing really was different. Except, of course, everything. Nothing was immutable, least of all that which she had unwaveringly believed was. She expected that everything would adjust to her inner being. For a volcano to erupt and cover it all over with liquid rock to form a whole new thing.

She thought about the small green and yellow placards nailed to the front of old houses all over New England. They declared the age of a house and its original owners. She thought of the drive to preserve old things, their value assumed to be somehow higher than anything anyone could come up with next. But if no one ever let the old things go, they'd never get to see the new things. Old things were new once, too.

Amy walked slowly through the rows and rows of flowers—all the flowers she could choose to create patterns in the small back garden of their building, shape constellations in living soil.

"Life goes on." Mom used to say. She never said it to Amy anymore. It would have been too cruel, but Amy recalled her mother's words. "Fight or flight" was another way to say it.

It was true. Hunger, the body, bleeding, breathing. The leaves turn and fall, then snow comes and jobs continue their relentless litany of demands and spring comes around again and Rachel outgrows her shoes.

Amy went to the mall with Heather and her kids to get Rachel new sandals for summer. It was early May and all the department stores were having sales for the first breath of summer. They pawed through tightly packed circular racks of clothes. Amy pointedly avoided the baby racks. So did Heather.

"Oh my God! Look at this, Amy," Heather said. It was a little brown jumper, perfect for a little girl. It was accompanied by a white short sleeve button-down shirt with a Peter Pan collar.

"Add a little orange tie and it brings you right back to Brownies," she said.

When she and Heather were little, they thought Brownies referred to the chocolate kind—they didn't know about the little imps.

"Remember how we thought it was so weird that a club would be named after a dessert?" She laughed. She laughed harder remembering more. She began to tell a Brownies story. It was a story they'd laughed at a hundred times, only funny to them. Heather gasped with laughter, tears in her eyes. She looked at Amy, her mouth open, her eyes happily squinted, but Amy wasn't laughing. Amy wanted to laugh; the corners of her mouth pulled up, but she forced them back down and held Heather's eyes. She didn't laugh. Heather stopped.

"I've got to look for those shoes," Amy said.

Heather looked away. "Okay," she said. They walked toward the shoe department.

Heather took what Amy gave her, which wasn't much. Amy was chintzy. The shabbiness fed the cold blood and kept it cold.

Amy measured her love for Sage by her grief and anger, the latter of which she doled out in generous helpings onto Heather's plate. Heather held out the plate to Amy with both hands and hungry saucer eyes.

In the humidity of the greenhouse, Amy meandered through the colorful flowers thinking her drab thoughts. She picked one up for Heather and thought, *She would love these flowers*. She wondered if maybe she could try harder. But guilt and fear rose up. If she gave into joy, let go of the anger, she betrayed Sage. She placed the flowers back down.

Not yet. A whisper.

~~~

Amy opened the windows at Déguiser and fresh air flowed into the stale, dusty space.

"We need to spring clean," Amy said to Sheila.

"When was the last time we even did a good dusting?"

"Feels like forever."

It had been a busy winter and now they were heading into the melee of the spring and summer wedding season.

"We're booked pretty solid from May through mid-September."

"Well, seeing that we have a small lull on our hands, want to help me clean the studio?" Amy asked.

"Do I have a choice?"

"Not really."

"Sure, then," Sheila said.

Sheila retrieved the vacuum from the small utility closet, an old workhorse that used to belong to Mom and Dad, and Amy grabbed an old cloth, dampened it and began dusting the shelves, windowsills, the desks and cabinets.

Amy kept a vase, blue and small and heavy, on the shelf with her design and art books. Heather brought the vase back for her from a college trip to Spain. It was cobalt blue with bright flecks of gold, crimson and green, sparkling like jewels. The base was round with a flat bottom; a graceful and narrow neck flowed upwards. It was hand-blown glass and fit perfectly in the palm of Amy's hand. The density of the orb pressing into her hand made her think of a heart beating.

She placed it on the highest shelf, safe from blundering, slippery hands. She took great care when she dusted the vase. Because she loved it.

She swiped away the dust from Matt's desk and the thick accumulation on the black plastic of the printer. She removed the vase and some framed pictures from the bookshelf and placed them on the nearby window ledge. As she dusted the bookshelf, she ducked her head a little to find an angle of vision where she could make sure the dust was cleared away. Some of the fine particles escaped her cloth and floated in the air. She could see them in the sunbeam from the window. The air that seemed so clean, so invisible. How much was floating that she couldn't see in the regular light from her everyday angles?

She placed the dust cloth on the windowsill and began to arrange the framed photos back into their places. She checked the angles and shifted things until they were right. She reached behind her back without looking and lightly grabbed the blue vase at the spot where the long neck met the blue orb. It slipped, slid down quickly through her dusty, damp fingers. Her empty hand flew out underneath the vase and the orb landed in the center of her palm with a heavy thump.

Adrenaline streaked through her; her heart beat wildly. She remembered to take a breath.

She stared at the blue vase in her hand and put it back where it belonged.

~~~

Amy's grandmother sewed a baptism gown when she was pregnant with Amy's mother, her eldest child. It was pure white, smooth polished cotton that had some of the quality of satin, but not as slick. The skirt was very long, extending three feet beyond an infant's feet. It had tiny, short gathered sleeves edged with lace. The bodice was smocked with three minuscule buttons resting softly on the chest. There was a simple bonnet to match which tied under the chin with white satin ribbons attached with impossibly tiny white satin ribbon bows.

At the bottom of the long dress, Grandma embroidered the names and dates of the births of her children in tight, precise stem stitch. Mom embroidered her children's names and Heather and Amy embroidered theirs. They all used thread from the same skein Grandma started with, a very pale silvery blue. They all pulled from that skein to inscribe in thread the names of their babies when they placed them in ritual into the hands of each other and God.

Each mother's stitch was different and distinct, but dug into the same cloth.

When Amy was a child, she was fascinated by the dress which to her looked like a tiny wedding gown.

"Mom, can we look at the baby gown?" Amy often asked.

Mom brought out the old cardboard coat box, removed the lid and carefully parted the brittle tissue paper. She let Amy touch the names and hold the little bonnet. Amy ran her finger over her mother's name, hardly believing she was ever so small.

"You wore this when you were a baby?" Amy asked every time.

"Yes. When you were baptized you wore it, too."

Amy ran her finger over her own name.

Now she wondered where the dress was.

She thought about the dress to occupy her mind because today they were going to clean Sage's room.

She wondered *What did I used to think about? Before the accident, what thoughts filled my mind?*

Simple things, she was sure. *What will we have for supper? Don't forget to take the clothes off the line before it rains.* Petty annoyances. *The girls are driving me crazy.* She cringed at thoughts such as these with shame and weighty culpability that she could have wasted any time frustrated with her baby. She remembered one time when Sage wouldn't nap and she fussed and cried and arched her back angrily away from Amy and she squeezed the child and hissed, "Stop it! Go to sleep!" Amy counted on nap time; she needed that break. Sage didn't seem any more upset by Amy's outburst than she already was, but Amy's body shook. She cried after Sage finally did fall asleep and called Heather to sob out the story to her and Heather laughed a little just because it was normal—she told Amy it happened to all mothers. Now, Sage dead, Amy wondered *How could I?* Sage had slept that day and woke smiling, elated to see her mama. Amy was breathlessly relieved.

Amy still talked to Sage. In her room, surrounded by her things, Amy relived moments of Sage's short life. Her smell still deep, deep in the fabrics if she closed her eyes and plunged all her being into the effort of retrieving the scent. *There. There it is.* In her room, Amy told her about the changing seasons and about Rachel and school. *Someday you'll go, too*, Amy told her, though she knew it wasn't true. She said it to protect Sage from the truth which was so cold and final and cruel. It allowed Amy to pretend it could be true. Just for a sweet moment she could believe; could almost forget. She might be gone but Amy would always be her mother. Only Amy's own death could wipe that conscious knowledge.

Amy and Matt often found each other, when the house was especially quiet, in Sage's still room. One morning very early, Amy watched the sun rise through Sage's window. She felt Matt's arms around her.

"Good morning," she smiled.

"Hi." His face in her hair, stubbly chin on her neck. He was warm and solid.

She spoke then—her voice, her mouth.

"Maybe we should put her stuff away," she said. These words were not planned. It happened as though her body formed them, the sentiment. She was the vehicle for some bigger thing.

Matt's breath was warm on her neck.

"I'm not going to go to the grave anymore. Well, not so often anymore."

She told him why.

She brought Rachel to school one day that week, then drove to the cemetery. She parked beneath the big oak tree and went and sat in the grass in front of Sage's headstone. The sun was warm and she touched the stone. It had absorbed the heat and was warm, too. The ground was soft again and the grass getting thick and very green. Last spring Sage was so small; not yet walking and she possessed few words. There was a language, but not the multitude of words she would have eventually accumulated. Amy recalled one morning when she sat on the floor folding laundry and watching Sage play. She could barely crawl, simply pulled herself around haphazardly. Her toys had captured her attention. But then she looked over and saw Amy. Her face bloomed into a huge smile and her eyes shone. She pulled herself across the distance to lay her head on Amy's lap; to smile up at her. This was the kind of gift she gave. Amy felt soft with the memory.

"I went to the grave because I'm her Mommy. Because she needed me, but she doesn't need me. I need her. I don't have to go there for her anymore," Amy told Matt, his face wet on her neck. "This weekend, let's put her things away." He nodded, his face up and down against her skin.

The day came to do it.

Alone in her room, up before Matt, Amy thought of the baptism gown. She thought of Sage's name stitched in the hem. She couldn't tear out the stitches simply because Sage was gone. She could, but the imprint from the needle would still be there. All those little holes and the faint traces of the thread's color. The ghost of the silvery blue. She could not remove her name; Sage could not be erased. She had been here on earth. She had worn the tiny dress. She was still here. Amy could remove the stitches, she could remove Sage's things, but the essence of Sage would remain imprinted in her. Amy could hold her there inside, forever her baby.

"Someday you'll stitch the names of your children," Mom said when Amy was a little girl.

Sage Angelina Sanders

Search

Amy and Heather have walked farther than they realized.

It's getting dark and the lights of the inns and homes twinkle at a good distance.

When they were children, there was a game Amy and Heather played over and over. They called it "shipwreck."

Shipwreck was created as a consequence of a cruise their parents took to Bermuda.

"What if you get caught in the Bermuda Triangle?" Amy had wailed tearfully. She's not sure where she had heard of it, but she imagined a giant swirling triangle of angry blue ocean water that sucked ships straight down, bow first, to the bottom of the ocean.

Mom, Dad and the ship returned intact and on schedule a week after they departed. They brought the girls petite embroidered handbags with cedar wood handles. With their parents safely home, they were free to explore the newly fascinating idea of cruises.

They gathered two babies each, diaper bags filled with the numerous changes of outfits they found necessary, blankets and doll strollers. They made sure the babies had everything they needed.

They played it the same way every time.

"Okay, let's pretend we don't like each other because you let your babies go in the pool and I don't." That was the only part that changed each time: why they didn't like each other.

The ladies meet on the deck of a cruise ship. It is a beautiful day, crisp blue sky, easy rocking waters.

"Hello! Oh, your babies are so cute," Amy says. Heather beams proudly.

"So are yours. Isn't this cruise ship beautiful? I was just about to take my babies to the pool. Want to come, too?" Heather asks.

They take their babies to the pool. Things begin to go wrong. There is criticism of parenting skills.

"You let your newborn in the pool?" Amy says.

Heather is indignant. "She is a very good swimmer. We took lessons at the Y. You don't let your baby swim? I think that's mean."

"No! They could drown or get sick. Only bad mothers do things like that." She tosses her head in disgust.

"Well, maybe we just shouldn't be friends!" Heather gathers her babies and stuff and stomps off.

"Wait," Amy hisses. "Doesn't your lady stay at the pool?"

"Oh, yeah." She stops.

"I am going to my cabin!" Amy declares.

"Like I would care." Hateful looks are exchanged.

Sometime in the middle of the night, the calm waters grow agitated. Wind whips the cruise ship through tidal-sized waves that have erupted in the middle of the ocean. The boat rocks, a toy in a tub. The two ladies frantically gather their babies. The deck is chaotic. They are ordered to abandon ship.

They throw a dark blanket over themselves, dark night, lack of visibility. And they run, run, run across the broad backyard, a rubber raft adrift in a vast violent ocean. They run until smack, they fall, the dark blanket of night covering them, their babies, the diaper bags and the strollers. The rubber raft is beached on some far-away shore.

In spite of the tempestuous journey, the ladies and their babies managed to fall asleep during the escape and they awaken slowly, with the first light of day. They stretch as their babies sleep soundly, *unaffected by the turbulent life-raft trip through one-hundred-foot waves, monsoon-force rain and wind.*

"Oh, my God, my babies!" The babies begin to cry, awakening.

"Oh! My little babies! You're okay," they croon.

Then they notice each other. They suddenly remember what's happened and realize with whom they've shared a life-raft.

"You!" Heather spits.

"Of all the people to get stuck in this raft with!" They storm off in opposite directions, babies, diaper bags and blankets filling their arms.

Life on the deserted island is not easy. Soon, the baby food and bottles run out and it is lonely on opposite sides of the island.

"Heather!" Amy calls from her side of the backyard. "Heather!"

"Yeah?"

"Let's pretend they make up."

This is the best part.

The babies and the baby stuff are moved to a space in the middle of the yard.

"Hi."

"Hi."

"How are you?"

"Good. You?"

"Fine."

An extended pause.

"I am so sorry," Amy gushes.

"I am so sorry, too."

They love saying 'sorry.' It's the zenith of the big build-up. Like Christmas Eve into Christmas morning. What's better?—the knowing it's coming or the moment it's here? When it's here, it means it's almost over.

"We should be friends!"

"Our babies would have so much fun! They're almost the same ages!"

And so the friendship begins.

After making up, the game dwindles quickly, the excitement fizzles out. The making up was good, but the moment before making up was better.

But here on this island, all grown now, Amy does not anticipate the moment of forgiveness. Instead, there are hot words on Amy's tongue. Their movement relieves the feeling in her belly where they have been growing hotter and hotter.

"Heather?" Amy stops. "Wait." She sits on a boulder.

Heather stops and looks back at Amy. "Yeah?"

Amy exhales a flame and steels herself. "What happened in the water? When I was in the bathroom. I need to know how it happened."

She walks toward Amy. "I don't know what you want to know." She sighs and sits.

"Everything. Every moment from the time I left."

Heather blinks hard. "You left. You saw us go to play. And when you were halfway to the bathroom, the sky started to get dark. Black. Really, really heavy. I could still see you. You were facing the sunny part of the sky. The blue. I almost called you back but I knew you wouldn't hear me and I thought I'd have time to get them all out. I called to them. The rain came so fast, in a sheet. The water was pounded by rain."

Her voice breaks up. Tears run from her eyes.

"I screamed and screamed to them to get to the sand. I grabbed Tara because she was clinging to my leg. I went to grab Sage and I couldn't see her," she sobs. "A couple of big waves broke right near us. I looked and looked. I ran through the water. The waves were coming in on the tide. They had gotten

bigger. The kids were walking back toward me, terrified. Back to the water. I didn't want them back in the water. I screamed at them 'get back to the sand.' I just couldn't find Sage. I just couldn't find her." She cries from her depths. Amy watches her sister gouged from the inside out.

When they were little, sometimes they pretended they were the pain monsters. Their own bodies did not feel any sensation inflicted upon them directly, instead the other sister felt it. As they jumped around in the waves, Amy felt all of Heather's sensations, and Heather all hers.

Heather tickled herself and Amy laughed like mad, falling into the water, coming up spouting.

Amy whacked herself hard on her left shoulder with her right hand and Heather grabbed her left shoulder and shouted, "Ow!"

"No, that wasn't one," Amy said. "That was a horsefly—it bit me."

"Oh."

Amy grabbed her nose and pretended to twist it hard. Heather grabbed her own, screaming in pain.

Heather always protected Amy when they were little. Even when Heather was still a tiny girl herself, only a year and some months older, she always provided a safe arm or voice or body in front of Amy's. As they grew, they caught up in size, knowledge, experience. But Heather never fully relinquished her position as protector. In adulthood, Amy reciprocated, fighting battles and injustices for Heather as earnestly as Heather did for her, but Heather never fully let the protective circle of arms drop.

They jumped in and out of the waves, laughing like crazy, and feeling the other's pain.

Now Amy stares ahead, heat pressing into her eyes from behind, making her dizzy.

"That's when you came back," Heather said.

It could have happened so many ways. That day could have been so many other kinds of days.

But it didn't happen any other way. Sage is gone. There is no other thing; no other day.

And here is her sister.

And here is her heart.

The shore possessed its particular seasons. Amy learned them when she was a child.

She remembered summers waiting, watching, learning the cycles. The shore had its own routines and ceremonies. She imagined it took great comfort in its own imitation, the years worked soft with repetition. In July, tiny rocks were strewn along the tideline. Walks were more difficult at this time. The rocks were about the size of large almonds. They rolled in the palm, nesting into the center of a cupped hand. The colors varied—grays, deeply-hued greens and blues, russets and browns, black, white. Amy had to watch her footing lest she step down hard with her heel or the tender center of an arch. Being careful was a cumbersome task in July. Scattered in among the rocks were shells, some whole, some in pieces. Scallop shells, quahog, some that were iridescent. The ones that looked like gross toenails. "These are sailors' toenails," Mom said. Amy and Heather were intrigued by them.

In August, the real seaweed arrived.

"It's so yucky," one of the girls lamented. They stood forlornly at the shore, their feet on damp sand, staring at the thick red surf.

"We're going swimming down there." Heather called to Mom, pointing down shore.

"Okay, be careful. Don't go past the last lifeguard stand."

"We won't," they said in unison, already trotting away. SWIM IN GUARDED AREAS ONLY. The signs were posted on all the lifeguard chairs. They were painted white boards with black hand-painted block letters, from square stencils.

The girls made their way toward the private beach where the water was usually clear.

When they were small, Mom pulled her beach chair down to the very edge of the shore. She read while the girls splashed in the shallows. Her eyes floated up frequently from her book to make sure they were okay. She was always right there.

As they grew, they were trusted on their own. They never did anything of which they weren't sure. They were careful children; they understood their limits, largely self-imposed as they were.

The water cleared enough for swimming several lifeguard chairs down from their spot—clean enough to swim in. It was a search. This always happened in August.

The beach had its rhythms to keep.

They skipped along the shore, in the clean, dry sand. It hummed and scattered beneath their feet. They kept their eyes on the water, searching for the waves breaking white and blue and clear.

"There!"

"There," Amy agreed. "Oh, thank God."

"I know."

They stopped at the edge of the water and Amy looked down as it came rushing up over her toes, her ankles.

"Okay. Today you just run in with me."

Amy looked at her, her face set. "I hate that."

"Come on. I'll hold your hand all the way." Amy held back. She stood several feet from her sister. That water would be cold.

"Don't be so wimpy, Amy!" She grabbed Amy's hand.

"Fine!" Amy yelled. "I'm not wimpy."

"Are, too," she muttered. "Okay, okay!" she said when Amy pulled away from her. "Let's go!" And she ran, pulling Amy along, her hand squeezing Amy's tightly. Water splashed at Amy, in her face, and she closed her eyes against it. Up to her shins, her thighs, her waist. She was slammed back a little by a wave. She opened her eyes as another wave crashed into her. She closed her eyes once more. She heard Heather laugh. Amy breathed in great gulps of air through her mouth. Then, without warning, she was underwater. Heather's hand no longer held hers. She tried to stand but couldn't find the sandy floor. Her mouth filled with water and she couldn't open her eyes. The ocean pulled and tossed her.

Another moment and her hand reached air. She followed it up, up. She gasped, opened her eyes, spun around, looking for the shore.

Heather's firm hand wound around Amy's wrist.

"Oh, you scared me! I couldn't find you," she said. Amy began to cry a little.

"Come on," Heather said. They dragged themselves out of the water and flopped down onto the wet sand at the shore. The warm shallow water moved over and off, over and off their legs and laps.

They were quiet.

"Want to go back in?" Heather asked.

Amy shrugged coolly. Her chest pounded. "Maybe later."

"Okay."

They got up and started walking back to Mom.

"You can take as long as you want next time," Heather said. Amy nodded.

"You girls back already?" Mom said.

"Yeah. It was still a little yucky down there," Heather said.

"Yeah," Amy echoed.

Amy and Heather didn't look each other in the eye.

"Maybe it'll be nicer later," Mom said.

They both agreed that, yes, anything was possible.

Three

Layers.

The early summer mornings were cool and dewy. Amy dressed in layers. Thin pajama bottoms, T-shirt, an old cotton sweater. As the day grew warmer, she peeled a layer and moved from the sunny seat to the shady one. She watched the sun rise out the family room window. No more morning coffee in her beloved kitchen; she was trying something new. There was none of the old comfort in the old ways, only pain and a growing hole emphasized by the scalding admission that nothing would ever be the same.

There was a part of herself that had evolved through habit. A self that built up, layer over familiar layer. Like an onion. What is at the center? The layers spoke to the layers, one layer informed the next. This was why transformation was painful. Peeling back layers of thick skin, callused and yellow, down to soft new skin. Baby skin. Blood bubbles up in vicious little blisters, the pulse visible, throbbing and rapid. She spent the winter peeling and discarding. As she pulled back a layer, she realized one was inextricably attached to the next. She surmised that to peel one was to peel all. To discard one was to discard all. A mass eradication.

But as winter was ousted, consumed by summer, the sun warmed her from her center and suddenly she wasn't sure about those peeling layers.

What could she keep?

That which she kept would be altered—this truth could not be avoided. She had tried to deny it, but it would not be refused. The pain was in fighting it. There were some things she needed to keep to sustain that which she wanted to sustain. To salvage some good from the rubble. The good: the life she and Matt had built so far, her little girl, her work, the places she loved. And the more sublime: a faith in the inherent worth of living, in cultivating a future, in the possibility of some happiness. She was sorting—the parts she could keep, the new she could forge.

Underneath these thoughts was another; the tiniest seed of a thought—she wanted her sister back.

Winter had taught her that no one can outrun the thing that burns to be run from. It was with her always. Would time soften it? Or would she slowly rework herself to accommodate it? Carve out a soft pillowy crevice in which it could nestle. She would cradle it and hold it, rock it and sing to it. And allow the layers to grow over it, unceasingly burying it.

~~~

Amy laid her stitched pieces on the studio work table. There were four half-finished pieces and several new ideas that she had recently sketched. A field of green with one flaming tree arousing autumn. An ocean of water, a blending of warm grays and coolness, all shades and depths of the colors. A woman uncertainly peeking out from behind a drawn curtain. The curving spiral of seashell starlings she'd begun last summer. And the spare dark stitching of the closed eyes. She turned them around, she fingered the unstitched silk, imagining the strokes of thread she might weave through it. She shuffled the paper that bore the sketches.

Amy heard the familiar creak of the studio door and turned to see her sister standing in front it, peering around the room.

"Heather?" Amy called out.

"Oh, hello."

"What are you doing here?" Amy asked, her tone curious, but not unkind.

"I left some of my equipment at one of the events last weekend. Your crew grabbed it for me. Matt said it was okay if I stopped by," she said, her words a breathless rush.

"Of course," Amy said. "We can ask him where it is."

"Heather!"

She turned, "Hey, Sheila! How are you?" They embraced.

"Sheila, do you know where Heather's equipment is?"

"Oh, the stuff you left at the Copley last weekend? It's right over in the office. I'll go grab it."

"Thanks," Heather said. She looked toward the window. "It's so sunny in here. I've always loved that about your place." Her eyes scanned the length and width of the windows and came to rest on the table.

"Are these for the show?" Heather asked and walked closer to the table.

"I don't know," Amy sighed. "Maybe I'm going to let that one go."

"Oh, you can't. These are so beautiful, Amy. So lovely."

"She still talking about bailing on the show?" Sheila asked as she handed Heather the bag that held her gear. "Why do you keep taking them out if you're certain you shouldn't do it?"

"It's two months away and all I have is several unfinished pieces and no coherent theme." She left unsaid that her inspiration and motivation had abandoned her since Sage died. She also left unsaid that suddenly there had been a stirring of both. Just the beginnings of stirring, like the quickening of a growing infant in the womb. She was almost afraid to speak of inspiration, which had been slowly creeping back. She was afraid to scare it away; she was afraid to admit she wanted it back, as if accepting its gifts meant accepting life itself and some part of her still wanted to refuse it. But, with a tentative hand, she had begun some sketches; she had threaded the eye of her needle with strands of colored thread, had pushed that fine filament of metal through the gently stretched silk.

Heather walked up to the table. "I see a pattern. The beginning of fall right here. The ocean waking before a storm. This woman seems as though she is contemplating something new; something uncertain. The starlings are like when the many become one, like a synchronization. When we wake from some coma and merge with something greater. Maybe those closed eyes represent the moment before we wake. I see it."

Amy walked closer and stood next to her. Maybe she could see it, too.

~~~

Summer pressed in with its fevered hands and hot breath.

A fist had pressed down on Amy's chest for nearly a year. Her breathing made shallow and her ribcage compressed. Strong fingers had clung to her flesh and held it tightly, but its grip had slowly loosened.

"How?" she asked her mother. She had done nothing but wait.

"It's time, " Mom said. "Time heals."

Amy could not deny this cliché. She hadn't been an aid in the process of healing. Just the opposite, she had done little to encourage it along. She had obstinately stood firm in its way. And yet now, as the summer drew in closer, her inability to breathe, to think forward, to feel anything but grief, was in some small but assertive ways, abating.

"I haven't done anything. I haven't forgotten her," Amy told her mother.

"Of course not. You never will."

"It still hurts, Mom. Like it was yesterday." Her mother only nodded slowly, her face tender with compassion.

Amy imagined her grief as a living, churning spiral in the center of her body. Once large, its revolutions rapid and lashing, it had settled into something more manageable.

"But you're becoming a new person."

"Will that make it easier?" Amy asked.

"Yes. It will never go away, but, yes, it will become easier."

Amy knew it would never go away. That was okay. She imagined her grief—some distant day—the size of a small, blue marble, nestled deep in her center. Hard and real and never forgotten. Not fed, but enduring.

It was late June and already hot. It was the kind of summer that came barreling in rolling over itself in heat and sun. There had been no rain or fog. No damp, only sun and warmth and blue sky.

One early morning, Amy sat by the window with her coffee, rich and hot, and read a nice, fat novel. Matt had left for work and Rachel was still asleep. She couldn't recall the last time she read a book uninterrupted. She never cared and wouldn't have denied her children a moment of her time, but she had forgotten how marvelous it was to read page after page. She remembered a time when this was not a luxury. There was a time before—there had been other ways of being, chosen with great care and consciousness and then abandoned—willingly discarded and in some instances forgotten entirely.

They'd been dropped in the path along the way, like Hansel and Gretel's crumbs, consumed, providing no way back. It seemed inconceivable that she could have forgotten all other incarnations of herself, and yet she had. But not the self she was with Sage—that could never be expelled.

"Mama?"

"In the living room, baby."

Rachel climbed into Amy's lap. They were still, Rachel's honey curls at Amy's chin. She breathed in Rachel's scent and held her small body, aware of her soft skin.

"What should we do today?" Amy said.

She opened her eyes wide and smiled largely, "School!"

Amy laughed. "You like school, don't you. But it's summer. There's no school in summer. What else should we do?"

"Umm..." she tipped her head, thinking, then looked back up at Amy. "The beach!"

Amy didn't speak.

"And I can bring my shovel and my bucket. And my dump truck!"

"That's...maybe we can. Let's have some breakfast, okay?"

Rachel ate oatmeal. Amy pretended to breathe.

Last week, Mom called and asked, "Would you want to go to Cattail for a little while? Rachel can play. We could go for a nice walk."

Amy sighed. "I don't know, Mom. I don't think so."

"Okay. Any time you want, I can go with you."

"I know. Thanks." But she wasn't sure she would ever be able to go there again. She wasn't sure she wanted to return.

As she scrubbed stuck oatmeal from the saucepan, she remembered: there were other beaches. *Of course there are*, she thought as relief coursed through her. She rinsed the last of the dishes and trotted to the living room where Rachel played with her blocks.

"Rachel. Let's get your bathing suit on. Then we have to pack the car for the..." she trailed.

"Beach!" Rachel shouted.

"This beach we're going to has a playground right in the sand!" Amy told her. She talked about all the things they would see. They drove out of the city, the hot sun pushing into the car. They crossed a small bridge and then bumped down a sandy road. The ocean came into view—sun dance and gentle ripples. The surf at this beach was mild, its sand a bit coarse and rocky, its shoreline short. *But, well, it will be good*, she told herself.

Rachel ran out ahead of Amy, her bucket bobbing from its smooth white handle. She plunked down in the sand and got to work. Amy set up a spot for them. It was just after noon and the sun was hot on her shoulders. She tugged a sunhat onto Rachel's head and sat down in her chair. She leaned back and closed her eyes for a moment. The sun pressed up against her, draped itself over her. With closed eyes, she absorbed the ocean sounds, the cry of the gulls, the voices of children, the smell of salt and seaweed and heated sand. She opened her eyes and watched the dune grass catching the salty breeze. She shifted her feet back and forth in the sand.

She could not deny it felt good.

They ate lunch and played together in the water.

"There's no bubbles," Rachel said, dipping her hand in and out.

"No," Amy said. "Only little ripples."

Only tiny ripples. Amy watched every move Rachel made. She shadowed her little girl as she practiced swimming. It was a frantic dog paddle, her head stuck out of the water from her stretched-out neck. She smiled broadly as she pushed herself into Amy's waiting arms. Amy remembered doing that very same stroke. They dried off and Amy read a book while Rachel played in the sand in front of her. As the sun made its way to the other side of the sky, the air cooled and Amy pulled a long-sleeve shirt over Rachel's head, slipped an old thin one over her own.

"Should we go for a walk?" she asked.

They rambled down the shore, Amy's feet in water, sand patterns decorating her ankles. Rachel fluttered back and forth; she found shells and rocks, chased seagulls. They came to a bend in the shoreline flanked by boulders. It was as far as they could go, there was no more sand, a harbor around the bend. Rachel found periwinkles stuck to the big rocks.

"What's these, Mommy?"

"Periwinkles. See?" She showed her how they suctioned to the wet rock. Amy sat on a flat boulder while Rachel explored, tipped her head back and felt the sun on her face. Boats moved in and out of the harbor, birds floated on the air, their feathers guiding their light bones.

Everything that happens in this life carries so much weight, is powerless to the relentless draw of gravity. All of it—pain and hurt and the petty slights of adolescence. All the things shared between people, at home and work, sitting in traffic, sitting across the globe. The worst, the events, the heartache, the joy are heavy in the present, their weight inescapable. But it all sinks down eventually; settles down and gathers dust. Amy wondered about that which was light enough to float to the surface. What rose up?

Rachel came over and climbed into Amy's lap, rested her head between Amy's breasts. She lifted her head and placed both hands on Amy's chest. Then she put her head down again.

Amy laughed, "What are you doing, baby?"

"Shhh, Mommy. I'm listening." She lifted her head and smiled broadly.

"Why?"

"It's like the ocean in there!"

They sat, Rachel's ear on Amy's heart, for a long time. She may have been listening to Amy's heart the whole time, or resting. Or maybe watching the boats.

Whether one or all, it didn't matter a bit.

~~~

Amy thought about her heart the entire ride home from the beach. She placed her hand on her chest to feel it beating.

Once Rachel was sleeping peacefully that evening, the salt and sand rinsed away, Amy went to sit on the balcony. Stars and crickets, a little city light, some city noise. The air was cooled down from the hot day and paired perfectly with her favorite butter-yellow, fat-weave cotton sweater.

Matt joined her. He laced his fingers through hers. "Tell me about your day."

"Mmm." She squeezed his hand. "It was really good. Not as hard as I worried it would be." It went unsaid that it hadn't been Cattail that she'd visited.

"I'm so glad," he said.

They turned on some quiet music and read for a while. Amy looked up from her book often, unable to fully concentrate.

Matt yawned. "I'm going to bed." He leaned down to kiss her.

"I'll be up in a minute."

She slouched down in the chair and looked up at the dimmed starlight. Much of it was obliterated by the bright city electric lights. Nothing like the Cattail summer sky. Her mind moved to her day at the beach. It had been almost as good and fine as she'd always known days at the beach to be. It was a dimmer version, but it was not bad. Amy wasn't exactly afraid to go to Cattail—she could not deny that she was fearful to see the place Sage died—but that was not the entirety of it. She was more afraid that Cattail had become *only* the place that Sage died. Afraid all the good was gone, replaced with only heartache. As long as she stayed away she could still harbor some hope that it could be more than that.

That is how it is with Heather. She sat up straight in the chair, her hands on the armrests. Is that how it was with Heather?

What do I want? she asked herself. She yearned for a revealed future. An assurance that she would heal. That she would be able to forgive. She needed to believe that there was some other side of this, some relief. To shed the desperate need to get past this while struggling just as desperately never to move on. Sage would never see a full life, why should Amy be able to love, to be happy? Why should Cattail give her happiness and peace? It didn't seem fair. Sage deserved Amy's life to be suspended—the price exacted for the loss of hers. If Amy were to live, at least it should be arrested at the moment of her child's death. This was the center of her grinding desperation to find the way out and the equalized fear that she might.

What else do I want? She sat back in the chair, her hands slid to her lap. She gazed up at the stars. Maybe there was nothing to know. Maybe she already knew—somewhere inside herself. Maybe she needed only to wait for it to rise up. These were the things that didn't have neat little answers. Maybe the answer *was* that there was no answer.

This can't be fixed. The thought surged.

This cannot be fixed with anything I've tried. What will fix this?

Amy slipped herself into the idea of being Heather. Tentatively, uncomfortably she felt around; she stretched out. How would it feel to be her? Amy looked at herself with Heather's eyes, Heather's heart.

For a year Amy had blamed her sister. If only she'd been more careful. Why had she never listened to Amy when she told her to be more cautious with the children? She always teased Amy to relax, that she was too high strung, too worried. How *dare* then had she allowed this to have happened?

Amy breathed slowly in Heather's body.

A small voice crept into her mind, a mosquito buzzing.

Did she let it happen?

No. Amy knew she did not.

But it was still cleaner to send the anger her way.

Mom's voice came to her. "You need to talk to her."

"I talk to her," Amy had said.

"You know what I mean."

Amy had only shrugged. "I even hang out with her. She comes over here. You've witnessed it."

Mom had said nothing, only looked at Amy evenly with unblinking eyes.

"Do it for yourself if you can't do it for her."

Amy never really heard, but now the words seeped in, a warm liquid that filled her out and trickled to all the ends. Suddenly, she was sure she wanted to do something to try. She wasn't sure why or how she had arrived in this place and she wasn't sure it mattered, just that it had come.

She got up and walked hurriedly to the phone.

"Heather? It's me."

Amy asked if she'd go to Martha's Vineyard with her. Heather said yes, tears swelling in her voice.

Open

They return to their room from their walk. Amy is hungry but doesn't feel like doing what needs to be done to get food.

The room is dimly lit by the light of one small table lamp. Amy picks up a brochure that lists summer events on the island. She scans through— Memorial Day through Labor Day.

"I always hated it when people had parties on Labor Day weekend," she says. "I always would rather have been at Cattail. I'd be so annoyed with the hosts all day."

"Me, too."

"It was the last real chance of the summer to go to the beach. You never seem to go after Labor Day, huh?"

Heather slowly shakes her head, agrees.

"The funny thing is, no matter when your last beach day of the summer is, you never know it. You never know it that day. You only realized it later. Like when fall had come. When I look back on it, I always think, yeah that was the last day of the summer. Like maybe I should have made more of it or cherished it better or something. But sometimes you just don't know."

She nods. Understands.

It is their last night at the inn.

It is dark. Amy looks out the window at the moonless sky. The stars are very bright in the impossible denseness of the black expanse. There is so little electric light out there. It's stunning. It seems as though she could inhale the stars and they would flow with her breath, dissolve into her. Staring out into that breadth, she doesn't feel alone; she feels a piece of something bigger, absorbed into something of which she is a part. She is not alone.

"God, we were so young when we were here last," Heather says softly from behind her. Her voice is so sad.

Amy nods. So much has passed unremembered since then. And, of course, everything monumental— marriages, births, deaths. The events that place their hands firmly and possess the power to reshape, molded like clay. A potter's wheel. We spin and spin, *Amy thinks.*

The first time they were here, there had been nothing but possibility. Life had been wide open— anything, everything. All of it; every dream. Where had they fallen short? Where had they compromised? What were the mistakes? Life hands it out randomly—plans be damned. It's what's done with it that matters. What has Amy done?

She wants to be little again; curl up on Mom when things get overwhelming—when the safest place you knew was your mother's warm, sweet-smelling neck. She told you it was okay and it was the easiest thing in the world to believe it. Simple problems, simple answers. It would be such comfort to curl up and know everything was okay; close her eyes tight and let someone else take care. Open her eyes and all would be better.

Heather cries softly. Amy still faces the window. She imagines her sister's tears falling to the bedspread. She knows how Heather's face looks when she cries. Amy knows every one of Heather's expressions.

"I wish it could be the way it was before," Amy says softly.

"It can never be that way. Whatever happens in life changes things, Amy."

Amy breathes quietly into the glass.

"Is it always going to be like this?" Heather sniffs.

"I don't know, Heather. I don't know what to do." She wants to step over the wall that stands between them. She can't name what it is that is stopping her.

Amy hears the bed squeak, then feels Heather's presence behind her. She is close, her warmth a solid block filling the empty space. She rests her face between Amy's shoulder blades. She shakes lightly and tears wet through Amy's thin cotton shirt to her skin. Something in Amy sinks a little. She reaches behind her back and takes her sister's hand. She has always loved holding her hand. It is the first, softest thing Amy can remember. Heather shakes harder, her head presses more heavily into Amy.

"Amy, I'm so sorry." It is like a soft wail. It comes from somewhere deep and soulful. Her remorse is a deep sting to Amy's insides. What has she put on her? Amy had wanted Heather to take this from her; bear the burden, the blame. As if it could diminish Amy's pain, her loss, bring Sage back. And Heather has taken it, held it to her like an offering, an infant, helpless; made it her own.

But it doesn't belong to anyone. There is no purpose for blame. It is a dead end, an endless road. Walking, walking, muscles cramping, eventually atrophying, deteriorating, going nowhere.

This is the road upon which Amy has placed her sister. Pushed her, prodded her on and forced her to bear the weight.

Amy feels something loosen in her and then it is like pulling a small stone from a wall of stones and there is a great rush. And she wonders at the power of one small stone.

She turns to Heather, her own tears falling. She is so sorry. Realization hits her, a hard blow to the stomach. *They embrace fiercely and sob together. Amy is flooded with a relief, like something heavy letting down. Her body is soft; all the hardness slipping away. She hadn't known she'd become this rigid.*

"I'm so sorry," she whispers after a while. She says it over and over. Heather says it, too. Their own sister mantra. They don't need to articulate their apologies. They know, as they have always known, without the need for words.

MELISSA CORLISS DELORENZO

PART 4

Her breath.

Floating under buoyancy of salt water with closed eyes and held breath, the ocean roars. Not like a lion—like the breathing of a thousand Goddesses. Floating beneath the surface with eyes closed, the body dissolves, more salt for the liquid's flavor, more salt to dry white powder on the brow, the knee. She remembers everything she is with crystal clarity. She forgets everything she is with glorious abandon.

She has always felt as though she has arrived, gotten somewhere, when she gets to water. It may seem that stepping into an ocean, large and unwieldy, mindful and willful, would engender fear. That she would be overwhelmed by the enormity, overly aware of her own smallness, the frailty of her body, her bones. But it never occurs to her to be afraid or think of herself as small. She feels instead diluted, accepted, cupped into a thing that is greater, that is infinite and sacred. Washed by salt, minerals, seaweed rubbing her skin sleek, smoothing the roughness, the sin.

Salt is curative.

Whenever she walks onto that beach, she is silenced. Her voice, her internal chatter. She never knows why and maybe the mystery is the source of its strength. She could lay her eyes upon it for great lengths of time and still never understand it. At the same time she knows the why doesn't matter. It is a coming home to self, to source, to infinity. There are places that are close to God. There are churches without floors and ceilings.

The ocean breathes at her in one giant endless lungful; ruffles her hair and cools her skin. She keeps waiting for it to take another breath but it does not need to. The breath flows over her body and penetrates somewhere deeper until her breath and its breath mingle in one giant shared belly-breath. Sand tickle-flows over the tops of her feet, across her ankles, sticking there, creating intricate patterns of the Universe. Hot skin and the breath of the infinite in all its forms.

You can write of water and all liquidy things and they will not flow from the page or leak slowly away.

Water is solid in words.

August Again

It is August again.

Déguiser is ready for Amy's vacation. Her stomach grows nervous every time she thinks about going.

"You know you can go and not worry," says Sheila.

"I know."

"I know you know, so is it that you don't want to go?"

She sighs. "I do. I don't. I do. Get it?"

"I don't. I do."

"See what I mean?" Amy laughs.

"It's understandable, Amy."

"I'm scared."

Sheila nods slowly.

"What if..." she sighs again. "I can't talk about the what-ifs anymore." She was tired to her bones of going through them.

"Maybe you just leap."

"Leap?"

"Yup."

"You're so wise."

"I know."

Amy puts a hand on Sheila's shoulder. "Seriously. I don't know how I could have made it this far without your help."

"Yeah, yeah. Say it in my paycheck. Words don't pay the bills," Sheila jokes and it lightens the air in the room and for that, too, Amy is grateful.

Amy laughs again. "Okay, let's go over the books so I can get out of here and commence to the leaping."

Once things are set at the studio, Amy meets Heather for coffee at their favorite café on Newbury Street.

They sit out on the sidewalk, the day growing ever-warmer. They peel off layers while they sip coffee.

"I want to try to go back to Cattail," Amy tells Heather. "I thought I never would, but I think I want to now."

Heather listens. Amy senses she wants to say something. Amy suspects Heather still holds back in speaking with her. That she still walks lightly. Amy remains quiet, hoping her open silence imparts her willingness to listen.

Heather says, "I went. I was convinced I'd never go back. But then I found myself there. I didn't head out with the idea of going. I was just feeling so lost one day and I took off from work and found myself on the road and I just kept going."

"When?" Amy curls her legs beneath herself.

"January. It was weird to be there during winter. There was a big pile of snow in one corner of the parking lot. And of course it was freezing. The water was frigid. Even I thought so." She smiles and so does Amy. Heather pauses for a few moments. "I sat in the sand. I didn't really know why I was there."

"Was it..." Amy can't find the words.

"It was..." Heather looks out into the street, searching her mind, "scary. At first. I thought it would be awful, but then it was okay. I was so afraid to go there. But mostly it was the same as ever. It made me feel the same as always. It did make me think of Sage. Of course. But it was okay."

"I've been afraid to hope," Amy says. "Well, that's not it really. I've felt badly about hoping."

"I know," Heather says. "But maybe you can have Cattail and have Sage's memory, too."

Amy sighs. "I think you're right. I just hope I feel it. You know what I mean?"

She closes her eyes and nods.

"Here's the thing: if you don't we'll figure it out," Heather says. "There are other beaches and we'll figure it out."

Amy meets Heather's eyes and smiles at her sister, who takes her hand and smiles, too. They sit in silence, the city moving around them.

"We've gone a few times this summer." Heather says shyly. It is part apology.

"I know, Mom told me. It's okay." And she really believes it is. It stings for a moment then subsides.

"We felt really weird about it for so many reasons."

"You shouldn't." But there is a part of her that is comforted because they feel this way. This year has taught Amy that everyone must heal in their own way.

"It's such a part of me. Of us—you know?"

Amy nods. "I can't imagine never going back. But I'm scared."

"Well, you know you've got all of us. To help." She pauses. "I'm glad you're thinking of going back. It could never be the same without you."

A sudden memory emerges. "I just remembered once a few years ago," Amy says, sitting up, "before I was married, I went to Cattail during winter, too. On a whim. I had some spare time so I drove out there."

It was never their habit to go to Cattail during the winter, spring or fall. In Amy's mind it slept, slept, slept when they weren't there. But then there it was, as always. Same clumps of long cord grass, same dunes, same large stones, same pounding water.

"Only difference was the bathhouse and snack bar were boarded up, the lifeguard chairs were gone and they put up those wooden fences to control the blowing sand," Amy says.

"Yeah," Heather nods. "All the human stuff."

"But the rest. It was all the same." *It just goes on. It just goes on and on*, Amy thinks.

They are quiet.

"I want to try going back," Amy says. "But I feel shitty about wanting it back." Her eyes fill. She swallows back tears.

Heather places her hand on Amy's arm. "Just because you go on doesn't mean you don't love her."

"I know. In my mind, I know. But happiness is hard. And peace is hard. I want those things but feel so lousy for wanting them. Like it's some kind of betrayal."

"I know," she says. She doesn't try to solve this for Amy. She simply allows her to speak, she listens. She knows and Amy knows that there is no answer. It simply is. It is exhausting listening to those who try to attempt to determine answers. Amy stopped a long time ago. But Heather offers no answers. Their relationship is still healing—there is work here. But some things never change.

"I'm so afraid it's not going to be the same. That it's ruined. That it's changed beyond recognition." These words have been piling up inside Amy. They burn as she speaks them.

"Maybe it won't be the same. Maybe it can't be. But maybe it can be different and still be good."

Amy nods her head.

She is beginning to believe that *different* might be alright.

She is beginning to believe in possibility again.

~~~

Since the day Sage drowned, Amy has not stepped foot on Cattail Beach. She once unwaveringly believed she would never go back. She spoke the word "never." But some of her has softened. And now she wants it back: the peace it offers, the version of herself that is somehow truer when she is there. Through grief and crippling guilt, she has yearned for Cattail. But it is tainted; it is stained. She knows it will never be the same. Maybe now she is ready to accept this truth and reclaim what good can be salvaged. The old familiar things no longer give her comfort and she recognizes that the rituals never were truly the same. She thought they were, but each day, each year plays out in small ways that can never be duplicated. Words, laughter, a bird flying through a particular sunset will never happen exactly that way ever again. It's only once. Specifics will be forgotten— what they laughed at, why it was funny at all, but that they laughed will endure. The essence endures. The comfort is in the essence. She always wanted something solid of those moments to hold in her hands. But of course she can't have that. If she could, the moments would be relegated to the merely ordinary.

Once she let go of her old habits, things began to come easier. Nothing is the same as before. Nothing can be—it is altered. She understands. Yet she is still afraid of what she might find when she steps onto the sand. Will she find Sage there? Will she still belong there? Is it still hers? Is she still its?

But she will try. Because not trying feels worse.

"Amy, Cattail is not perfect," Mom reminded her recently. Amy had told her mother that it might be ruined for her forever. This, her ideal place.

One day, a few summers ago, they had planned to meet at Cattail when Mom called.

"The beach is closed." She'd seen it on the news that morning. High levels of bacteria—unsafe for swimming.

She reminded Amy. "And don't you remember the summer we kept finding hypodermic needles on the shore?"

Garbage, too, washed up from the open ocean. Big dead fish sometimes rotted in the sun and dry sand above the tide line.

One day, a large man collapsed in the sand not far from where Amy was sitting. She remembered a tremor through his knees and he fell to them neatly, then—not so neatly nor gracefully—fell forward onto his large barrel of a belly. He wasn't wearing a shirt, but socks and topsiders with his bathing suit. His friends called the lifeguards who streaked across the sand. Soon, an ambulance made its way to the tar path and down the stretch of sand reserved for emergency vehicles. The man did not stir. And the entire time, a crowd of people encircled him, spectators in this man's intimate moment. More people spread out past the circle. They stood on their toes and used their hands as visors, wobbled back and forth trying to get a look. The guards had to tell people to move out of the way so the EMTs could move the man, now on a stretcher, into the ambulance.

Amy watched peripherally. She told herself she only wanted to know when it was over. She felt terrible that this poor man had become a spectacle. She didn't want to participate.

At first, Amy was disgusted by the behavior of those onlookers, as if they couldn't get enough of the man's misfortune. The attention they gave it was perverse. The same thing happened whenever there was a surf rescue. But then it occurred to her that it might simply be fear—fear of death. The actuality of it, the inevitability and, of course, the finality. Did people possess an innate need to gawk at glimpses of death in this way? A craving for a closer look, a moving in and pulling back—a small taste from the safety of distance.

Yes, here where death was for the old and the infirm, the unlucky. In places where death was everyday, a regular occurrence, and none were exempt and luck was for no one, those people might be more likely to turn away from death. Not to outrun it, because it is understood everywhere that to do so is an impossibility. But because they would also understand that they are entitled to no better—no different. *We try to pretend we're not mortal*, Amy thinks. The others know they are. They know they are not above it.

These are things that can be understood rationally, but to know them in the bones is different.

Amy chose not to recall these things about her beloved beach. She confined them as incidental, not fundamental, aspects of Cattail.

Maybe now, because of Sage, she can see all of it—not only that which she chooses. She wonders if this is a gift and knows only time will tell.

Time will tell so much that she cannot know yet.

The time comes to pack the car for vacation. On the way out of the city, she fights rising anxiety. Her throat is tight, her hands rolling over each other. Matt glances at her and rests his hand softly over hers.

"You okay, babe?" he asks.

"Just a little nervous." She says this as lightly as she is able.

"Can we take the back roads to the cottage?" she asks. The highway goes right past Cattail and she's not ready to see it yet. Driving past it without stopping, without taking those first steps onto the sand, seems wrong. When the time comes, she must drive through the gate, park the car and walk on strong legs, with sure steps onto that beach.

But she must begin slowly.

They drive past houses, trees, flow over curves in the road she knows by heart. An overwhelming sense of familiarity washes over her. It rises and sticks in her chest until she remembers to take a breath. The road curves to the left and the earth falls off and rolls over hills and clumps of tall green trees. The meandering stone walls frame it. The green quenches her like water in a dry throat.

They pull up to the short road that leads to the cottage, bump over the crushed shells and small stones and pull onto the grass out front. The car shudders to a stop, the music from the stereo silenced abruptly.

When Amy, Matt and Rachel arrive, they dump their stuff on the grayed wood of the porch. The look of it, all the smells and sounds, nestle deep inside her, settle in. Resonate a hum that she knows by heart. It feels good to hear it. She stands on the graying wood planks of the deck, uneven but firm beneath her feet, and inhales the familiar scent of heat, of tar, of burning stone, of things growing impossibly from sand. It touches some place deep inside. A place of comfort and knowing that is only accessible through odor or touch and memory—not words, not organized thought, not through bumbling attempts, but only by organic unraveling. She thinks she feels happy. She thinks she feels hopeful. She thinks she feels a small coming together inside her body, inside her spirit. This feeling has no dimension, it simply pervades.

It is different; of this there is no question. At first, it panics her. Was this supposed to be some sort of epiphany? Some small part of her hoped she would be instantly healed simply because she came back. But the larger part of her knew this would not happen.

Nothing is so simple. She is learning to accept what is and stay open to what unfolds.

"Sweetheart!" Mom says. They greet each other. Heather comes out and hugs her, too.

"Should we head to the beach?" Mom asks.

"It's getting kind of late," Amy says. "It's already after three. You guys go. I'll get settled and make supper for tonight." No one asks her why or tries to convince her otherwise. They head off to Cattail.

Amy takes stock in the kitchen, finds very little to work with, and decides to drive to the local grocery store. She devises a menu and grocery list in her head on the drive over. Everything is so lush and green— trees, grass, bursting hydrangeas. She glances at the old houses, placards affixed attesting to their antiquity, 1879, 1825, 1902. It is all so beautiful, so known. It carries her back to a safer time, a time when she was sure she knew: herself, her family, her world. Now she is relearning. Letting go, holding on, sifting, sorting. Sand, seashells, tiny rocks, heavy stones, water. Sifting.

She is working at being.

She thinks of her family down at the beach. Matt offered to stay with her, but she told him to go and relax, play with Rachel. Being alone feels right to her. She needs to find her feet in that cottage. Feel the floorboards, reach out to the walls, push into the ceiling and feel out the corners.

The air in the grocery store is, as always, frigid. Mom keeps a couple of sweatshirts in the trunk of her car particularly for this store. Of course, Amy, as always, forgets about the cold until she walks in the door. She shivers in her short sleeves as she wanders the aisles. Orzo, chickpeas, zucchini, carrots, golden raisins. One of her weird concoctions that they initially laugh at but then gobble up.

The cottage is silent and still when she returns. She puts the grocery bag on the table and turns on some music. She smiles when she opens the CD player—Heather has already popped in one of the old favorites. Amy presses play and turns it up loud. She shakes to the music as she sautés onions, slices zucchini. She drinks a beer, very cold and good. Beads of condensation build up on the brown bottle almost as soon as she removes it from the fridge.

As the food simmers, she has a few moments to relax. She goes to the deck and sinks into one of the chairs. She spreads her body out and breathes. She sips the beer, breathes in, exhales. And it seems that the poisons that have been burrowing and nestling into her flesh, her organs, are starting to loosen, to rise, to flow out with the stale air in the bottom of her lungs. The air takes them, absorbs the toxins, pushes them out to the sea. An offering her ocean can bear.

Dinner is almost ready and everyone returns. They take showers, drink beers, eat the food. They put the children to sleep. The adults wander off to bed, yawning, their skin glowing and warm from the sun. Lights go out.

"Matt? Are you sleeping?" Amy whispers.

He takes her hand.

"What was it like?" she asks.

He rolls to face her. She can see his face awash in the blue-hued moonlight from the double doors of the Juliet balcony.

"How was it?" she asks again.

He sighs a little, but smiles. "It was...okay."

"Okay?"

"It was hard in the first moments. All I could see was her and think about everything. But then it was okay. I didn't think it was going to be easy, but I've always thought it really didn't matter. She's gone and going there or never going there is not going to change that."

"I'm sorry I wasn't there with you," she says.

"It's okay. I was okay. I know it's harder for you."

"Oh, I'm sure it's not," she says.

"Cattail is."

"Yeah, maybe Cattail is."

"Think you'll go tomorrow?" he asks and rubs her shoulder gently.

"Maybe."

She tries to imagine what it might be like, but fear warbles through her. It's the thing she knows she needs to do to find peace. Whether she finds it benevolent or intolerable, she must know one way or the other.

"Yes," she says. "Maybe tomorrow."

~~~

The house is silent. Everyone is asleep. It is very late, and Amy listens to the cooing of children, the stirring of adults in their sleep, a fan swooshing steadily in one room. She closes the cottage door silently and drops into one of the chairs on the deck. It slopes and cups her back, and her head tilts skyward as she slides in more comfortably. She breathes. The chair holds her solidly, is rooted beneath her. She looks up. In the back corner of her eye, the very edge of one pointy eave of the cottage is visible, its white trim. She can see the silhouette of her own nose. She shifts her awareness from these earthly things, from herself. Stars everywhere puncture the blackness of the sky. The moon, low on the horizon, is two-thirds full and bright orange, almost red. It's a Harvest Moon. The Milky Way winds in pearly spirals. Venus shines brightly; twinkles clearly. Amy takes it all in.

For the first time, she understands why she must return to Cattail. It is not simply because it is vacation time or because going there is what they have always done. What they've always done supports her only so far these days. She needs to return to Cattail to reclaim the good.

There is good.

While everyone showered earlier, Amy worked on her final embroidery piece for the art show.

Heather joined her at the kitchen table, hair wet from a shower and sweet-smelling.

"Is this your sixth piece?" she asked.

"Uh-huh," Amy smiled.

"So you're going to do it."

Amy winced a little. "I think so?" she said in a squeak. "I mean I haven't pulled out. So, I think so."

Heather laughed. "You seem so very sure!"

Amy laughed, too. "What if the work is not good enough?"

"Amy, it is more than good enough."

"I've been so scattered this year..."

"And everything you've got is in those pieces. They're so real. Let me see this one."

Amy held it up for Heather to see. Amy had hand-dyed the silk a watercolor blur of blues and purples. In colors deep and rich, a family of three encircled their arms around a green and brown earth. A large star like a satellite sparked in the sky around them.

Heather's eyes filled with tears. "It's beautiful. How could you wonder if this is good?"

Amy looked up at the ceiling and tried to hold her own tears. "I'm still trying to be sure," she whispered.

They looked at each other for a few suspended moments. "Well," Heather said, "it is better than good so you need to do this show. Say, 'yes, I'm doing it.'"

"Yes, I'm doing it?"

"No, like without the question mark: YES, I'M DOING IT!"

"Really? I have to?"

"Yes, you do."

"Alright...YES, I'M DOING IT!"

"Girls..." Mom called from down the hall.

"We're not fighting, Mom!" Heather called. "God..." she growled.

Amy sits in the dark of midnight now, and realizes this is one of the things she has learned: there is good.

There is pain and sorrow and desperate yearning. But there is also good. There is Matt. There is Rachel's head on Amy's heart. There is her sister. This is what she must learn to see again. There was life before, there was life with Sage. There is still life. There will be more life. It can never be what it was, but maybe it can still be good. This is what she is trying with Heather. She must try and try, because it is worth it and she wants it.

The knowledge that life goes on used to make her angry; used to make her cry. Sometimes it still does. Maybe it always will. But here is the truth: she is here.

She is.

She knows why life goes on. This is why life goes on. Peering up at the stars, she knows she is small. It's not an original thought, but she feels as though she now understands what it means to be small. This, the moon, the stars, the ocean crashing softly behind, is all that will be left. All that will endure. What of her pain? What of her life? What of her? She will not be here. She could never forget all that has happened, but she can choose what to let go. Only now in her smallness can she understand this. She possesses the power. She matters; all that has happened to her matters. Her baby matters. But what she chooses to keep is what makes *her*.

This is knowledge. Knowing is different from believing, but maybe it is the first step.

This is a truth she believes; a truth that resonates in her bones. The sensation feels fine and good. She breathes into this chair she has sat in for many years. She absorbs the blackness, the stars, the fading orange moon into her skin. Venus sinks into her skin. She feels all at once that maybe she can learn to reside in this skin again. A return to her own body. It will take time, but it is a start.

She breathes.

The moon rises, pale orange.

Venus winks.

~~~

Everyone readies for the beach. The towels are pulled from the line, tri-folded and left waiting in the sun of the deck. The open cooler is filled with waxed-paper-wrapped sandwiches, plums and grapes, cantaloupe spears in the tall Tupperware container. Sunscreen is slathered over already-tanned skin.

This is not the time for Amy to return.

She needs to do it alone. There is a right way to do this.

"I think I'll stay here for a while," she says to Mom and Heather in the kitchen.

"Stay?" Mom says.

"Okay," Heather says and smiles at Amy.

Matt smiles, too, when she tells him. He knows. She has told him how she needs to do this.

She spends the day reading on the deck. She naps like a cat and when she awakens goes for a long walk. She walks down the bumpy crushed-shell road and notices that the house on the corner got an addition over the winter. The new section is covered with weathering cedar shingles. Crisp and clean and blond. The older part of the house grayed and defined with age. The new shingles will take time and seasons and weather. But eventually they will blend in—she has seen it happen—and then it's difficult to remember where the new and the old once met.

This is time. Its measure.

Time is the shore she walks along, the soles of her feet getting wet. Time is the ocean moving in and out. Endlessly. The sandpipers and gulls. Born and reborn and aging and dying. Every year only seems the same: a flock of birds doing the things they do, the water that rushes over her feet, that she swims in, the sand she walks upon. Never the same water, never the same sand, moving and changing, but most of all enduring. The water rinses the sand from her feet and ankles over and over, erases her footprints.

This sublime perfection.

Amy often thinks about perfection now—how difficult it is to find it, to grasp it, to hold onto it. Can it be real? Even there in the moment when she thinks perfection is attained, she realizes only the idea of it is perfect. Life is harder than that. It takes ideas of golden flawlessness and tarnishes them. Green-hued corrosion edging copper. The gray of weathered shingles. This is true beauty, nature's hand, when it can be perceived that way.

Beauty sometimes is dead-on. Sometimes you live in it. Bathe in it, warm liquid, not too hot. You are in the soft petals of the flowers. You are a part of it. You get it. Beauty is in your face; you can't miss it. Other times it eludes you. You almost have it, but it wriggles out of your hand. You can't get a look. It is right behind you or right in front of you and when you turn your head toward it you catch a shimmering edge of it escaping around the corner. What is around you is what's left—dull, ordinary. Everything you wanted, everything that was meant to comprise perfection. And there it all is.

So maybe that's it. Maybe that is perfection.

The time passes slowly—she is very aware of its pace.

She is waiting.

Her family starts to filter back from the beach. One carload and then the other. The sun is at that place in the sky—the right place.

"I think I'll go down for a quick swim before supper," she says. She attempts casualness and doubts anyone buys it, but they act as though they do. Matt kisses her. "Okay," he says.

"See you in a bit," Heather says. She kisses Amy, too. She tastes of salt.

Amy drives over to the beach slowly and turns into the open gate. All the workers are long gone for the day. It's free to get in at this hour in the afternoon. She parks in the far south lot, locks the car and makes her way up the boardwalk.

The smell comes to her first. She stops, closes her eyes and opens her senses. The scent carries Amy to that safe place, that good place. A simplicity, a clarity. She listens to the ocean and can tell from the sounds of the water how big the waves are, how frequently they flow in. She opens her eyes and her legs carry her to the edge of the sand.

What rises up is not pain, not reminders, but the remembrance of beneficence. She says in her mind to Sage: *Feel it? Do you feel it? I miss you. I will never let go. I don't have to. You are here. Where I am, you are.* Amy sees the images of Sage's death as a wraith, a double exposure against the sunny backdrop that has been a part of her entire life. But the clear picture is the sun at her favorite angle, the dark blue water, the white caps, the sand warm-spun sugar beneath her feet already decorating her toes and ankles. She wiggles her feet in it. She digs her heels in as she walks over it. She feels it. Not only her skin, but something deeper. The sand, the stones, the water in her feels it, connects with it.

She feels herself.

She pulls her shirt off, tosses it and her towel in the sand and runs to the water.

She doesn't take her time—she plunges in. The water roars, it holds her. She moves through it, with it.

It is a womb to contain her, to revive her. To make her as whole as she can be. Whatever whole means, whatever it is. And maybe she will be reborn. Or maybe she already has been. Or maybe she doesn't need to be.

She smiles tentatively.

Her body and spirit open, guardedly, to joy.

She allows herself to feel at home.

In this moment, she is *her*.

That is all she can be.

She swims and dives under and feels it all around her.

She dissolves.

They giggle, crowded in the small bathroom, and pull their clothes onto their bodies. They wear sweatshirts hanging loose over thin, worn flannel pants. They cover their mouths with their hands, laugh because they're supposed to be quiet.

It's early when they slip out of the cottage. Everyone is asleep. They close the door soundlessly.

The long wet grass dampens their ankles, the bottoms of their pants, as they cross the lawn. Its color is a saturated green as if it could not possibly be more green. Night clings to the sky behind them, the round vapor moon hangs, holds the last breath of night.

They reach the shore. The sun, low over the ocean, drips light onto the rippling water. Bright spots ride small waves. They skip down toward the water and kick off their sandals. The raspy sand rubs their bare feet, tender skin aware of the texture in the contrast of softness and grit. Their hair curls wildly when it meets the ocean air; tendrils escape from their loose ponytails. The air floats, a soft stream that pushes their pants to outline their legs.

Amy looks at the dark blue of the water between the shifting light. It stretches toward the horizon and down the beach. She thinks *the ocean is so big* but not in words.

The damp salt air makes their fingers sticky.

Amy holds her sister's hand.

Little again.

ABOUT THE AUTHOR

Melissa Corliss DeLorenzo is the author of the
novel *THE MOSQUITO HOURS* (2014). She received
a BA in English literature from the University of
Massachusetts and a Master's of Fine Arts in Creative
Writing from Naropa University. She was a Senior
Editor at Her Circle Ezine. Currently, she is a
homeschooling mother, yogini, avid reader, novel
writer and part-time librarian. She loves books and
matcha green tea beyond measure. Melissa lives in
Massachusetts with her husband and children. You
can find her blog and more about her work at
www.melissacorlissdelorenzo.com
and her co-authored book blog at
www.readingatthekitchentable.com

Made in the USA
Las Vegas, NV
28 April 2021

22122624R00184